FIRE DANCER

Also by Victor Kelleher

———————•———————

FIRE DANCER
VICTOR KELLEHER

VIKING

Viking
Penguin Books Australia Ltd
487 Maroondah Highway, PO Box 257
Ringwood, Victoria 3134, Australia
Penguin Books Ltd
Harmondsworth, Middlesex, England
Viking Penguin, A Division of Penguin Books USA Inc.
375 Hudson Street, New York, New York 10014, USA
Penguin Books Canada Limited
10 Alcorn Avenue, Toronto, Ontario, Canada M4V 3B2
Penguin Books (N.Z.) Ltd
182–190 Wairau Road, Auckland 10, New Zealand

First published by Penguin Books Australia, 1996
10 9 8 7 6 5 4 3 2 1
Copyright © Victor Kelleher, 1996

Typeset in Plantin 12/13pt by Midland Typesetters, Maryborough, Victoria
Made and printed in Australia by Australian Print Group, Maryborough, Victoria

National Library of Australia
Cataloguing-in-Publication data:

Kelleher, Victor, 1939– .
Fire dancer.

ISBN 0 670 87111 7.

I. Title.
A823.3

This project has been assisted by the Commonwealth Government through the Australia Council, its arts funding and advisory body.

Permission to use words from the article 'Neanderthals' by Rick Gore (*National Geographic Magazine*: Volume 189, Number 1, January 1996) in the blurb and preface of *Fire Dancer* has kindly been given by *National Geographic Magazine*, Washington D.C., USA.

O, wonder!
How many goodly creatures are there here!
How beauteous mankind is! O brave new world,
That has such people in't!

THE TEMPEST (5.I.184)

The Neanderthals were an ancient race of humans who died out tens of thousands of years ago. What happened to them nobody knows. Perhaps they came into competition with our immediate ancestors and were destroyed, either through conquest or disease. Perhaps they simply interbred with modern people and were absorbed into the mainstream of human history. Whatever the reason, all trace of Neanderthal life suddenly ended, their culture gone – vanquished or absorbed . . .

Part 1

A FOREIGN SHORE

1

It looked nothing like a ship to Ivan, with its heavily reinforced body and outjutting observation decks. But then, as the guide continued to explain, there was no need for aerodynamics where they were going.

'In the time routes,' he told the assembled travellers in his slightly lecturing tone, 'it's not heat or air-drag you have to worry about. The real problem is staying clear of heavy objects that may once have occupied your chosen space.'

'What if we *do* bump into another object?' Ivan asked impulsively, and all the other travellers turned in his direction, making him redden and duck his head. One girl in particular, someone roughly his own age, gave him a doubtful look, reminding him that he didn't really belong amongst these well-to-do people.

'It'll have to be something pretty big to do any damage,' the guide answered with a laugh. 'But again that's not a real worry. We've explored this time route on numerous occasions, and it's completely

3

clear as far back as we need to go. There are no volcanoes, no landslides, nothing like that. The mountain and the lake you can see outside this building remain more or less unchanged right back into palaeolithic times.'

He paused, giving them time to gaze through the nearest window at the glitter of the lake in the afternoon light.

'Now,' he went on briskly, 'if there are no more questions I suggest we start to board.' And he gestured towards the waiting ship perched high above them on its raised platform.

Singly and in pairs, talking excitedly amongst themselves, the travellers began to mount the stairs. Ivan didn't rush to follow, his mouth suddenly dry at the thought of what lay ahead. Nervously, he was just about to join the last group when someone spoke to him from behind.

'You're not scared, are you?'

He turned and stared into the bored but undeniably attractive face of the teenage girl he had noticed earlier.

'No, not ... not scared exactly,' he lied.

She shrugged and eased past him, blocking the way. 'So how come you're on your own? Why aren't you with family like everyone else?'

'I live with my aunt,' he admitted, 'and she would never have agreed to come. She's too old. She couldn't afford it anyway. I won this trip as a sort of prize.'

The girl arched her eyebrows knowingly at him. 'I see. So you're one of these brilliant scientist types who know all about physics and stuff.'

He shook his head. 'There was an essay contest and I won, that's all.'

The guide was waving them up to the entrance of the craft, but the girl pointedly ignored him, lounging against the side rail of the stairs as though they had all the time in the world.

'An essay?' she queried, and Ivan could tell she was only pretending to be interested. Her real aim was to annoy the guide. 'What was it about?'

'Neanderthal people.'

She suppressed a yawn. 'Yeah, that makes sense. For you to see the genuine article I mean. Though personally I find the thought of goggling at a bunch of primitives about as interesting as watching grass grow.'

She was interrupted by a middle-aged woman who stepped abruptly from the craft above them.

'Josie!' she barked out. 'You get in here before I lose my temper.'

'Speaking of primitives,' Josie muttered under her breath, and shot Ivan a fleeting smile as she led the way upwards.

The interior of the ship was as much of a surprise as the heavily built exterior. Ivan had expected it to be bare and spartan, almost laboratory-like; whereas it resembled nothing so much as the plush lounge room of an expensive hotel, with deeply padded armchairs and couches arranged around the ports.

'Just a few pieces of information before we set out,' the guide announced, and Ivan slid quickly onto a couch beside Josie. 'As I'm sure you're aware, this trip will occupy hardly any clock time. We'll arrive back only a split second after we leave. However, it won't seem like that to us. From our point of view the trip will last some hours. So I suggest you sit back and enjoy yourselves. I must remind you, of course, that for anyone here to interfere with the past would be dangerous in the extreme. We're strictly observers. But for all that I'm sure you'll find the whole experience fascinating. To witness your own kind in their primeval state is a privilege reserved only for the lucky few.'

'D'you call this luck?' Josie asked languidly, and received another angry glare from her mother.

'Say what you like, young lady,' the guide insisted, 'we're still privileged. To look through the window of time and observe our palaeolithic ancestors in their daily lives – that's something most people can only dream about.'

'Some dream,' Josie commented, refusing to be put down, and winked at Ivan. 'By the sound of things it'll be more of a nightmare. Especially if those ancestors of ours decide to take a pot shot at us.'

'Josie!' her mother growled, and glared at Ivan too, as though Josie's silent wink had somehow involved him in the argument.

'No, it's all right, madam,' the guide said placatingly. 'Let me reassure these young people once and for all. There's really nothing to fear. For instance, the stone weapons of our ancestors could barely scratch the surface of our hull. As for their intelligence! They're primitives, you understand. Quite stupid on our standards. No match for us and our technology.'

It was on the tip of Ivan's tongue to point out that the brains of Neanderthal people had in fact been larger than our own; but by then there was such a strong air of disapproval in the plush interior of the cabin that he decided to remain silent.

'Right,' the guide concluded, and beamed at his audience. 'There's nothing more to detain us. I would advise you, therefore, to prepare for the adventure of a lifetime.'

His announcement must have acted as a signal to the pilot in the sealed compartment because straight away the engines hummed into life and the ship rose slowly through the opening in the roof of the building.

Ivan, sitting tense and still on the overstuffed couch, felt the thrust of the ship beneath him. Far below he glimpsed the lake and the adjoining mountain, the expanse of land between them lined by row upon row of red-roofed dwellings. Then the light didn't so much dim as change its quality, and everything outside the ship faded into a grey-white blur.

How long that fade-out lasted he couldn't tell. There was something timeless about it, like the stroke of midnight when the sleeper lies poised between one day and the next. Except that he wasn't asleep; merely held in a state of suspension, the same as everyone else in the cabin, their faces blank and unknowing. Even Josie, when he glanced towards her, had momentarily lost her look of quiet assurance.

Then, with a kind of swooping sensation, the light brightened to full day and the lake and mountain were back, spread out beneath them. The same, but different. The lake larger than before; the mountain slightly less craggy; and the expanse of land between ... !

A communal sigh rose from the assembled travellers, and Ivan strained forward in his seat for a better view. Yes! There was no mistake. All trace of the red-roofed dwellings had disappeared, replaced by a band of dense forest that hugged the shores of the lake and formed a dark green fringe around the upper slopes of the mountain. The only break in the canopy was down near the lake, where a great outcrop of rock seemed to hold at bay the enclosing trees; and from that small clearing a single tendril of smoke, blue-grey against the forest backdrop, curled lazily skywards.

'That, ladies and gentlemen,' the guide said grandly, pointing to the telltale wisp of smoke, 'is our destination.'

Again his words must have served as a signal to the pilot because the ship immediately slipped sideways and down, falling so fast that Ivan had to swallow hard to control his churning stomach. The engines roared, and as the ship banked and steadied just above the treetops, the travellers were given their first sight of the cave dwellers – a ragged group of women and children clustered fearfully together near the entrance to one of the caves.

'Homo Neanderthalensis,' the guide said even more grandly than before.

But Ivan needed no such explanation. The identity of the people below was written all too clearly in their thick-boned limbs, in their great brow ridges, and in their heavy hands and feet. These, unmistakably, were true representatives of the Neanderthal people he had read about, studied, tried so hard to picture in his mind's eye. And here they were! The real thing! Only ten or fifteen metres away and gazing straight up at him, a look of fear in their deep-set eyes.

'Wonderful!' he breathed, and heard a murmur of disagreement.

It was Josie, an expression of total disgust on her face.

'You call them wonderful?' she said incredulously. 'Those ugly brutes down there? Look at them! At how filthy they are. Horrible! Not really people at all. Just *animals*! Filthy animals!'

Ivan was about to protest when the scene below changed slightly. As if responding to a command, the women and children scuttled inside the cave, and at the same instant a man burst from the forest and ran across the clearing, his long hair and skin tunic streaming out behind. He carried a stone-headed spear which he hurled skywards, the point striking tinnily against the underside of the ship.

The faint 'ping' of its impact sounded so feeble from inside the craft that most of the travellers broke into laughter. But already other men were running from the forest, their eyes fixed intently on the ship. They were also armed, their clubs and spears rattling like fine hail against the ship's outer shell.

This time the pilot didn't wait for a signal. The engines roared, the craft banked to the left, and within seconds it was far out over the lake, the clearing no longer visible.

'As you've just seen,' the guide said, 'these people are no real threat. On the other hand it's Government policy not to disturb them unduly. So from here on we play more of a waiting game.'

That 'game', as the pilot soon demonstrated, consisted of gliding silently back across the lake, only a metre or two above the surface, and coming to rest in the shallows beside a tall bluff. There, hidden partly by cascading vines, partly by the deepening shadow cast by the bluff itself, they had a clear view of a narrow sandbar that angled out from the encroaching forest.

'The cave dwellers come down here to fish and to collect water, especially in the late afternoon,' the guide explained. 'From past experience we've found that this is a good place to wait and watch. I'd say they should start arriving in half an hour or so. In the meantime I suggest you enjoy the light refreshments we have on board.'

Within moments a steward appeared from the aft cabin bearing trays of food and drink. Ivan, too tense to eat, and feeling the odd person out once again, sauntered over to one of the observation decks that jutted wing-like from the side of the craft. During flight these had been closed off by airtight doors, but now they stood wide open, and he ventured out.

Although the whole deck was enclosed by plastic walls, the plastic itself was so clear that he felt as if he were stepping free, out into the mysterious world of the distant past. Wonderingly he gazed about him: at a brightly coloured dragonfly that shimmered by, almost within arm's reach; at the tiny wavelets that slopped against the craft's side right there at his feet. As he watched, something stirred on the sandy, weed-strewn bed of the lake: a long sinuous shape that might have been an eel, but might equally have been something far more ancient and sinister.

He crouched for a better look, so intent on whatever lurked in the murky water that he didn't notice the person moving up beside him.

'What's down there?' Josie asked, making him start and rock back on his heels.

'I'm not sure,' he replied shakily. 'Maybe an eel.'

'Yuk!' She wrinkled her nose. 'Mind you, even an eel's a pleasant change after all those oldies in there. God, my mother! She's such a bore! She was the one who ... '

'Hold on a second.'

Ivan had straightened up, distracted by something outside the ship.

'What is it?'

'Over there.' He pointed to the far side of the bay, where the bushes at the forest's edge were being agitated by more than the wind. 'I think someone's clambering down the bank.'

Sure enough, only moments later one of the Neanderthal people pushed aside a leafy bough and stepped onto the spit of sand that ran out from the shore. She was a young woman, short and thick-set like all her kind, and she wore a baggy dress of animal skins that reached almost to her knees. Her face, framed by shoulder-length black hair, was marked by the usual heavy brow ridge; and her other features were as broad as the hand with which she waved aside the midges that clustered about her head. Yet in spite of her sturdy build and bony features, she moved with surprising delicacy, something fawn-like about the way she ventured warily across the sand and knelt in the shallows.

'Wow, what a dog!' Josie said, and laughed. 'You wouldn't date her in a hurry.'

Ivan winced at Josie's tone. He felt that here in this world of the past, where he and Josie were the interlopers, they had no right to stand in judgment.

'She's not exactly beautiful,' he conceded, 'but I wouldn't really call her ugly either.'

Josie let out a snort of disbelief. 'Oh come on! Look at that face! Those hands and feet! You're not going to tell me they're things of beauty.'

He shook his head. 'No, all I'm saying is that she's – I don't know – different.'

'I'll say she is,' Josie agreed, and reached up to click on one of the external sensors.

11

The sounds of the outer world immediately flooded in: the sigh of the breeze across the lake; a faint background clatter of insects; and as a kind of undertone, a hoarse throaty noise which Ivan failed to identify.

'Hear that?' Josie said disparagingly. 'She's singing. How'd you fancy having *her* serenade you?'

Ivan listened hard, and realised Josie was right. The girl *was* singing. Moreover there was a definite rhythm to the sound, her voice rising and falling in a way that wasn't wholly unpleasant, despite the hoarseness of the tone.

'She sounds almost happy,' he murmured in surprise.

'Well, she doesn't look it,' Josie countered.

Again Ivan had to admit Josie was right, for the girl had broken off her song and risen cautiously to her feet. Her dark eyes glinting in the late afternoon sunlight, she swung her head from side to side, scenting the breeze. Whatever she detected obviously alarmed her. And not just her, because the bushes shook once more and a man sprang out onto the strand. He was much older than the woman and armed with a spear which he flourished in a show of warning.

'Waark!' he muttered throatily – or that was how it sounded to Ivan – and the woman scuttled across the sand and crouched beside him.

Like the man, she was gazing out across the bay in the general direction of the ship.

'I think they must have seen us,' Josie said nonchalantly.

'I doubt it,' Ivan said. 'The sun's at our back. It's dazzling them.'

'You're forgetting they're just animals,' Josie

argued, 'and animals can detect things human beings can't. They can probably hear our voices.'

'But the ship's supposed to be sound-proof.'

'Let's test it and see,' Josie said, and before Ivan could stop her she thumped the plastic wall with the heel of her hand.

The response was instantaneous, the heads of both the man and the woman swivelling around slightly. Now they really *were* gazing straight at the ship. And all at once it occurred to Ivan that the original cause of their alarm must have been something else altogether, something hidden by the trees beyond the shoreline.

He barely had time to formulate the thought before the foliage on the near side of the bay parted suddenly and a huge grey shape charged into the shallows, headed directly for the ship.

'Oh no!' he heard Josie moan, and then they were scrambling madly towards the open doorway.

Before they could reach it the deck erupted beneath them, the dome-shaped walls buckling and splintering under a heavy impact. A trumpeting cry rang out overhead; and as massive grey limbs blundered past, Ivan felt the cold touch of water swirl up around his waist.

The deck was gone from beneath him now, the churned water strewn with wreckage; and unaccountably the ship seemed further away, its air-tight doors firmly closed. Even as he struggled to understand what that meant, the huge creature blundered past once again – a nightmare vision of tusks and fur and chunky limbs – the wash from its body as it headed for the shore buffeting Ivan aside. He staggered and nearly went under, a blunt fragment of plastic smashing into his forehead. Dazed, he lurched upright and saw with dismay that the ship had already drifted well out into the lake.

'Stop them!' he heard Josie sob, and felt hands pluck at his sodden T-shirt. 'They can't ... they can't ... !'

That was when he registered the steady throb of the engines and realised that the ship wasn't just drifting. It was being *driven* clear of the shore. More alarming still, the pitch of the engines had begun to change, rising to a roar and then to a scream.

Tearing himself free of Josie, he made a despairing lunge forward, but found his way blocked by floating wreckage. In any case the ship was hopelessly out of reach by then – a long silver shape that lifted slowly from the lake, hovered for a few seconds, and finally blurred at the edges and vanished altogether.

'Gone!' he muttered, struggling to take in the awful truth. That he and Josie had been left behind. Abandoned. Marooned in a past so dim and distant that already he felt lost for ever.

2

'Bastards!' Josie screamed, and shouldered Ivan aside, her clenched fists raised above her head. 'Bastards! Bastards! Bastards ... !'

Because he was still in a state of shock, there was little conscious thought in what Ivan did next. More as a reflex action than anything else, he clamped one hand over her mouth and dragged her under, simultaneously kicking free of the sandy bottom and driving out into the lake.

He was surprised at how strong she was, at how she fought him there in the greenish depths. He needed all his strength just to hang on, his legs kicking more and more feebly as long threads of bubbles looped from their mouths. Her breath, it seemed, lasted longer than his. A deep roar sounded in his ears, like an inner alarm, and all at once she had broken away and angled upwards.

He surfaced a few seconds behind her, forgetful of everything but the need for air. There was a moment of sweet relief as he took his first long breath, and then she was shaking him for all she was worth, her features distorted by a mixture of rage and despair.

'What the hell were you trying to do?' she shouted furiously, the volume of her voice reminding him again of the peril they were in. 'Drown me? Finish what those bastards started?'

Her hands were so tight about his throat that he couldn't answer, and she shook him again out of sheer frustration. 'The damned animal had already gone!' she continued no less desperately. 'In case you hadn't noticed, we're alone here! We're ... !'

He managed to break free and gasp out, 'Not alone ... the cave people!'

That quietened her, the shock of realisation replacing her anger. Together, their heads low in the water, they turned towards the sandbar, but thankfully it was empty, the man and woman having vanished back into the forest.

'D'you reckon they saw us?' Josie whispered fearfully.

'Hard to say,' he murmured, treading water to stay afloat. 'They may have run off when the animal charged the ship. If we're lucky they don't even know we're here.'

'What if we're unlucky?' she said, her voice cracking under the pressure of trying to sound calm. 'What if ... ?' She had to pause to collect herself. 'Supposing they saw the observation deck break up? What then?'

'That ... that may not be so good,' he admitted, his voice as unsteady as hers. 'They could be dangerous.'

Her immediate answer was to sink beneath the surface, as if hiding herself from prying eyes. She surfaced seconds later, her face a little paler, her hair slicked back by the drag of the water.

'You were the one who said they were human beings and not animals!' she whispered accusingly. 'So if they're like us, what is there to be worried about?'

'Being human doesn't necessarily make them like us,' he said, and even this whispered conversation sounded perilously loud to him now, his eyes making a frantic search of the shoreline. 'They're palaeolithic people. Early stone age. To them, we're ... we're ... '

'Aliens?'

'Kind of.'

'Oh, great! That's the best news so far! It wasn't enough just to be dumped here in the year dot. Now we have to beat off a bunch of savages, or at least hold them at bay until the ship comes back!'

'Shush!' he broke in as something slapped the water over to their right.

'What's that?' Her face had grown paler still.

'A fish maybe. But we're tens of thousands of years back in time. I haven't a clue what lived in these waters then.'

'God!' she groaned, and began swimming furtively towards the shore. 'I don't believe this is happening to me! I really don't!'

He followed close behind, periodically sinking beneath the surface to search the greenish water in their wake. Fortunately nothing rose from the depths – no snouted head or gaping jaws – and soon he felt the reassuring touch of sand beneath his feet.

They waded ashore in silence, as wary of the waiting forest as they had been of the lake, but again nothing emerged. The bluff loomed above them as before, though now its shadow reached nearly to the far side of the bay.

In the yellowish light of late afternoon they climbed the bluff, using its hanging fringe of vines to pull themselves up the steepest places. From the top they could see right across the lake which remained ominously empty. The only sign of movement was an arrow-shaped formation of birds that winged their way homeward through the fading day.

'Bastards!' Josie muttered again, and sank down despondently on the lip of the bluff.

They didn't speak for a while after that, too miserable to do more than sit there with the forest at their backs, drinking in the last of the sunlight which felt pleasantly warm after the chill of the lake.

'So why did they clear off and abandon us?' Josie said at last, as much resentment as anger in her tone now.

Ivan shrugged, already sensing where her questions would lead and wishing she would keep quiet. 'It was emergency procedure,' he admitted grudgingly. 'They had no option.'

'How d'you mean, no option? We were passengers, for God's sake! It was their duty to look after us!'

'It's all set out in the regulations,' he explained. 'You should have taken time to read them.'

'Quite the little expert, aren't we?' she said mockingly. 'Well, go on then, what do these precious regulations have to say?'

'That if there's damage to the ship's hull, the automatic pilot kicks in. The main thing is to prevent any contamination from outside. Bugs and germs and stuff from the past that might ... '

'Hang on a minute.' She waved aside the rest. 'Are you telling me they left us behind because we've been contaminated by direct contact with this place?'

'Something like that.'

'But they *will* come back for us, right?'

'I expect so.'

'Yeah.' She nodded, as if to reassure herself. 'They're probably rigging up an isolation chamber right now. How long d'you reckon it'll take for them to get back here? Another hour maybe?'

It was the question he had been trying to avoid ever since they had waded ashore; and now, forced to confront it, he couldn't help shivering slightly.

'Oh no, don't tell me we have to spend the night in this dump!' she groaned, misinterpreting his silence.

Already the sun hovered perilously close to the horizon, and he stood up in an effort to still the sudden trembling in his limbs.

'I think maybe you're overlooking something,' he said. 'The trip itself doesn't take any time at all. Not clock time. Technically speaking they can choose to arrive here whenever they please. It's just a question of programming. They could have reappeared a split second after they'd left if they'd wanted to.'

'So why didn't they?'

'There could be lots of reasons.'

'Such as?'

He hesitated, and then took the plunge. 'The ship may have been badly damaged in the collision.' There, he'd said it, and he wiped clammily at his forehead. 'It may not even have made it home.'

'It didn't look too badly damaged to me,' she objected, refusing to share his gloom. 'It lost one of its observation decks, that's all. Anyway, it isn't the only ship the Company owns. They could have sent out another one. They're sure to have some kind of emergency drill – you know, a rescue team or something, all ready and waiting in case a ship doesn't turn up.'

'I didn't think of that,' he admitted.

'So think about it now,' she said impatiently. 'What else could be keeping them?'

'Nothing, unless ... ' He paused as a particularly unwelcome idea occurred to him.

'Unless what?'

He had to take a calming breath before going on. 'Unless they have no way of programming in exact times of arrival. I don't know how precise their instruments are.'

'You mean they could be an hour or two out? Or even a day?'

'Maybe a lot more than that,' he said in a small voice.

She stood up and took him roughly by the shirt. 'Are you talking in months? Years?'

'I just don't know!' he very nearly wailed, and watched in despair as the sun dipped below the horizon and long shadowy fingers reached across the water from the distant shore.

She let him go and stepped away, her expression half hidden by the falling dusk. 'I see. For all we know they may be out there now, searching the time routes.'

'It's possible.'

'I'd say that's a bit like looking for a needle in a haystack, wouldn't you? I mean, how do you go about finding just two people when you're not even sure what year they're stranded in?'

He had no answer to that, and she gave a forced and bitter laugh.

'Well, let this be a lesson to you,' she said recklessly. 'Don't get involved with people as rich and powerful as my mother. Follow their lead and you'll end up in a godforsaken hole like this, with nothing but a tribe of savages to keep you company.'

She stopped short as the sharp crack of a breaking twig sounded from further up the hillside.

Ivan, responding instinctively, had dropped into a low crouch.

'What was that?' Josie demanded, looking so conspicuous in the failing light that he tugged her down beside him.

'Listen!' he whispered, and past the steady hum of insect noise they heard it – the furtive tread of someone or something, moving slowly through the forest towards them.

3

With the way straight ahead blocked off, they took the only escape route open to them, and that was to climb down the sheer side of the bluff. In the thickening dusk it proved harder than they had bargained for. Twice Ivan grabbed at slender vines that broke away in his hands; and when he was still several metres from the ground he lost his grip completely and fell headlong, crashing into Josie directly below.

With a swish of breaking stems and a great splash they landed in the shallows together.

'You trying to get us killed or something?' Josie hissed fiercely, and scrambling clear she waded through the shallows to the narrow strip of sand that bordered the bay.

By then it was all but dark, the edge of the forest like a black wall that warned them off. On the other hand there was nothing to be gained by staying on the beach. With the lake at their backs they were too exposed, too obvious a target for any creature with passable night vision; and already there were signs of movement up on the bluff, the silhouetted trees stirring suggestively. A formless shape rose against the eastern sky, and with one accord they ducked their heads and pushed through the outer fringe of bushes into the forest.

The utter blackness of it startled them both, and for the first few seconds all they could do was cling to each other.

Josie was the one who broke the spell. 'We can't go on meeting like this,' she murmured in a feeble attempt at humour, and one behind the other they groped their way forward.

The lie of the land was their only guide now, and through a process of trial and error they worked steadily up the slope – sometimes bumping into trees, at others catching their feet on coiled roots that sent them sprawling in the soft litter.

More than anything else it was the noise they were making which worried Ivan. And sure enough when next they paused to listen, there were definite sounds of pursuit: a rustle of leaves from below, followed by the same furtive tread as before.

'How the hell did I ever get into this?' Josie groaned, and plunged on, leaving Ivan to catch up as best he could.

Yet no matter how rapidly they pushed through the darkened forest, still the unseen presence dogged their heels. Desperately they changed direction, zigzagging up and down the slope in an erratic pattern, but that achieved nothing either. It was as if their pursuer had some prior knowledge of what they would do next because always, when they stopped to rest, it was there below them.

On one occasion it came so close that they heard its panting breaths and caught a whiff of unfamiliar body scent. That really spooked them, and they ran off through the flimsy undergrowth, with bushes and young saplings catching at their hair and clothes and leaving deep scratches on their exposed skin.

One of the giant forest trees finally halted their progress. Hand in hand they slammed into it and fell backwards, stunned. Ivan, struggling to clear his head, actually saw lights before his eyes as he stumbled to his feet.

'God, what is that thing behind us?' Josie moaned.

For the moment, however, Ivan was more worried by the illusion of flickering lights than by thoughts of pursuit. Even when he rubbed at his eyes the lights refused to disappear, dancing in the blackness. Wildly, he remembered stories of deaf people plagued by constant noises in their heads. Well, was this what it was like to be blind? To be forever haunted by visions of non-existent lights? And if he *was* truly blind, what chance would he have against ... ?

The renewed sound of padding footsteps brought him to his senses, and all at once he saw the lights for what they were.

'The Neanderthal camp!' he breathed, and groping for Josie in the dark he hauled her up beside him. 'Over there!'

She resisted feebly. 'What if they're the ones who're following us?'

'Then we've got nothing to lose.'

'But ... '

Another whiff of unfamiliar body scent drifted up through the trees, silencing her protest, and again they were running, across the slope this time, guided by the twinkling lights.

For all their terror they both stopped short of

entering the camp. Crouched just outside the last line of trees, they listened first for telltale sounds of pursuit. To their relief there were none – merely an unbroken clatter of insect noise; and at a deeper level altogether, the husky tones of a singing voice, the rise and fall of the notes not unlike the murmur of wind through the canopy.

Together they turned and peered into the camp itself. A small circle of people was seated about a central fire. Just one person stood in their midst – the same young woman they had seen down by the lake earlier in the afternoon – and it was she who was singing, in full throaty tones that somehow blended into the night. She accompanied the song with gestures as she acted something out. A scene of terror apparently, for she opened her eyes wide and pushed her hands outwards as though fending off some invisible enemy.

'What's she up to?' Josie breathed, her hand cupped about her mouth to prevent the words from carrying.

Ivan waited before answering. In the uncertain firelight there was something both grotesque and also oddly beautiful about the scene before him; the woman so graceful in everything she did, and yet so heavy and thick-limbed.

'I think she's acting out what she saw this afternoon,' he whispered in reply.

'So she *did* see the ship.'

'Not necessarily. It could be the animal she's singing about. Look, she's acting scared. And listen to her now.'

The woman's voice had taken on a low grunting tone, more animal than human, which rippled out past the fire and seemed to stir the forest into uneasy life. There was the merest hint of an answering grunt from somewhere in the outer dark – or was it just an echo of the woman's call? – and then the song came to an abrupt end as a man ran from the forest on the far side of the clearing.

'Waark!' he barked out, followed by a stream of word-like sounds, and Ivan recognised him instantly as the hunter who had accompanied the woman to the lake. Except that now his face and chest were streaked with sweat; and there was a wild-eyed look about him as he shook his spear in Ivan and Josie's direction and repeated the same warning as before, the waark-sound again standing out from the other words.

This time there was no doubt about the response from the dark – a snuffling half-growl that set the hairs tingling on the back of Ivan and Josie's necks.

The people in the clearing had drawn into a tight protective circle, with the warriors forming an outer ring, and the women and children clustered at the centre. A single figure stepped clear of the circle: a middle-aged woman draped in a garment made almost entirely of feathers. Feathers also decorated her long grey hair, together with animal teeth and fragments of shell and bone. Yet it was her face which commanded most attention – the great brow ridge accentuated by a thick band of red-brown ochre; similar bands of yellow encircled the eyes; while her mouth was outlined in a ghostly blue-grey. The overall effect was both compelling and terrifying, especially there in the pool of shadowy light cast by the fire, where she looked more like some bird spirit risen from the earth than a creature of flesh and blood. And Ivan and Josie, despite their fear of the outer dark, drew back from her in awe.

Reaching inside her feathery robe, she produced a length of bone, yellow with age. She held this towards the fire as though she intended tossing it into the flames, but then shook it threateningly in the direction of the forest. Three times she performed this ritual, which ended with a sharp bark of command.

Again there was a snuffling grunt from the shadows, so perilously close to where Ivan and Josie crouched that they flattened themselves to the ground. An instant later, with the faintest of rustlings, the creature was gone. They didn't actually hear it withdraw, but now they could sense the emptiness of the forest immediately behind them.

The people in the clearing must also have sensed it, for with a roar of approval and much stamping of feet they pushed forward to the outer limits of the clearing, defying the night. Glancing up from where he lay in the twiggy undergrowth, Ivan could see the triumphant glint in their eyes; detect a sweaty tang of fear as they raised their arms in victory.

'Waark!' they chanted, 'Waark!' But now it was directed not at themselves. Clearly it was intended as a warning to whatever lurked within the forest. Take care, they seemed to be saying. Approach this clearing at your peril.

Their warning once given, they soon drifted back past the fire to the caves which showed as black openings in the huge boulders that blocked off the clearing's upper edge. Only the young woman and her ageing warrior companion lingered in the firelight – she, to perform a brief shuffling dance, her bare feet raising powdery spurts of dust as she moved around the fire and also disappeared.

Alone, the warrior moved to the centre of the

clearing and sat cross-legged on the bare ground, his spear resting upright against his shoulder. In that attitude, with his mane of hair fallen about his shoulders and his heavy features curiously expressionless, he reminded Ivan of a primitive carving he had seen once; an ancient talisman set there to guard against the untold evils of the night.

Silently Josie crawled up beside Ivan and pressed her mouth to his ear.

'Shouldn't we clear out while we've got the chance?'

His only answer was to glance across his shoulder at the murky backdrop of the forest.

'Yeah, I see what you mean,' she responded, and made a brave attempt to recapture her typically cool manner. 'It's like being caught between a rock and a hard place.'

He shook his head. 'No,' he murmured, his eyes never leaving the man in the clearing, 'I feel safer here. These people are survivors.'

'People?' she took him up quietly. 'Who are you kidding? Look at that goon over there. At the face on him. He's only one step removed from all the other animals in this damned place. Me, I'm out of here the first chance I get.'

For all her talk, however, she made no attempt to move off. Instead she snuggled down in the undergrowth – she, as much as Ivan, reassured not just by the nearness of the firelight, but also by the stony-faced figure seated some twenty or thirty paces away.

More than once in the course of the next few hours Ivan parted the undergrowth to satisfy himself that the man was still there. On each occasion the fire had burned a little lower, the night had grown a little cooler. At the very last, some time around midnight, the fire had subsided to a dull red glow; and by then Josie had drifted into an uneasy sleep, her body twitching spasmodically as she relived, in dreams, the terrors of the day. Yet still the man continued his vigil, as immoveable as the night itself.

Or so it seemed to Ivan. 'Waark,' he muttered, in imitation of the man, as though that one shared word could somehow bring them closer. And lulled by the simple sound of it, he also succumbed to weariness and slept.

4

They awoke chilled to the bone and soaked by fine rain that drifted through the canopy and whispered against the surrounding foliage.

In the uncertain light of early dawn the forest looked the least inviting of places, its bright greens reduced to a uniform grey, the column-like trunks of the trees stained black by the mist and rain. The clearing was now empty, the sentinel having also taken refuge in the caves. The only evidence of the Neanderthals' presence was a feeble rag of smoke which rose from the burned-out fire and mingled with the mist drifting between the trees.

'If hell exists,' Ivan groaned, 'this must be it.'

Numb from cold and stiff from sleeping on the hard ground, he and Josie rose groggily to their feet. Like the forest, they seemed to have been transformed by the darkness and rain. Their faces were drawn, their clothes mud-spattered, their arms crisscrossed with scratches.

'Talking of hell,' Josie observed in a whisper, 'you look as if you've just spent the night there.'

'People in glass houses ... ' Ivan began, but she immediately held a finger to her lips.

It was a timely warning for only seconds later someone drew aside a crude curtain of skins covering one of the cave entrances. Before anyone could appear Ivan and Josie had scuttled off into the misty grey morning.

Finding their way back to the lake wasn't difficult. The slope of the hillside was signpost enough, and in less than ten minutes they were again perched on the headland that jutted out on the western side of the bay. It was the obvious place for them to hide: its thick bushes and vines protected them from prying eyes, while its height gave them an uninterrupted view of the lake. They even managed to find a tiny nook in the lee of a craggy tree, and there, reasonably protected from the drifting rain, they set themselves to wait.

'To think how I used to scorn breakfast!' Josie said through chattering teeth. 'Right now I'd kill for a plate of bacon and eggs. What about you?'

When Ivan didn't answer, she nudged impatiently at him with her shoulder.

'Come on,' she urged, as if purposely trying to irritate him. 'You look a morning kind of person. What would that doting old aunt of yours be busy cooking for you?'

'I get my own breakfast if you must know,' he answered shortly. 'Anyway, this isn't the time to start thinking about food.'

'Why? Because there isn't any? Or because we may have a long wait ahead of us?'

'There's just no sense in it,' he said doggedly. 'It'll only make us feel worse.'

'Not nearly as bad as we'll feel tomorrow though,'

she insisted, continuing to niggle at him. 'If we're still here, I mean. We'll be really hungry by then. And hungrier still in a few days' time. Maybe hungry enough to start acting like those primitives up there.'

He rose to his knees, thoroughly unsettled by her. 'Look, just leave it alone, okay! The ship'll arrive soon. You'll see.'

'And if it doesn't?'

'It *has* to.'

'Yeah, but what if it doesn't?' she pressed him. 'What's your big plan of action? You're the one who read all about this period. What do you mean to do?'

He was aware that he was being tested, but still he couldn't help the tears starting to his eyes.

'I don't know,' he confessed miserably, and sank back down. 'I haven't a bloody clue.'

If he had been expecting sympathy, he was soon disappointed.

'I don't believe this,' she responded with a sigh. 'Of all the people I could be marooned with, why does it have to be a ... ?'

Before she could finish he was on his feet, intending to march off into the forest; but as he turned away he caught a flash of movement at the corner of his eye. He thought for a second it was the ship, waiting for them down in the bay, and he very nearly cried out with joy. Then he pulled aside a sodden bough and saw the thing for what it was: a raft of saplings, buoyed up with bladders, being pushed out through the shallows by a group of Neanderthals.

They sang as they worked, a rhythmic song which continued even after they were clear of the bay, the dip of their scooped paddles keeping time to the rise and fall of their voices. A second craft soon followed, the two vessels creeping further and further out into the lake until they were lost in the haze of rain. Only the song persisted. Amazingly cheerful on that dank morning, it sounded clear across the dawn-still waters, a timely reminder that this was not wholly a place of despair.

'I can tell you this much,' Ivan said quietly, taking courage from the sound. 'We're not going to die here. Somehow we'll manage to survive.'

'Yeah, but how?'

He thought quickly, trying to translate his change of heart into practical terms. 'The Neanderthals are successful hunters,' he said with sudden determination. 'We'll steal from them if we have to.'

'From them!' She pulled a face. 'You can count me out. I'd rather starve.'

'We'll see about that,' was all he said, and again settled beside her, the two of them huddled together in an attempt to keep warm.

By mid-morning the sky had begun to clear; and by early afternoon they were warm and dry, basking in bright summer sunlight. Through the dazzle of the day they could see the fishermen far out on the lake, their stocky figures periodically stooping as they thrust long spears into the water. Most of the time they were unsuccessful, their efforts greeted by silence. Only occasionally was there a flash of silver as a hunter held aloft a fish, followed by a roar of approval from his companions.

'It looks as though some things never change,' Josie observed, and shrugged contemptuously as the men's voices again rang out through the stillness of the day.

'Meaning what?'

'Well, listen to them. To the racket they're making. Doesn't it remind you of the boys' day out at the footy?'

Ivan listened hard to the last of the shouts. There was a raucous element of triumph in the voices it was true, but also something else. An air of celebration, and of childlike joy, which he had never thought to hear in the voices of grown men.

'They just sound happy to me,' he murmured, and felt a sudden and unexpected pang of envy.

'Happy!' Josie scowled at the glittering waters of the lake. 'Any cretin can laugh. Personally I don't see much to laugh at around here.' She gave Ivan a sharp probing glance. 'We're stuck in this primeval dump, aren't we? Be honest.'

'I wouldn't say that,' he hedged.

'What *would* you say?'

'The ship'll find us,' he insisted, trying hard to keep the doubt from his voice. 'They need time, that's all.'

'Time!' She gave a snort of dismal laughter. 'It's the one thing they've got plenty of. Not us though. We're running out of time fast.' She indicated the towering forest at their backs. 'What chance do we have against that? Sooner or later something in there's going to get us. That's if we don't starve to death first!'

The mere thought of starvation caused Ivan to cast longing eyes towards the rafts. The men on board had given up fishing for the day and were now paddling their catch back towards the shore. As they passed slowly beneath the bluff the two watchers had a clear view of them – of their beetle brows and ragged skin clothes and hulking hands and feet. They were still singing softly amongst themselves, a lilting melody which again seemed to blend with the mood of the day.

Having beached the rafts, they dragged them into

the cover of the forest and set about the business of gutting and scaling their catch, which they did with flint knives. Before they had finished, a small party of women and children emerged from the forest, led by the middle-aged woman in her cloak of feathers.

She appeared less forbidding than she had the night before, yet still there was something awesome about her. Her decorated face, her long hair with its array of shells and teeth and bones, retained some of their other-worldly quality despite the brilliant sunlight. Advancing on the hunters, she pointed to the distant reaches of the lake as though drawing attention to some invisible object hidden by the glare. Then she stretched both arms out before her, held them quite still in an act of invocation, and finally flung her hands up to the sky. There was an answering 'Aah!' from her audience, and she repeated the same miming ritual a second and a third time, always with the same response.

'What's going on?' Josie hissed. 'Is the ship out there or something? Can she see it?'

Ivan shook his head, sensing what the woman was about. 'I think she's acting out the ship's disappearance,' he whispered.

'So they *did* see it!'

'Yeah, but maybe not yesterday. Judging by the way they're carrying on, the ship's a fairly regular visitor. From their point of view it may have been coming here for years.'

'Don't say that,' Josie whispered bleakly. 'Not years! If the time route's that broad the ship'll never locate us.'

She fell silent as the ageing hunter who had stood sentinel the night before suddenly swung around and gazed in their general direction. For one terrible moment it seemed that he must have heard them, and they both froze behind their flimsy screen of foliage.

'Oh God!' Josie breathed.

Ivan, crouched dead-still in a pool of sunlight, felt a cold trickle of sweat snake slowly down his back.

Yet apparently the hunter had been distracted only by a bird calling from the treetops; for with a half-smile of recognition he soon turned his attention back to the shaman-like figure of the woman who now pointed to the morning's catch.

At a word of command from her, the biggest of the gleaming fish was taken from the rest and held up towards the sky, its body turned from side to side so that it flashed silver in the sunlight.

'What are they doing now?' Josie muttered, mystified.

Ivan, however, had again sensed the woman's purpose. 'The fish reminds them of the ship. They're the same shape and colour. And look at that.' He nodded to where one of the warriors had taken the fish and placed it on a slab of rock at the water's edge. 'They're leaving it there as a sign.'

'A sign of what?'

Ivan shook his head. 'I'm not sure. Maybe it's to entice the ship back.'

'Or to keep it away,' Josie suggested ominously.

'Yeah, that too.'

Whatever the reason for their offering, the Neanderthal people began filing back into the forest, obviously satisfied with their day's work. As always it was the ageing warrior who brought up the rear. Before leaving the beach he paused, glanced questioningly at the surrounding scene – as if probing the rocks and trees, willing them to give up their secrets – and then with a dissatisfied frown he also stepped from view.

'The bastard knows we're here!' Josie said in a shocked voice, and flopped down in the wispy grass.

'I doubt it,' Ivan said. 'He'd have come after us if he'd known.'

'Then why did he look round like that?'

'He's a hunter. That's what these people were ... *are*, I mean. They know how to read the signs. He probably feels that something's wrong, but he's not sure what.'

'So how long till he finds out? Till he realises we're here and tracks us down?'

Ivan shrugged uncomfortably. 'Hard to say. We haven't used their paths, and in any case last night's rain would have washed most of our footprints away. So as long as the ship locates us in the next day or two we should be ... '

'Yes of course, the ship!' Josie interrupted, and stood up. 'That's the answer. If the Neanderthals can be made to believe that it's paid them another visit – you know, that it's maybe picked up anybody it may have left behind – there won't be much for them to get suspicious about. As far as they're concerned everything'll be back to normal.'

'How can we convince them of something that hasn't happened yet?' Ivan asked cautiously.

'Easy.' She pointed at the fish on its slab of rock. 'That's a kind of offering, right?'

'I suppose so.'

'Well, if it disappears they'll assume the offering's been accepted. Even brutes like them can work that out. They'll think the ship's been back to settle unfinished business. It's what I'd believe, wouldn't you?'

'Not necessarily. An animal could take the fish just as easily.'

'No way,' Josie replied, with a show of confidence Ivan would have given almost anything for. 'Animals leave tracks behind, and this time there won't be any. Watch, I'll show you.'

Before Ivan could stop her, she had slithered down to the water and begun wading across the bay. She reached the slab of rock without once setting foot on dry land, and minutes later she was back, flinging the fish onto the ground between them.

'There, the ship's been and gone,' she said triumphantly. 'All we have to do is bury the evidence.'

She was already scooping a hole in the dark soil when Ivan reached into his pocket and pulled out a small Swiss army knife. 'I have a better idea,' he said quietly, and opened the main blade. 'We can eat the evidence.'

'What! Raw?' She gave him a disgusted look.

'I read once that people will eat just about anything after a few days without food,' he said, and made his first cut into the side of the fish.

Yet for all his brave words he was taken aback by the way the silvery exterior parted to reveal the bloody flesh within.

'Yuk!' Josie exclaimed, and backed off. 'I'll wait a day or two more if you don't mind.'

He made his second cut and eased a sliver of raw flesh off the bone. He had to admit it didn't look at all appetising. On the other hand he was seriously hungry. There was an unpleasant hollow in the pit of his stomach, and ever since early morning his mind had kept veering back to the subject of food no matter how hard he had tried to think of other things. He looked again at the bloody fragment on the knife blade, braced himself, and was about to raise it to his lips when Josie reached out and stopped him.

'Maybe you shouldn't.'

'Why not? We have to eat something.'

She wiped hungrily at her mouth. 'Yeah, but not that,' she said, and pointed at the scrap of meat. 'In any case maybe it would be better if we didn't . . . you know.'

It was the first time Ivan had seen her hesitate or look really unsure of herself.

'Didn't what?' he prompted her.

She let out a nervous laugh. 'I was just thinking that it might be risky to eat anything at all while we're here.'

'Because of disease, d'you mean?'

'No, not that.' She waved aside the idea. 'Before we left, my parents were talking about something called the . . . the butterfly or the beetle effect. I was only half listening so I'm not certain of the actual title, but it's a scientific theory which says that any changes to the past alter the future. Have you heard of it?'

Ivan nodded. 'And you think that eating this fish might alter *our* future? Make it impossible for us to get back?'

She gave him a sickly smile. 'Something like that. Or . . . or worse.'

'Worse how?'

She turned away, as though unwilling to let him see her face as she made her next admission. 'When you were cutting the fish it struck me that . . . that just by being here we may already have changed everything. And maybe that's why . . . ' She paused and took a deep breath. ' . . . that's why they haven't come back for us. Because they can't. Because the future isn't the same as when we left. There may not be any ships. People may not even have discovered the time routes, not in the future as it exists now.'

'Listen.' He pulled her round to face him. 'I know the theory you're talking about, and it's not really scientific. It's based on a science fiction story, that's all. I haven't read it, but it's something about a time traveller who crushes a tiny bug back in the past. That small change multiplies through the years, pushing the future into new paths.'

She gazed straight at him. 'So it's only a story? It isn't true?'

'People thought it might be true at first,' he admitted, 'when they began exploring the time routes. But they soon discovered that the stream of time can't easily be deflected. Small changes don't make any difference to it. The past absorbs them and everything stays the same.'

'And big changes?' she queried. 'What about them?'

'It all depends how big.'

'What about our being here all this time? Is that important enough to make a difference?'

'I wouldn't think so.'

'Eating this fish then,' she insisted, 'or anything else that's edible. What about that?'

'No, it's like crushing a bug – the same as in the story – nothing more. Think about it, the ship probably kills tiny life forms every time it lands here.'

But he could see she wasn't convinced.

'So what would be a big change? The death of a human? Such as one of us dying in this place?'

'Yeah, that might cause a few ripples,' he conceded.

'Well, I don't see it that way,' she responded. 'Why

should we be more important than a fish? What makes us so special? If you ask me we'll be just as much at risk once we start eating things. If we act as if we belong here, then this is where we'll end up. There'll be nowhere else for us to go.'

'You certainly won't go anywhere else if you starve yourself to death,' he pointed out. 'Our first duty is to stay alive, and to do that we have to eat.' He held the piece of fish out towards her. 'Look at it. Do you seriously believe this is going to change the course of time?' And to show how confident he was, he put it into his mouth and tried to swallow – tried, but failed, because the raw taste made his stomach rise and his mouth fill with saliva.

'Phaugh!' He spat it onto the ground and wiped a hand across his mouth. 'You're right about one thing anyway. I'm not hungry enough yet for raw fish.'

She didn't laugh as he might have expected. Already she was deepening the hole she had begun earlier, her face unusually pensive.

'It's not a question of hunger,' she said, tossing the fish into the hole and covering it with earth and grass. 'It's a question of belonging. If we give ourselves to this world – if we start eating and acting as though we're a part of it – it'll absorb us. We'll become people of this past, not of the future. This'll be the only home we can claim for ourselves.'

'Yeah, you could be right,' Ivan said vaguely, too worried about their immediate situation to go on arguing, and for perhaps the hundredth time that day he scanned the lake, searching in vain for a glimpse of silver.

He was still searching those outer reaches some hours later when, in the early evening, several Neanderthal women descended to the lake to collect water. Excited by the disappearance of the fish they ran hooting back to camp and were soon followed down by the rest of the small community. Gathered on the fringes of the lake they burst into song and began to enact some form of ceremony which suddenly broke off as the ageing warrior raised his voice in what had become a familiar warning.

'Waark!'

Unlike the rest of his people, he had left the shore and waded knee deep into the water where he gazed intently at the sandy bottom.

'He's spotted your footprints,' Ivan hissed.

'He can't have. They'll have been washed away by now.'

'There'll still be traces. Like I said, these people were great hunters. They're skilled in reading signs.'

Ivan and Josie fell silent as two other warriors waded into the lake. Shading their heavy brows against the setting sun, they also inspected the area around the rock and seemed to come to the same conclusion as their companion for they barked out similar warnings. One particularly broad-shouldered young man jerked his spear up in an attacking stance and swept it slowly around the whole curve of the bay as though daring whatever lurked there to show itself. Then, with none of their former excitement, the whole community filed quietly back into the forest.

'Damn that old fool!' Josie muttered as the last of the people disappeared. 'Now they *know* someone's here. They'll probably be out looking for us tomorrow.'

'I'm not so sure about that,' Ivan said. 'They seemed pretty scared to me.'

'The young one didn't seem scared. Not when he

pointed his spear in this direction. You don't have to be Einstein to guess what he'd do to us given the chance.'

'He didn't look very friendly,' Ivan half agreed, 'but he's a lot less threatening than other things I can think of. The animal that stalked us last night, for instance.' He saw Josie shudder at the memory and he went on quickly. 'It'll be dark soon. I don't want to get caught out here again. Like it or not the Neanderthal camp is still the safest place around.'

She nodded reluctantly, but before they could descend from the bluff there was a stirring in the forest and a number of giant shapes lumbered onto the beach. In size and appearance they resembled the modern elephant, except that their tusks were far more weapon-like – long and straight, jutting before them like spears.

'They could be what attacked the ship,' Josie whispered, so softly that she was sure she wouldn't be heard; yet still the keen hearing of the lead animal picked up the sound, for it raised its head and scented the breeze, its tusks gleaming. For several long minutes it held that stance – the sun, meanwhile, dipping towards the horizon – and only when it was satisfied that all was well did it allow the herd to plunge into the shallows.

Crouched on the nearby bluff, Josie and Ivan hadn't dared to move until then. Now, under cover of the splashing and sighing from below, they stole silently inland. But already, in a last burst of light, the sun had sunk from view; and with a suddenness they were unprepared for, the night descended, falling upon the forest like a pall.

Here, in the deep shadow of the trees, it was altogether too dark, too forbidding. Wherever they looked they were met by a wall of inky blackness. And even as they groped their way forward, even before the first threatening snarl issued from the darkness ahead, they knew in their hearts that they had delayed for too long and that the Neanderthal camp, apparently so near, lay beyond their reach.

5

'Shush!' Ivan whispered, the sweat standing out on his forehead despite the coolness of the evening.

The snarl sounded once again, and Josie's hand tightened on his.

'This way,' she murmured, her voice as unwavering as her touch; and numb with fright he allowed her to lead him back down the slope.

Except there was no escape in that direction either, not with the elephants still wallowing in the shallows. When Ivan and Josie stopped to listen, they could hear pig-like grunts and splashes drifting up from the lake's dusky shores.

At the thought of being trapped there in the dark, Ivan felt a rush of panic. Where now? he tried to say, but the words refused to come out, his mouth bone-dry, his lips too stiff to move freely. And in the midst of his terror it occurred to him that words were useless in this ancient world. They had lost their power to shape events. At that particular moment he would gladly have given all the words he would ever utter for . . .

For what?

Desperately he groped for some saving idea, but all that came to mind was an image of the ageing warrior, spear in hand, and of the feather-cloaked woman shaking a bone at the surrounding dark. Yet how could they possibly help from up there in the camp which now seemed star-distances away? Light years from this all-pervading darkness and terror. In another universe almost, one characterised by warmth, light, and above all, safety.

The animal snarl and Josie's voice broke through his despairing thoughts together, vying for his attention.

'Come on, this is the only way,' she whispered hoarsely, and pushed him against something hard and rough. Immovable.

Dimly he registered what it was – a tree, one of the giants that reared above the forest floor – but in his panic-stricken state he had no idea what she expected him to do next.

'Climb, damn you!' she demanded, so loudly that there was a rumbled reply from the surrounding dark – the wordless threat of that other voice rendering him more helpless than ever.

'Do it!' Josie screamed into his ear, and slapped him hard across the face. 'Now!' All the weight of her body pressing him upwards.

Somehow he managed to respond. With unwieldy limbs he reached for handholds, found them, heaved himself up, and reached for more, all the while dogged by the dreadful certainty that something – some unnameable beast of the night – was about to leap upon him; to tear him from his precarious hold on life and hope, and send him plummeting down to the unforgiving earth.

He glimpsed a ravening, tooth-edged mouth, imprinted there in the waiting dark, and then Josie's voice again broke through.

'Faster!' Pushing at him from below, her frantic hands urging him on and up. 'Faster! The bloody thing's right behind us!'

He could hear claws scrabbling against the flaky bark of the tree. So close! And all his panic issued into a sudden storm of energy. He felt a new kind of strength surge through his arms and legs, impelling him upwards, to where a bough curved out from the main trunk.

How high was he now? he wondered fleetingly. But it hardly seemed to matter because he was on his feet, *running* out along the bough! To a point in the outer dark where the bough dipped and groaned beneath his weight and the solid feel of the tree gave way to a smother of leaves and twigs that broke in his hands.

One final blundering step and the bough was gone. Only a frothy mass of foliage sustained him – that and the terror inspired by another of those low snarls, followed by the pad of soft feet on the bough at his back.

'No!' he sobbed, and reached for the night itself; for the outer blackness that defined this place. His arms arced across a gulf of emptiness. His body pitched outwards and down. His hands clutched on nothing until, with a gasping rush, he encountered the swish and tangle of more leaves, more twigs, that snapped and tore and eventually held as he floundered amongst them.

His outstretched fingers located a thickish branch and he hung on; anchored himself to this stable part of the night until he had regained his breath. Through his hands he could feel the tug and sway of the tree, and he took courage enough from the solid feel of it to inch his way along the branch. He reached a fork and wedged himself into it, listening now, past the sound of his own heart, for another of those throaty growls.

Thankfully it reached him from some distance away, much fainter than before and accompanied by a fresh scrabble of claws. By the sound of things the animal was descending the tree. The thud of a heavy body striking the ground confirmed his suspicion. And after that nothing but the insect-shrill silence of the forest at night.

'Josie?' he dared to whisper after some ten minutes had passed, and was answered from higher up and well over to his left.

'I'm here. You all right?'

'Kind of.'

'You must be on one of the outer limbs like me.'

'Yeah, I think so.'

'Well, just stay put. We seem to be safe where we are.'

Yes, Ivan thought dismally, but where were they? And how long could they withstand the trials of this ancient place? He felt that another fright like this was more than he could bear. Yet still they had the whole night before them, and after that another day of uncertainty, with no relief in sight. Just a slowly fading hope that the ship would find its way back to one particular day in all the many millions of days that lined the time route.

'Don't worry, they won't leave us here for ever,' Josie whispered, as if able to read his thoughts. 'If we hang on they'll get to us.'

For the present at least, hanging on was something he had to do literally, because every movement of the tree threatened to dislodge him. He tried wedging himself more firmly between the forked branches, but they were too flimsy and eased apart under the pressure. Fully alert, and with both arms wound about the nearest branch, he was reasonably safe, even when an occasional gust of wind rippled through the canopy. What worried him were the hours to come, when he would have grown too tired to cling on. And what if he were to doze off!

It was that prospect which prompted him to loosen his belt and rebuckle it around the branch. Fastened like that to the tree, with no room to move and no way of changing position, he was soon in an agony of discomfort; but at least he was secure, whatever happened, and as the hours passed he clung to that one certainty as much as to the tree itself.

From time to time he heard Josie groan softly to herself high above him, and he assumed that she was also having a bad time. Periodically, too, she called down; brief whispered messages or enquiries, intended more to ease the sense of loneliness than anything else.

At one point she whispered, 'You okay?' and to his amazement she sounded sleepy.

How could she fall asleep so soon? he asked himself. But less than an hour later he also drifted off, sinking into a dream-plagued sleep in which he fled endlessly from nameless horrors.

⋆   ⋆   ⋆

He awoke to a world of grey light and drifting mist. Every part of him seemed to ache, and his first conscious movement sent pains shooting through his cramped limbs. Far more worrying, though, was the precariousness of his situation, for even in the dawn light he could see that he was perched at the outer extremity of the tree, on a branch that sagged dangerously. What's more, he was facing *towards* the main trunk, not away from it.

That puzzled him for a moment. He had no memory of turning back to face his terror. How on earth had he got into this position? Then, with a cold feeling in the pit of his stomach, he realised what had happened. In his panic he had leapt from one tree to another! There, higher up in the neighbouring tree, was Josie, still sound asleep; and nearer at hand was the bough he had leapt from, its foliage half torn away where he had crashed through.

A glance at the mist-wreathed ground far below told him how close he had come to death. Only by sheer good fortune had he landed on this present branch. Half a metre either way and he would have fallen into empty space. Luck, that had been the deciding factor. Blind chance.

Unless of course he was missing the point entirely! Was that possible?

A conversation he had had with Josie on the previous day came back to him. The stream of time, he had told her, can only be deflected by major changes. Well, what about his own death, would that have been important enough to alter the future? Or ... (He hesitated before continuing with the thought, the audaciousness of it unsettling him.) ... or was he somehow being protected by the stream of time itself? Could it be that his existence in the twenty-first century was so fixed, so established, that he couldn't possibly die here in the past? In which case this ancient world was powerless to harm him. It could merely threaten, like some caged lion. Finally, whatever they chose to do, he and Josie were immune to all its dangers. They truly *belonged* elsewhere, in another time and place; and for that reason alone, perhaps, it was inevitable that the ship *must* return, *must* rescue them.

But no, to think like that was tempting fate. If he opened himself to this distant past only to find that he was wrong, he would be defenceless. It was better by far to practise caution.

Still, even the faint possibility that he and Josie were destined to return to their own time served as a comfort. The grey morning seemed less desolate, his aching joints were more easily endured. Gritting his teeth, he unfastened his belt and made the hazardous climb along the branch to the main trunk of the tree; and that, too, tested him less than it might have done otherwise.

From there he called up to Josie, waking her. She yawned and gave him a sleepy, lopsided smile, her face half veiled by a tangle of hair.

'This isn't exactly my idea of five-star accommodation,' she said with a groan, and eased herself stiffly away from the branch she had been clinging to. 'Mind you, it beats the hell out of being eaten by some wild animal.' She gave a mock shiver. 'But speaking of wild animals, what *was* that thing chasing us through the dark?'

'Some kind of big cat, I expect, judging by the way it could climb.'

She pretended to laugh, only her eyes betraying her. 'Whatever it was, it certainly brought out the monkey in you. How did you get over there? Did you jump or something?'

'Look, about the way I panicked last night ... ' he began awkwardly, wanting to get his apologies over

51

with, but she refused to hear him out.

'Panic? I thought you were just saving your skin the same as me.'

'No, you were the one who did the saving,' he insisted.

She groaned once again, though not from discomfort. 'Let's not get into all that I-owe-you-my-life stuff. Please. I couldn't bear it this early in the morning.'

'It's true all the same.'

She clicked her tongue impatiently and began untangling her hair with the fingers of both hands. 'Listen, I tell you what we'll do. If you go down and make sure there's nothing nasty waiting for us at ground level, we'll call it quits. Debt repaid. Okay?'

He knew she was only humouring him, but could think of no ready answer, and he stared down through a haze of mist at the ground far below. When there was no sign of movement, he reached for a nearby vine and lowered himself hand over hand until his feet sank into the soft litter at the base of the tree.

Here, where the ground mist was at its thickest, dampening even the distant sounds of birdsong, the forest felt extraordinarily still, as if waiting breathlessly for the intrusion of the sunlight. As he glanced about him, he was aware also of a sombre beauty in the scene. The trees stood like watchful sentinels in the grey light, their upper branches like protective arms spread above him. And despite his night-time fears, he felt for the second time that morning that this place posed no real threat. Not ultimately.

'All clear,' he called, and minutes later Josie dropped to the ground beneath the neighbouring tree.

'You know something?' he told her. 'I have a good feeling about today.'

'I'm glad someone has.'

He shook his head. 'No, seriously. I have this feeling that everything's going to change for the better. Just wait and ... '

What made him stop was the Neanderthal hunter who stepped from the mist at Josie's side. As Ivan gasped and swung around, two other hunters appeared, each bearing a flint-headed spear.

'That's some feeling you had there,' he heard Josie mutter shakily.

Then someone grasped him from behind, someone with hands so strong that he winced under their pressure and stumbled forward to where, still half hidden by the mist, he could just make out the figure of the ageing warrior.

6

The mist swirled and parted as the warrior approached, his long hair beaded with tiny droplets. Close up, the skin of his face was etched by deep lines, like a wooden mask weathered too long in the wind and sun; and faint but intricate tattoos decorated the bony protuberances above his eyes. For several minutes he did nothing but examine the two captives, his eyes swivelling curiously from one to the other.

'What do you think this dumb bastard wants with us?' Josie breathed at last.

'Whatever it is, he's not dumb,' Ivan pointed out, for there was no denying the glint of intelligence in those deep-set eyes. 'If you ask me he's been onto us since yesterday, when he spotted your prints on the lake bed.'

'Well, you're the expert on these primitives,' Josie said. 'How do you suggest we ... ?'

She broke off as the broadest and fiercest of the young hunters grunted out a warning and cuffed her across the mouth.

'Hey! Cut that out!' she demanded, trying to stare him down, and received another light blow for good measure.

Ivan, too wary of the hunters' spears to intervene, thought for a moment that she was about to return the blow, her whole face flushed angrily; but the ageing warrior stepped forward and settled the matter, by placing a pacifying hand on the shoulders of Josie and the hunter alike. It was a curiously restrained gesture, as was his soft-voiced command. Ivan didn't understand the words themselves, but the tone suggested something like, 'That's enough, be still'.

'So what do you want from us?' Josie asked, challenging the warrior directly now, and he responded by pressing one hand to his heart and then pointing off through the mist-draped forest.

'I think he's offering us safe passage,' Ivan said.

'If it's so safe,' Josie objected, 'why the spears? I reckon it's a case of come with us or else.'

As if to show she was right, the young hunter frowned and prodded her in the side with his spear. A quick tentative jab, it wasn't intended to hurt: merely to indicate that he wanted her to move off.

'See what I mean,' she said with a false jauntiness that caused the young hunter to glare and prod at her again; and this time she followed the ageing warrior who led the way silently between the trees.

Ivan brought up the rear, flanked by two hunters, the strong animal smell of their bodies blocking out the freshness of the morning. He hadn't been prepared for them to smell quite so rank. Was this their natural body scent, he wondered, this less than human odour? But before he could decide, the Neanderthal camp came into view, the tall outcrop of rock visible between the trees.

Just before entering the clearing, the warrior paused briefly, pointed to a single footprint beside the path, and nodded at Ivan.

'What's he on about now?' Josie asked.

'He knows we were here the night before last.'

Josie shrugged. 'So he's the Sherlock Holmes of the ancient world. What do I care?'

She showed far less indifference some moments later, when they stepped into the clearing and were met by the enticing smell of baked fish. Ivan could see the fish themselves, laid out on hot stones that had been bedded into the coals of the central fire, and he would have rushed forward if the fierce young hunter hadn't raised his spear and barred the way.

'Hey!' Josie protested, and was also threatened with the spear, the young hunter glaring at her from a face even more heavily tattooed than the warrior's.

Forced to control his hunger, Ivan noticed then the presence of the shaman, her stocky figure wreathed in smoke from the fire. She alone occupied the clearing, the rest of the people clustered fearfully in the cave mouths. Dressed in her usual finery, and with her face freshly painted, she shuffled towards them in a half dance, singing hoarsely all the while.

'I suppose this is the floor show,' Josie began, and received more than a threat this time, the young hunter striking her so hard across the shoulders that she fell to her knees in the dust.

A nervous sigh rose from the assembled people, and the shaman, apparently emboldened by the hunter's action, shuffled nearer and pressed her thumb first to Josie's forehead, and afterwards to Ivan's. In each case she left behind a smear of clay.

That done, she turned and raised her face towards

the treetops, where the mist was rapidly dissolving in the early sunlight. As the last shreds of it tore and vanished, the moon became visible in the dawn-pink sky, just above the trees. There in the burgeoning morning it looked pale and worn, unreal almost, like some ghostly relic of the night. And even as the woman sang and watched, so the wind blew, the trees tossed their heads higher, and the moon slipped from view.

Straight away, as though to acknowledge its passage, the woman dipped her thumb into a tiny stone pot she was holding and marked the two captives with fresh clay, smearing it thickly across their brows.

'Is she crazy or something?' Josie muttered from the corner of her mouth.

But Ivan had already worked out what was going on. 'They saw the ship fly here,' he whispered in reply. 'They think we've come from the moon.'

'Then what's the clay for?'

'She's making us look like them. She's turning us into creatures of the earth.'

Only as he mouthed the words did he understand their full significance, and without further explanation he lowered himself to the ground and pressed his hands, his face, his whole body into the fine dust.

'Have you gone crazy too?' Josie hissed, but he ignored her, rising slowly to his feet with his skin and clothes now covered in a powdery coating.

It had exactly the effect he had hoped for. The people sighed once again, far less fearfully than before; and the woman turned towards the sunlight, stamped both feet in the same dust, and began what could only have been a victory dance.

As her voice lifted in song, Ivan determined to

complete the ritual for her – to offer final proof that he was indeed a flesh-and-blood creature. His mouth already running with saliva, he walked eagerly across the clearing, snatched up one of the fish, and crammed a handful of the flesh between his lips.

That first taste of food was like heaven. He was vaguely aware of people cheering and singing in the background, but for some minutes all he could do was eat, with a single-mindedness that blotted out everything else.

When at last he came to himself he was ringed by laughing people. On every side their heavy faces peered curiously into his. Through the throng he could see Josie, her eyes flickering hungrily from him to the fire.

He picked up one of the fish and held it out to her. 'Go on, take it,' he called above the surrounding noise.

She shook her head and advanced slowly through the dancing people. 'I don't want to be trapped here,' she said. 'I want to go home.'

'You will,' he promised, and meant it. 'One day the ship will come back for us, but we have to survive until then. If we don't eat we'll die.'

Again she shook her head, though she had begun to waver, her lips moist with longing as she gazed at the fish in his hands. 'It'd be like death anyway, to get stuck in this place, and if I start acting like I belong here, there'll be no going back.'

'It won't make any difference,' he assured her. 'Trust me.'

He held the fish out for the second time, and in spite of her hunger – in spite of having eaten nothing for nearly forty-eight hours – still she resisted him.

'I can't!' she wailed. 'It'll make me the same as

these other brutes.' She waved a hand at the people all around. 'Once I've shared their food, I'll be part of this. There'll be nowhere else to go.'

'What about me?' he challenged her. 'Am *I* stuck here now? Will *I* have to stay behind when you head out on the ship?'

It was the clinching argument, and all at once her resolve crumpled. Snatching the fish from his hand, she hunkered down and began cramming it into her mouth, eating with a desperation he had never witnessed in anyone before. Cries of encouragement rang out from the onlookers, but she merely hunched her shoulders, shutting them out, intent upon the shreds of flesh which she wolfed down.

She straightened slowly once the worst of her hunger had passed, an expression of utter dejection on her face. Try as he might, Ivan could find no trace in her of the haughty young woman who had confronted him on the steps of the ship, so long ago it seemed, in an unbelievably distant future.

'That's it then,' she said miserably, and wiped a greasy hand across her mouth. 'It's over. From now on this is all there is. This!' And she pointed to the towering forest, its canopy tipped with sunlight.

Part 2
THE CLAN

7

Ivan crawled from the cave a little after dawn. Hunched against the early morning chill, he drew the skin cloak around his shoulders and joined Josie and the clan at the central fire. Altogether they numbered barely a dozen souls, a small bedraggled group which looked especially down-at-heel at this time of day.

Having lived with them for over a month now, Ivan had grown used to their heavy features and ragged appearance. He and Josie hardly looked much better in their torn and stained clothing. They had even come to share the clan's distinctive body scent, which resulted from a heady blend of wood-ash, forest herbs, and animal fat, all worked together and then rubbed into the skin to ward off mosquitoes and other insect pests.

'Phooh!' Josie had complained at first, rejecting the fatty substance out of hand; but after being badly bitten by mosquitoes two nights later, she had changed her mind and smeared herself from head to toe.

Ivan glanced across at her now, at the way she

crouched, blinking sleepily, at the fire's edge. With her long-limbed body hidden by a skin cloak, and with her hair matted and uncombed, she could almost have passed for a true member of the clan. What set her apart wasn't so much her fine-boned features as her habitual scowl of discontent. For although she remained convinced that the ship would never return – that like it or not this was where they belonged for the rest of time – still she found it almost impossible to come to terms with her new existence.

'You call this a life?' she had complained bitterly on one occasion. 'In that case I'd rather be dead.'

In spite of that she struggled on, day by day, sustained more by anger and resentment than anything else.

Not so Ivan. Josie's brand of brooding anger was foreign to his nature. He was sustained at least partly by hope, because unlike Josie he clung to the belief that they would be rescued. Each day without fail he made trips to the lake on the off chance of sighting the ship. And always, after every disappointment, he told himself the same thing – 'Next time ... next time ... ' – refusing to give up his slender hold on the future.

Yet it wasn't hope alone that kept him going. For all its squalor, he had to admit to a secret fascination with this primitive world. So much about it caught and held his imagination. There was the fiercely guttural language which he was gradually beginning to understand, thanks to the patient teaching of various clan members. And more fascinating still were the many songs and dances performed around the fire. All had a rough vitality about them that he had never encountered in the safe, humdrum world of the twenty-first century. Here, each new dawn presented fresh challenges, not all of them pleasant (he had to admit that too), the hours ahead like an untold promise.

This present morning was no exception, though for the moment the clan was at rest.

As the sunlight finally pierced the canopy and speckled the dust at their feet, Kharno, the ageing warrior, picked up a stick and poked at the fish cooking slowly on the firestones.

'The waters have been plentiful this year,' he sighed. 'We will eat well when the winter comes.'

His son, Lheppo, frowned and rubbed irritably at his brow ridge, making the tattooed pattern stand out more clearly.

'Other clans will fare better,' he growled. 'When the snows begin to fall, they won't have two useless mouths to feed.'

Kharno clicked his tongue and nodded towards Ivan and Josie who were struggling to follow what was being said. 'These moon people aren't like us,' he chided his son gently. 'You've watched them. They're helpless, the same as children, and as with all children they should be seen as a blessing, not a burden.'

'They fell from the sky like rain,' Lhien added – she was Kharno's wife and the clan's shaman. She shook her head wonderingly, the tiny bone ornaments in her hair clinking softly together. 'It is not for us to question the rain, and neither should we question their presence amongst us. They are here, that is all. Think of them as a gift from the moon.'

'I would rather have the moon tears our mountain brothers gave us,' Lheppo retorted, and reaching inside his leather tunic he drew out a small droplet-shaped piece of once molten silver which he held lovingly in his palm. 'This is a true moon gift. A thing of unearthly beauty. Not like these ... these ... ' He flapped one dauntingly muscular hand in Ivan and Josie's direction. 'These creatures have no beauty. Look at them! At their puny limbs and ugly faces. Nor do they possess the skill and courage of our people. What good are they to us? The monkeys in the lowland forests are quicker to learn and more eager to please than these things from the sky.' To illustrate his point he shoved roughly at Josie, sending her sprawling in the dust. 'You, thing with no name, bring me food,' he ordered her.

Ivan, who had understood that last rough gesture more clearly than any of the words, readied himself for what would happen next. It was the same every morning. Always Lheppo and Josie ended by snarling at each other, or worse, nearly coming to blows.

Yet for once Josie didn't retaliate. Sloughing off her cloak, she rose submissively to her knees and made as if to scoop one of the cooked fish from the stones.

'You see, she learns,' Kharno murmured.

Even Lheppo seemed satisfied. With a grunt, he sank back on his heels, momentarily off guard.

That was when Josie acted. Rising and turning in a single motion, she snatched the silver droplet from Lheppo's hand and leaped across to the far side of the fire.

There was a shrill cry of delight from Tharek, one of the three children in the clan, followed by an angry roar from Lheppo.

'Give it back, moon-sprite!' he demanded – his voice suddenly in keeping with his name which, as far as Ivan could gather, meant something like Hunter of the Night.

66

Josie stared haughtily across the fire at him. 'You pathetic animal,' she said in English, 'I'll teach you to mess with me.' Then, more falteringly, in the language of the clan: 'This ... moon tear ... mine.' And as proof of ownership she closed her fist on the silver.

'Take care,' Kharno advised her in a whisper – also living up to his name which translated as The One Who Walks Softly.

It was sound advice because Lheppo immediately lunged across the fire. His great fists, however, merely closed on air. Josie, far quicker and more agile than anyone had expected, slipped beneath his groping hands, snatching a burning stick from the fire as she did so.

'Let's see how brave you are now,' she said, and waved the brand in his face.

He backed off a pace or two, his shoulders hunched and knotted, his eyes searching for an opening.

The whole clan by then was on its feet, the two young hunters and their wives grinning nervously. One of the nursing babies whimpered in fright and reached for its mother's breast; while Aghri, Kharno and Lhien's daughter, looked apprehensively from Lheppo's clenched fists to Josie's superior smile.

'Don't be a fool, Josie,' Ivan breathed. 'Give it back.'

'Like this, you mean?' she responded, and held the silver droplet out before her, only to jerk it away when Lheppo reached for it.

Incensed, he let out a choking cry and stepped around the burning stick. He almost had her then, his hands closing on her shoulders.

There was a sudden smell of burning as she jabbed the stick against his tunic, a cry of pain from him, and once more she had ducked and twisted free.

'Josie . . . !' Ivan began, and never finished.

'Whose side are you on anyway?' she sang out, retreating to the edge of the clearing. 'You want him to have it? Here, *you* give it to him.' And she tossed the droplet high in the air.

Ivan watched it arc upwards, a speck of purest gold as it caught the sunlight and seemed to hover above him. Then it was speeding downwards. He felt it slap into his open palm, slither out, and land with a faint plop in the dust. Where was it? Frantically he scrabbled on the ground, finding stones, pieces of bone and twig, everything but the droplet itself. Already Lheppo's heavy tread was audible above his own quick heartbeats; Lheppo's shadow there on the earth, darkening the spot where his fingers finally closed on the smooth shape of the silver.

'Leave him!' he heard Aghri cry out, and her shadow seemed to intertwine with Lheppo's.

He looked up, directly into the sunlight, and saw two silhouetted shapes struggling together. There was the sharp sound of a blow, a moan of pain, and the smaller of the shapes fell away and became Aghri, her shocked face almost hidden in a smother of hair. Lheppo, equally shocked, gazed down at her, an expression of utter disbelief distorting his heavy features.

Aghri flinched and scuttled out of reach. Lhien, meanwhile, swept off her cloak and stood bare-breasted in the sunlight, her eyes fixed upon Lheppo.

'You know the law,' she said accusingly. 'The clan is one family, and no member of that family must raise a hand against another.'

Lheppo inspected his blunt-ended fingers in wonderment. 'It was the hand that did it,' he protested.

'In my thoughts I was hitting the nameless thing.'

'Then the hand must pay,' Lhien replied, and plucking another brand from the fire she pushed it towards him.

He took the hot end without flinching and held on until a wisp of smoke rose from his charred fingers. 'The hand will remember,' he said at last, and let his arm fall to his side.

Wincing at what had just occurred, Ivan approached Lheppo. He expected the tattooed face to turn fiercely upon him, but Lheppo hardly registered his presence – even when Ivan pressed the silver droplet into his good hand.

'Here, it's yours,' he whispered. 'Keep it.'

Lheppo glanced down at the fragment of glistening metal and then looked across at Josie, seeking her out from all those present – his broad features strangely impassive, his eyes narrowed against the glare of sunlight.

Josie, hovering at the edge of the clearing, had flung her own stick aside in disgust. All her haughtiness had disappeared, her eyes locked onto Lheppo's. For a minute or so they might have been alone, everyone else silent, watchful, with just Josie and Lheppo staring at each other in wordless challenge.

Then with a breathy grunt Lheppo crumpled to his knees and squeezed both eyes shut. Two plump tears formed on his dark lashes and rolled down the hollows of his cheeks. They were tears of passion, there was no doubt of that, but Ivan could not have said what *kind* of passion – whether rage or pain or merely a bitter sense of defeat.

High in the trees a parrot screeched out a welcome to the new day, breaking the spell. Nearer at hand

Aghri whimpered and sidled closer to Ivan, seeking comfort from his presence. And as the clan settled around the fire to eat, it occurred to Ivan that if Josie were right – if they were destined to remain in this ancient world – then this morning's confrontation was a foretaste of what it truly meant to belong here, to be caught up in the life of the clan. A life as passionate as it was bewildering.

But no, he refused to accept this as his destiny. Josie could vent her life in anger and resentment if she wanted to. Let *her* become a victim of this passionate and bewildering place; let *her* be foolish enough to think she could take it on and win. As for himself, more than ever before he preferred to pin his faith on the ship; and ignoring his own hunger, ignoring Aghri's gentle pleas for him to sit and eat, he hurried from the clearing and ran headlong down the path that led to the lake.

8
·

No shimmering steel craft awaited him when he reached the shoreline. The lake was empty, the same as on every other morning, its wind-ruffled surface troubled by nothing larger than a pair of otters cavorting out there beyond the shallows. He had half known it would be like this even as he ran down the path, but still he felt a sharp pang of disappointment.

Where were their rescuers? What was keeping them? Was Josie perhaps right when she argued that their remembered future no longer existed – that their protracted stay here in the past had changed the future for ever?

On balance he couldn't bring himself to believe that. It didn't seem likely that his and Josie's absence from their own century was enough in itself to alter the whole temporal scheme. They simply weren't important enough. In all probability the ship was still out there somewhere, still searching for them in the long limbo of the time route. It *had* to be.

'Come, come, come, come,' he intoned, willing the ship to return – and realised with a guilty start that he was acting like Lhien who also resorted to spells and incantations at times of crisis. Well, he knew better than to believe in magic. He, after all, had the benefit of having lived in the future; of having experienced the real power of science. He *knew* that magic was so much mumbo jumbo.

Even so, there was no denying how comforting it was to sit at the water's edge and conjure the ship. To pretend that he had the power to will it into being. It was a way of combating his helplessness, of holding it at bay.

Maybe that was also why he derived such comfort from listening to Lhien's murmured songs and spells. She, too, was trying to control her unruly world; to bend it ever so gently to the clan's needs.

As always the thought of Lhien's songs gave him a feeling of inner warmth, of security. Which was odd considering how he had reacted less than half an hour earlier, back at the camp. Then, he had fled from the idea of being drawn into the life of the clan. Yet now, crouched on the sunwarmed spit of sand that thrust out into the lake, he visualised an even more disturbing possibility.

What if Josie and Lheppo's resentment of each other erupted into open conflict? Were that to happen, he and Josie might be cast out altogether. Already, in the eyes of the clan, they were creatures who had fallen from the moon, nameless people with no guiding spirit, no underlying personality. Forced to choose between such beings and one of their own, the clan might well decide to give them back to the moon, to reject them completely.

Ivan shivered at the prospect and huddled closer to the sand. To be utterly alone here! To have nothing and no one to protect them from the beautiful but sinister world of the forest. He shivered again, remembering their two nights of terror a month or more earlier, and glanced fearfully at the towering trees that crowded the lake's edge.

Previously he had made a point of visiting the lake in the company of one of the hunters. This morning, for the very first time, he had set out on his own. What's more, apart from the Swiss army knife in his pocket, he had come unarmed, with not even a club for defence.

Out on the lake there was a loud splash as the otters disappeared. In pursuit of fish? Or startled perhaps by some hint of danger? Nearer at hand a bird shrieked and flapped up towards the canopy. And suddenly alert to the sights and sounds of the forest, Ivan rose and turned to face the trees.

Behind him the otters surfaced with a hiss of breath, one of them cradling a mud crab in its paws. But that was of little reassurance to Ivan now. Having been awoken to the hidden dangers of this wooded hillside he wasn't sure whether to stay where he was, exposed on the open sand, or to make his way back to camp.

The bird shrieked again, a long warning note – as if to say, 'Beware!' – and without consciously intending to, Ivan found himself running. Along the open spit, his feet sinking nearly ankle deep into the sand, and up into the trees, where he lost his footing and fell. For two or three seconds he lay on the path, his pulse racing, listening to the creak and groan of the trees as they bent in the wind. Other, less identifiable sounds also filtered down through the wind-haunted silence, and he sprang to his feet and scrambled up the steepest portion of the path on all fours. Once on the flatter sections he sprinted for all he was worth, with the dappled sunlight pursuing him leopard-like through the leafy undergrowth.

His whole body damp with sweat, he burst into camp and sank to his knees before the fire. A fish had been left for him on the stones, but for the moment he was too unsettled to eat. From over near the cave Lhien eyed him thoughtfully and called Kharno who emerged soon afterwards.

'It is better to go armed than to tremble,' he advised Ivan softly, and drove a stone-headed spear into the ground beside him.

One of the young hunters, by the name of Orhnu, also emerged from the cave. 'Be like the other no-name,' he added with a toothless grin. 'Carry a weapon when you venture into the forest alone.'

The other no-name?

Ivan looked questioningly at Kharno. 'Where ... is she?' he asked, struggling with the guttural sounds of the words.

'You mean the moon woman?' Kharno shrugged and laughed. 'She thinks she is a hunter. Lhien and Aghri told her, no woman has the strength of arm to hunt, but she wouldn't listen.' He laughed again, at the strange follies of these moon people. 'So I gave her a good spear. This will keep you safe, I said. The power in this spear will protect you, not that stick of an arm.'

'Even Lhien's spells couldn't put strength into a body as skinny as hers,' Orhnu agreed, and slapped at his own ample forearm to show what a hunter's limbs should really be like.

But Ivan was looking only at Kharno, an expression of disbelief on his face.

'She ... hunts ... now?' he asked in a shocked voice, aghast at the image of Josie creeping alone through the forest, with heaven-knows-what stalking her in the leaf-green shadows.

'Pshaw!' Kharno dismissed the notion out of hand. 'She only plays at hunting, to anger Lheppo. She is a woman, and as weak as the moonbeams that stain the ground at night. Whereas you ... ' He eyed Ivan critically, hesitated, and decided to be kind. 'You are a man, born to hunt.'

Ivan wasn't at all sure about that, but Kharno, his mind made up, was already urging him towards the largest of the caves.

'Come,' he said encouragingly, 'we must prepare you for the hunt.'

'No ... Josie ... ' Ivan protested.

'J-os-ie,' Kharno repeated, mouthing the word with difficulty. 'This is no fitting name for a human being. It means nothing.'

'The no-name,' Ivan corrected himself, hanging back despite Kharno's urgings, 'you must ... help her. Danger ... in forest.'

'I've told you,' Kharno reminded him, 'she has my best spear to keep her safe. And Tharek is tracking her. She will come to no harm.'

'But Tharek is ... is a child.'

Kharno shook his head. 'Only in years. Compared with the moon woman he is wise in the lore of the forest. He will be there if she needs him.'

With that final assurance he led the way into the cave.

After the brilliance of the morning Ivan could see nothing for a while and had to rely on Kharno's firm grip to guide him through the dark. At a sharp turn in the tunnel he spied a smoky flame some way ahead, and after stooping beneath a rocky arch they emerged into a high-ceilinged chamber lit by a row of rush flares.

It was a weird place to come upon so suddenly, the walls and ceiling decorated with scores of paintings. Gazing about him Ivan spotted the ponderous shapes of elephant and bear and bison, the less bulky outlines of antelope and wolf, a single low-slung tigerish creature, and interspersed amongst them, the upright figures of Neanderthal hunters. All were vividly depicted in rich earth colours that gave them a disconcertingly lifelike quality, their limbs appearing to move in the flickering torchlight.

'This is where the hunt begins, here amongst the spirits,' Kharno whispered, and pointed to the far side of the chamber where Lheppo was crouched before an unfinished painting of a shaggy buffalo-like creature.

Lheppo glanced across his shoulder and frowned as they approached.

'Why do you bring this thing in here?' he growled, one hand poised above the great curved horns of the animal in the painting.

His other hand, Ivan noticed, the one Lhien had burned, hung at his side.

'He must learn the ways of men,' Kharno answered simply.

'What use are our ways to him? He is a thing of moonshine.'

'Yet he has chosen the earth,' Kharno pointed out. 'If he is to take his place amongst us and win a name, he must understand the power of seeing. No one can survive long in the forest if he doesn't make peace with the creatures he hunts.'

Lheppo swung aggressively towards them. 'So this thing is to come with us? You want the mark of his hand here on the spirit-likeness of the chosen prey?'

'He will perish on those horns otherwise,' Kharno

argued, nodding at the painting. 'You know that.'

'I know also that he is not a man,' Lheppo said, and reaching across to Ivan he pulled aside the collar of his torn and filthy shirt, to reveal the pale skin beneath. 'How can he bleed like us? There is no blood under this skin. Look at it. It's as white as the belly of the catfish buried in the mud of the lake.'

'Even the catfish bleeds when you cut it,' Kharno replied. 'Why should our moon cousins be any different?'

'Because they fell from the sky and suffered no harm.'

'That was before the earth accepted them. Before Lhien touched them with clay she had moistened in her mouth. They are mortal now, the same as the rest of us. That's why we cannot deny this nameless thing the right to place his mark upon the painting.'

'I would sooner share the painting with a child like Tharek,' Lheppo said, but he moved grudgingly aside just the same – watching with brooding eyes as Kharno picked up a thin tube of root, chewed the end to a feathery pulp, and handed it to Ivan.

'The animal spirit awaits our making,' Kharno instructed him in a solemn voice. 'Set your mark upon his likeness and he will have no power over you. Like a true hunter you will be his liberator, for here he will find sanctuary – here in the work of your hands – when his body dies out there in the forest.'

Aware of the importance of the occasion, Ivan made a careful inspection of the small stone pots grouped beneath the painting. They contained a variety of colours, and he hesitated for some seconds, glancing from the unfinished painting and back to the pots, before finally dipping his 'brush' into the black. The animal's head was what fascinated him most, with its curving horns and large liquid eye which seemed to gaze longingly from the wall as if pleading for its spirit life; and steadying the brush with both hands he darkened the outline of the eye, giving it an even more soulful quality. Next he strengthened the ridges near the base of the horns, applying alternate stripes of black and creamy white until they glistened realistically.

He was caught up in the excitement of the painting now, so engrossed in creating the likeness of this wild creature that for a while he lost all sense of his surroundings. He might almost have been somewhere in the murky depths of the forest, intent upon some half-made shape that flitted through the shadows ahead.

It was Kharno who brought him back to the reality of the smoky cavern.

'You see,' he hissed. 'The spirit answers to his call. It comes when he beckons.'

'He may have the gift of seeing,' Lheppo conceded, 'but that alone won't make him a hunter.'

'What is a hunter if he has no eye?' Kharno countered.

'And what use is an eye without a strong arm?'

Kharno sighed and tipped his face to the gallery of paintings that crammed the walls. 'He will find strength enough when the time comes,' he murmured, and rested a calloused hand on Ivan's shoulder. 'In his heart he is a man, I know it.'

He spoke with such quiet confidence that Ivan couldn't bring himself to say otherwise – to admit that the idea of the hunt made him quail inside. It sounded too brutally real, too hazardous; and already, after only weeks in this ancient world, he had no illusions about the extent of his courage. Here in the cavern it was different. Here where the brush and the heavy earth colours answered to his bidding, he felt strangely at home, in control. Whereas out there in the deeps of the forest! Confronted by flesh and blood animals!

He shut that thought off just as Lheppo spoke.

'I don't care what you say, this moon thing has no stomach for the hunt. Look into his face and you will see it.'

'I have read his heart, not his face,' Kharno answered stoutly.

'Then why is he silent? Why doesn't his heart speak aloud?'

'Use your eyes, not your ears,' Kharno admonished him. 'The no-name has spoken through his hands. Look.'

And together with Lheppo, Ivan looked and saw with a faint sense of shock that the painting was complete. The final touches he had made to the head had brought the animal startlingly alive, its lowered horns and flaring nostrils so real that it seemed about to paw the ground or snort in protest at these two-legged intruders.

'It is a thing of wonder!' Lheppo admitted, genuinely impressed. 'It awaits only Lhien's blessing to join with its spirit self.'

'Then do not keep the spirit waiting,' Kharno ordered him, and Lheppo lumbered off to return some minutes later with the rest of the clan, Lhien amongst them.

She had donned her feather cloak for the occasion, and there in the lamplight she used Lheppo's collection of colours to decorate her face. When she was ready she began to dance, stamping her feet in time to a gourd rattle. As the tangy scent of raised dust filled the cavern she broke into song – one of her throaty incantations which, to Ivan's ears, seemed to rise and fall like some fitful wind.

Yet in contrast to her other songs, there was nothing restful about this one. It conveyed a definite hint of challenge, of danger, which kept the whole clan keen-eyed and alert. And watching them as they strained forward, taking in every word, every note, Ivan was impressed yet again by how closely they resembled his original mental picture of Neanderthal people. This was how they *had* to look to survive here. With their stocky frames and weirdly savage features, in some cases more apelike than human, they were true inhabitants of these old times. Lheppo especially – his jutting brow emblazoned with tattoos, his great hands dangling loosely against his thighs – appeared fierce and daring enough to withstand almost anything the primeval forest could pit against him.

Glancing covertly from one rapt face to another, Ivan lost track of the song for a while, so he couldn't have said exactly when he became the centre of attention. One minute he was a spectator, looking on; the next he was conscious of the song being directed straight at him. Lhien's stamping dance had brought her to within a metre of where he stood; and with a quick thrusting gesture she shook the rattle in his face, driving him towards the painting.

He could sense it at his back, its single painted eye fixed upon him. While all around, the people sighed and took up Lhien's song, the chorus of their twined voices swelling out into the far spaces of the cavern.

It had suddenly grown unbearably warm in there, the atmosphere stifling. He wiped at his eyes which smarted from the mingled smoke and dust; and at each breath he found himself nearly choking, the air tinder dry in his throat.

'This is the likeness I grant to you,' Lhien droned. 'This is the gift of the people. Take it, take it.'

Again the rattle was shaken in his face, directing his gaze to the painting itself – his eye and the eye of the buffalo meeting for the first time, or so it felt.

'Who are you?' the creature seemed to ask him silently. 'What do you want of me?'

The answer came in the form of a flint knife which Lhien pressed into his hand. 'Put your touch upon the beast,' she instructed him in song. 'Claim it as a brother.'

A brother? He didn't understand. For the moment all he could do was stand open-mouthed and confused while the people sang and the painted beast, more fully alive than ever, waited expectantly in its rocky niche.

But waited for what? What kind of brotherhood could he offer this animal of his own creating?

'Give it a sign,' Lhien chanted. 'Mark it with your lifeblood.'

He understood what was expected of him then, and he looked at the scalloped edge of the knife and pushed it quickly away, rejecting it.

'Aah,' the people sighed.

And Lhien, her feet like the drumbeat of his own heart: 'Tie the beast to you with blood. Make it answer to your bidding.'

'Do it,' the people trilled. 'Do it while the song lasts.'

But already, in his mind's eye, he had seen the jagged wound the knife would leave, and although he raised the blade to his arm he couldn't bring himself to make the cut.

'No,' he muttered faintly, and let the knife slide from his fingers.

The song broke off abruptly. Lhien, clearly shaken by his refusal, stooped for the knife and offered it to him once more.

'Be careful,' she whispered, as though fearful that the shaggy outline of the buffalo might hear. 'If you turn away, the beast will claim you for itself. *You* will become the prey.'

It was a warning more than a threat, and he tried to steady himself, intending to obey her this time. But while he still hesitated, Lheppo stepped forward and plucked the knife from her hand.

'The no-name is not of this earth like us,' he said contemptuously. 'You have seen the colour of his skin. He has milk in his veins, liquid moonlight, and what use is that? Only blood is strong enough to bind the spirit world to us.'

So saying, he lifted the knife to his shoulder, waited for the song to resume, and then, as the voices rose around him, drew the blade across the tensed muscle. Red-black in the torchlight, blood welled up from the open wound and trickled down his arm.

'Do it,' the people sang as before. 'Do it while the song lasts.'

And he dabbled his fingers in the wound, turned towards the painting, and with quick swiping gestures made bloody marks on the animal's throat and just above its shoulder, which was the closest point to the heart.

'It is done,' Lhien chanted. 'The creature is bound to you.'

'. . . bound to you,' the people repeated, the song slowly dying away.

In the ensuing hush all that could be heard was a

child's fitful cough and the occasional shuffle of feet. No one looked at Ivan. All eyes were turned to Lheppo.

'You are the hunter,' Lhien pronounced at last, and was about to shake the gourd at him in a kind of blessing when a patter of footsteps sounded from the tunnel and Josie emerged into the chamber, a dark object draped across her shoulder.

'I ... hunter ... too,' she declared defiantly, and slipped from beneath her burden which landed with a thud at Lheppo's feet.

One of the rush torches flared up briefly, revealing the object for what it was: a young deer, its head thrown back, its throat freshly cut.

'She killed it!' Tharek blurted out from the back of the chamber, his face vacant with wonder. 'I was there. I saw her throw the spear.'

'What of the creature's spirit?' Lhien demanded, rounding on her. 'There was no chosen painting for this beast, nowhere for its soul to journey when you took its life.'

'I don't care a damn about your paintings,' Josie answered in English. 'Like I said,' and here she rammed the butt-end of her spear into the dust and reverted to the language of the clan: 'I ... hunter ... too.' Her gaze remained fixed all the while on Lheppo, as if daring him to contradict her.

His only reply was to stare broodingly back at her, the light from the flare reflected in his eyes.

9

Ivan pulled hard on the woven rush cord that held the spearhead in place, knotted the cord tightly, and sealed off the rough ends with hot pitch. Yes, that was plenty firm enough, he decided as he flexed the joint to test the strength of the binding. The spearhead itself was already complete, and more than adequate for its task. He had made it on the previous day, from a sharp splinter of flint which he had worked on for hours, chipping away the excess stone to produce the kind of arrow shape he wanted. The shaft still required some attention, however, and he set about stripping off the remnants of bark and then rubbing the exposed wood with handfuls of sand until the surface felt smooth and even.

All that remained was the balance of the weapon, and he weighed it in his hand. A little too much weight in the tail, perhaps, and with another piece of sharpened flint (he was always careful to keep his steel knife hidden) he began to whittle away the last few centimetres of the shaft.

At this type of work, which required attention to

detail, he was a match for many members of the clan. He had shown himself far more skilful than Josie, for instance, who was too slapdash and impatient. Where she outstripped him was in the actual use of the weapon, in those more active pursuits where ...

No, he corrected himself mentally. That wasn't entirely true. In their practice sessions he consistently out-threw her; and he was also more accurate, hitting the mark time and again. The real difference between them had nothing to do with skill: it was a matter of attitude. She was the one who had put her skills to use; who had gone to the forest alone in order to test herself. Testing situations, in some ways, were her natural element. She didn't exactly revel in them, yet always, no matter how tight the spot, she managed to retain her self confidence and her cool.

And he?

He was good at running away. He had proved that within seconds of his arrival here, when he had dragged Josie clear of the shore; and again barely an hour later when he had led their mad scramble through the darkened forest. And when he couldn't run? Like the night they had been trapped down near the shore? He had frozen then. Gone into a blind panic, and only Josie had saved him.

So when the pressure was on, as it would be in the upcoming hunt, was running away the only thing he could be relied on to do? He hoped not, though a small voice of doubt whispered otherwise. To still that voice he stopped whittling for a while and hefted the spear in his hand, allowing the weight and balance of it to steady him. When the time came he would stand his ground. He was determined about that. For unlike Josie he didn't resent his new life. A part of him felt a real attachment to both this place and its people. Which was why it was so important to succeed; why he desperately needed to prove himself before the ship returned and took him away.

Josie, of course, no longer believed in the ship. For her, hunting was basically a means of demonstrating how superior she was to the Neanderthals. It also provided her with an outlet for her anger, enabling her to strike back at this land which held her captive.

He had only to glance sideways at her now, to where she worked beside him, to see the anger in her face – the way she bit her lip and frowned when the binding of her spearhead refused to hold.

Cursing under her breath she tossed the weapon aside and glared moodily at Aghri who had just emerged from the forest, a gourd of water propped against one broad hip.

'Here comes your girlfriend,' she observed as Aghri deposited the gourd near the cave and walked over to join them. 'Look at her, she can't take her eyes off you.'

Although Ivan knew there was no point in answering in kind, he couldn't help himself.

'You can talk. What about Lheppo?'

'What about him?'

'I wouldn't say he ignores you.'

'That's because he hates me. Can't you see that?'

Ivan shrugged, too committed now to draw back. 'Love, hate, who can tell?'

'I can tell.'

'Lucky you,' he added sarcastically, and wished he hadn't.

'Listen, you creep!' she whispered, leaping to her feet and standing over him. 'Don't you ever, *ever* link me with that ... that ape! That *barbarian*! Not unless you want to end up as cat's meat. D'you understand?'

He pretended to be puzzled. 'So how come you're free to link me with Aghri?'

'Oh get lost!' she responded, and grabbing her unfinished spear she headed off in the direction of the lake.

Once she had gone the pointlessness of their exchange struck home. For one thing he had no interest in making her more miserable than she already was. For another, he didn't mind being singled out by Aghri. Something about the Neanderthal woman's homely features made him feel relaxed, less on edge. Perhaps it was the fact that she showed no sign of being critical of him. Like now, the way she squatted at his side, beaming up into his face.

'The moon woman is angry?' she asked, in a voice he had become so accustomed to that he hardly noticed its huskiness.

'I think ... this is so,' he replied, trying to act unconcerned.

'What troubles her?'

He had to think about that. 'She yearns for ... for her moon life,' he said at last.

'Ah yes.' She nodded to herself. 'This moon life, what is it like?'

Again Ivan had to pause for thought, to cast his mind back to the days of his safe suburban existence. How far off those times seemed now, though by the clan's reckoning less than two moons had passed. He had to make a positive effort to visualise his aunt's Victorian cottage with its broad veranda and tiled gables; and even when he had brought it vividly to mind, still it was like a fragment of someone else's memory – someone he knew intimately and well, but had grown away from.

It was the same when he recalled his aunt: her face was clear enough, as was her soft voice and uneven temper, but she too had become like an inhabitant of someone else's past. Disconcertingly, he remembered angry words she had spoken to him once, a year or two after his parents' death. 'I'm too old to take the place of your mother,' she had complained, turning away. 'I've brought up one family and that's enough. Why, we're not even blood related.' They were sentiments she had never repeated, never once. For the most part she had treated him with ... well, not exactly love, but with kindness and consideration. So why remember that single moment of rejection? Unless, perhaps, it told him things about his past life; signalled to him that he wasn't as firmly anchored in those future times as he cared to believe.

'Does it pain you to think of your moon life?' Aghri inquired, breaking in upon his silent reverie.

'Pain me?' He shook his head in hasty denial, while secretly acknowledging that she had a real talent for reading his thoughts from his face. 'Our moon life was ... was happy.'

'Then why do you frown when I speak of it?'

He hunted through his limited vocabulary for words to express himself. 'Some moon people were ... were happier than ... than me. Josie – the other no-name – she was ... ' He stumbled over the idea of wealth, and said instead: 'She had ... many spears ... many cloaks ... many caves. She ... she weeps for ... for these things.'

Aghri gave him a puzzled look. 'But why? She has these things still. What is ours is hers. And why should anyone mourn for many cloaks? We can wear only one garment, sleep in only one cave.'

He had no ready answer to that. 'The moon people

are ... are different,' he muttered lamely.

'Like this, do you mean?' she asked, and ran her fingertips tenderly across his brow. 'Is this how all your people look?'

He nodded, and she smiled indulgently at him. 'Lheppo says the flatness of your face is ugly, but not to me. I told him, the animals of the forest have their own beauty, and so do the moon people. We must accept them for what they are.' As she spoke, she took his hand and raised it to her own much heavier brow which was decorated with a single flowery line of tattoo. 'What about my face?' she asked him shyly, pressing his fingers to the swell of bone. 'Do you find that beautiful too?'

For once his expression didn't give him away – partly, perhaps, because he didn't actually find her ugly. As she herself had just said, all creatures have their own kind of beauty, and he had dwelt with the clan long enough to realise that on their standards she was far from plain.

'Yes, you are beautiful,' he told her, taking refuge in a half truth.

'As beautiful as the other no-name?' she pressed him.

For once a lie came readily to his lips, Josie's angry dismissal of him still fresh in his memory.

'If the ... the sun and the moon were ... were sisters,' he began, struggling to translate his ideas into this foreign tongue, 'then you ... you are the sun.'

Nothing could have been sunnier than the smile she gave him at that moment.

'You speak like Lhien,' she said modestly.

That took him by surprise. Lhien had fascinated him from the outset, and yet he had never tried to

89

copy or be like her. What's more, since the episode in the cave he had felt that she disapproved of him. On her terms he had blasphemed; he had turned his back on the spiritual path she had presented.

'I don't think Lhien likes me,' he muttered, thinking aloud; but Aghri, ready as ever to placate him, waved aside the suggestion with a sweep of one broad hand.

'Lhien fears for you, that is all,' she whispered earnestly.

'Fears for me ... how?'

Aghri glanced across to where Lhien was sunning herself in the entrance to the nearest cave, and she dropped her voice even lower. 'Since you rejected the spirit of the beast, she has it in her mind that it will seek you out on the day of the hunt. It will claim you for itself.'

The hunt again! In recent days it had shadowed every hour of his waking life, and despite the sunlight he edged closer to the lingering coals of the fire.

'Do *you* think the beast will ... will claim me?' he asked quietly.

'Not if you placate it in your heart,' she assured him. 'Not if you honour its spirit self and reveal yourself to it.'

'How ... how can I ... do that?' he queried – and wondered at the same time why he should be taking any of this seriously. It was all nonsense, primitive mumbo jumbo, and he would have stopped the conversation there and then if it hadn't been for the look of utter conviction on Aghri's face. For her and her people the mysterious connecting links between the human and the animal worlds were as real as the ground beneath their feet. And the longer he dwelt amongst them, the harder it was to ignore their beliefs or contend that they exerted no influence over him.

As though aware of his inner conflict, Aghri delayed her answer until his flickering gaze had steadied.

'Tonight,' she said, and took his hands in hers, 'when we prepare the warriors for the hunt, that will be the time to show the beast your secret heart.'

'Yes, but . . .'

'Trust me,' she interrupted. 'And trust the moment.'

Then before he could question her further, she rose and returned to the cave.

After that he only pretended to work at the spear, distracted by Aghri's closing words of advice. She was asking him to put his trust in each passing moment, whereas back in his former existence he had done the very opposite. There he had planned every aspect of his life: how to spend his money and his free time; when to work or study; what to wear for this or that occasion – everything. The trouble was, none of that forward planning worked here. True, the clan made every effort to plot a safe course into the future – the cave paintings were proof of that – but still their existence was too precarious, too hand-to-mouth, for them to know with any certainty what the next day would bring. Finally they had little control over the great forest that hemmed them in. Their only option was to trust the moment, as Aghri had said; and while he, Ivan, shared their plight, it was his only option too.

So was nothing constant or dependable in this place?

Aghri maybe . . .

He dismissed the idea irritably. In the end she was

as foreign to him as nearly everything else. And rocking back on his heels, he gazed up at the cloud-streaked sky. That at least was totally familiar, unchanged over the millennia. He could rely on that.

Or could he? Hadn't Lhien pointed out that he and Josie had fallen from those skies? And wasn't she in a sense right?

Utterly confused, he resumed work on the spear. Head down, he hacked at the shaft until the flint knife broke in his hands, cutting him, and a drop of his own blood – as deep red as blood had ever been – stained the shaft of the spear like some secret sign.

*   *   *

The moon had set early, and even the stars were few in number, blocked out by the thickening cloud. The night, black and still, was like some wild creature which seemed to watch from the unknown depths of the forest. All that the clan could set against it was the fire, a great heap of wood they had spent the last hour of daylight collecting.

It blazed up towards the heavens now, crackling and roaring in the stillness, with the clan gathered about it, their rapt faces bathed in its lurid light. Yet for all its power, it wasn't the fire alone that held them mesmerised: it was also the bird-like silhouette of Lhien who moved slowly before the backdrop of the flames, caught up in the ritual retelling of an ancestral story.

Draped in her feather cloak – the clan's tribute to its bird totem – she was enacting the story in a mixture of dance and song, her performance so measured and intense that even Ivan and Josie were

92

held by it, though the intricacies of the language itself often baffled them.

'In the beginning,' she sang to the assembled audience, 'we, the people of the clans, were nothing.' And she shrank down inside her cloak and crouched close to the ground, as small and featureless as a rock or tree stump. 'We were a part of the forest,' she droned on, rising and shuffling perilously close to the flames. 'Like most of its creatures we lived in fear. By day we huddled beneath the roots of the great trees; and by night we hid high in the canopy with the apes and monkeys. They were our cousins then and shared our terror.'

Her dance changed at that point, to a kind of monkey prance that brought murmurs of nervous laughter from her audience.

'We were also tiny in those far-off days,' she informed them in a husky whisper, 'because we had no time to search for food. Always we were running.' Here she scurried to the edge of the clearing and back again. 'Always we were hiding, escaping from our common enemy. He is out there still. We, the people, know him well and do not forget his name.'

'The leopard spirit!' her audience sighed in ready response.

'Yes,' she agreed. 'None other. In the days of his victory he was lord of the forest. This clearing was his home. These caves were his sleeping place. With tooth and claw he held them against all intruders. In the arrogance of his heart he knew that none could withstand him.'

The clan had bunched closer; the children cast terrified glances over their shoulders at the dark mouths of the caves.

'Then one day,' she informed them in a high trilling voice, 'the sky spirits grew tired of his arrogance and pride. "We will humble this creature of the night," they said, and sent lightning down to fire the forest. But they had forgotten about the caves, and the leopard spirit slept there safe while all the other creatures fled before the fury of the flames.'

Lhien herself might have been a part of those legendary flames as she pirouetted slowly before the central fire, her craggy body all but merging with the blackened shapes of half-burned trunks and branches.

There was a whimper from one of the children who was quickly hushed by its mother.

'We were numbered amongst them,' she sang on, 'those many fugitives who fled before the roaring demons of the fire. We made our way to the treeless slopes where our true cousins live to this day, and there we prayed to the bird spirit who had soared above the fire, untouched by it. "Give us power over this demon fire," we begged, "and we will honour you always."'

'Always,' the people echoed her.

'The bird answered our prayer,' Lhien continued, and flapped the wide wings of her cloak to simulate a bird in flight. 'It gathered red-hot embers before the forest cooled, wrapped them in moist clay, and brought them to us. It made us the new fire masters. Henceforward, it told us, fire would spill from our hands as it does from the hands of the sky spirits.'

'And then ... ? And then ... ?' the people sang, their voices breathy with excitement.

Lhien had snatched a burning brand from the flames. 'And then we made fire sticks for ourselves,' she declared triumphantly. 'With those sticks we drove the leopard spirit from these caves.'

'Yes!' the people sang. 'Yes!'

'Since then the caves have been ours, and the leopard has borne the marks of our burning upon him. You have seen his coat, with its black and yellow markings. It is a sign, set there by our hands. Proof that he now belongs in the forest, a creature of sunlight and shadow; and that we belong here within the circle of the fire.'

There was a drawn-out communal sigh, immediately disrupted by a shouted challenge. The suddenness of it caught Ivan and Josie by surprise.

'Now the leopard spirit claims the forest for itself!' someone cried.

'Never!' the people answered fervently.

'He claims the animals every one.'

Again the word 'Never!' rang out into the surrounding dark, and was repeated as each animal was mentioned by name.

'Monkey . . . horse . . . antelope . . .'

At the mention of the word 'buffalo', the loudest shout of all rose from the onlookers, and with a snort a shaggy, monstrous shape lumbered into the firelight. It was Aghri, draped in a buffalo skin, complete with horned head; but from the outset her performance was such that Ivan and Josie felt as if they were confronted by the live animal. Aghri didn't so much copy its movements as become the creature itself. Each toss of the head, each stamp of the foot, had a wild unbridled quality about it. And when she stood at bay and glared at the audience through the tiny eye holes, she might have been some old bull making a last stand against its ancient and mythical enemies.

'Who calls to me from the spirit world?' she demanded in a deep voice. 'Who is it that lures me to my painted likeness?'

95

'He comes,' the audience responded, and Lheppo stepped into the firelight, a blunt-ended stick in one hand.

'I have called to you,' he answered readily. 'I have named you brother.'

The lowered head swung slowly towards him, acknowledging his presence, and then away again.

'There is another here who called to my spirit through its likeness,' Aghri insisted, and let out a wild snorting cry. 'One who denies our brotherhood. Which is he?'

There was a real tension in the air now, a whiff of fear that made everyone but Lheppo cower back. And with a lurch of the heart, Ivan realised that he was the one being summoned.

Close beside him Josie wiped a hand across her mouth and turned away, wrenching herself free of the illusion that bound the rest of the audience.

'That's your cue,' she whispered, a forced note of laughter in her tone.

Yet even her attempts at mockery couldn't shatter the illusion for Ivan.

'Mine?' he muttered through stiff lips, and shuffled further back into the shadows.

He had never been any good at acting, but that wasn't really the point here because he wasn't being called upon to act a part. Like Aghri he was expected to *become* his role. This firelit clearing was both itself and also some forest glade; and the classic meeting of hunter and prey was about to take place.

'Where is this nameless one who calls to me in spirit?' Aghri roared, and gouged the air with her horns. 'Why doesn't he stand forth? Is he shamed to call me brother?'

'You heard the lady,' Josie murmured, and pushed

96

him forward. 'Don't keep your audience waiting.'

Before he could draw away, other hands clutched at him, urging him on; others again forced a blunted spear into his grasp; and all at once he was standing alone in the firelight – alone, that is, except for the buffalo shape that rose like a humped black shadow against the flames.

Lifting her buffalo head, Aghri made a show of testing the breeze.

'I smell no common blood-scent,' she declared, the words rumbled deep within her throat. 'There is no brotherly bond between us. Why is this?'

He tried to answer, but couldn't, and someone spoke up for him.

'Because he spurned the knife. Because he did not tie you to him with his own life-blood.'

Aghri raked theateningly at the ground. 'Then you are not my brother, and yours is not the weapon I need to fear. You and I, we are both of us in peril on this day.'

So saying, she lowered her head, blew noisily in the dust, and readied herself to charge.

Caught in the blaze of firelight, dazzled by it, all he could do was watch, horrified, as the buffalo shape shambled across the clearing towards him – one half of his mind telling him all the while that this was just a pantomime, a play for children; and the other half refusing to listen, aware that in some vital sense this *was* the hunt. This was exactly how it would be off in the dark reaches of the forest. And with that knowledge he forgot the assembled people, forgot this firelit scene, and imagined himself in some forest glade.

The buffalo was almost upon him now. Nothing stood between them but the blunted spear and the strength of his own arm. He tried to jab forward, to fend the animal off, but couldn't. Nor could he turn and run, the lingering memory of the assembled people like a wall at his back. As on the night Josie had saved him from the leopard, he froze. Stood there petrified until the hulking head and shoulders of the animal filled his vision; until he could smell the grease and dust embedded in its coat.

Only when it was too late did he raise the spear. Not in an attacking move. He was incapable of that. His upward jerk of the arms was nothing more than a reflex; his body's instinctive desire to avert disaster. Then with a jarring impact the broad head and curved horns struck him full in the chest and he went down in a smother of reeking fur.

The fire had been blotted out. He was lost now in a real dark, a mass of limbs and skin pinning him to the dusty earth. He could hear tortured breaths close beside his ear; feel the pressure of a heavy body. Yet for some reason those terrible horns did not bore at him. The creature remained curiously inert despite his helplessness; a deadening weight that gasped and sighed like a high wind in the trees.

He was plucked free before he had puzzled out what was happening; hauled up into the firelight by Kharno, and greeted by the cheering people.

He saw then the reason for their joy. The 'beast', in the form of Aghri, lay sprawled at his feet. She hadn't risen because she was too breathless, her whole body curled around his blunted spear which had accidentally struck her in the stomach.

Kharno took Ivan's hand in his and raised it high. 'The painter and the hunter are one,' he declared, and was again greeted by cheers of approval.

'He has claimed the beast for himself,' Lhien added from the sidelines.

Of all the people, their faces bathed in firelight, only one continued to eye him doubtfully.

'This moon thing is a danger to us,' Lheppo growled. 'He has failed to understand the ways of the hunt. No man wrestles with the spirit of the buffalo and lives.'

'How can you say that?' Lhien asked sharply. 'You have seen him do it here tonight.'

'Yes, we've seen it all right,' Josie responded in English – her voice floating out of the dark, followed by a knowing chuckle.

'What does she say?' Lhien queried, turning to Ivan. 'What is the meaning of these moon words?'

But it wasn't the words themselves that concerned Ivan. It was Josie's laughter and what *that* meant. Or rather, what it told him about himself. The real truth beneath this sham of victory.

10

The dawn-hushed forest was clear of mist when Ivan emerged from the cave, the sky skimmed with pink by the unrisen sun. He had hoped to have this morning hour to himself, but already Gunjhi and Ilkha, the wives of the two young hunters, were busy cooking at the central fire.

'You should still be asleep, moon boy,' Gunjhi called cheerily to him. 'You will need all your strength today.'

'The days of the hunt are long like the forest paths,' Ilkha agreed, fanning the coals around the cooking stones. 'Go back and rest while you can.'

'I'm rested enough,' he answered shortly, not wanting to stop and talk, and made his way to the path which led up and around the great outcrop of rock that housed the caves.

By rights he should have taken a very different path, the one that led down to the lake's edge, but there was no time for that. Not on this particular morning, even though the question of rescue had never been more pressing.

'Please let them be there,' he muttered as he reached the top of the path and emerged onto the lookout point high above the caves. 'Please let them. Please.'

But as always he was disappointed, the lake completely empty – or at least as much of the lake as he could see. Tall trees screened off the near shore, so he supposed it was vaguely possible that the ship lay hidden from view. That after all was where it had anchored on the afternoon of their arrival. For all he knew his rescuers might be down there at that moment, waiting to whisk him away. Maybe the only barrier to his escape was his own lack of faith in the future. If he were simply to turn his back on all of this, the hunt included, and take that other path, the one to the lake, he might yet come across the ship, dull silver in the dawn light, floating at the edge of . . .

No! He shook his head in disbelief. He was clutching at straws. For them to arrive now – on this day of challenge when he needed them most – was too much to hope for.

'Damn!' he swore softly, doing his best to contain his disappointment, and sank despondently onto the vine-strewn rock.

It was no good pretending any longer: he would have to go through with the hunt. Perhaps in the end it wouldn't be as bad as he expected. He had yet to discover, for instance, whether he could come to any harm here in the past. A few scrapes and bruises, that was all he and Josie had sustained so far. With luck they might be immune to anything these ancient times could throw at them, their fate written elsewhere.

It was an idea he often reverted to when he was feeling down, but always, in his heart of hearts, he knew it was wishful thinking. Like his secret hope that the ship would zoom in and rescue him at this the eleventh hour. Things didn't work out that way. Whether he liked it or not the hunters would depart within the hour, and he would be expected to go with them. He could refuse, of course, but then he would be publicly shamed, and for reasons he had yet to get clear in his mind he dreaded that prospect more than the hunt itself. To have Josie laugh at him as she had the night before! Or worse, to have Aghri, his one staunch ally, turn against him! Again he shook his head, as though answering to some unseen judge. On balance, now that the moment of decision had arrived, he preferred to take his chances with the hunters.

With a sigh he stood up. Far below he could see various members of the clan emerging from the caves. One of them, a heavily set figure whom he took to be Lheppo, seemed excited about something because he was waving his arms about and shouting. At that distance it was impossible to decipher his actual words, but clearly he was angry. And that other figure – was it Josie? She also looked angry, her voice floating tinnily up through the stillness of the morning.

What were they fighting over now? he wondered. And why did they feel so bitterly opposed to each other? Whatever the cause, this was no ordinary argument. He could make out that much even at this height – partly from the way a third figure (Kharno?) pushed between them and forced them apart.

Ivan gave a resigned shrug. He had too many problems of his own to worry about their squabbles. Let them get on with it, he decided, and was about to turn away when Lheppo lunged past Kharno and struck Josie to the ground.

The dull 'thock' of the blow reached right up to the lookout point, and Ivan crouched at the very lip of the rock, straining to see. Josie was obviously hurt; stunned maybe, because for some seconds she lay quite still. Then, as Kharno knelt beside her, she sprang to her feet and snatched something from the ground near by. A spear! Now she was the one lunging forward, with Lheppo backing off as fast as he could. But only in order to pick up another spear – the two of them facing each other across the fire, with the rest of the clan looking on.

'My God!' Ivan breathed the words aloud as he turned and scrambled for the path. What the hell was Josie thinking about? Didn't she realise that Lheppo could ... that he was strong enough to ...?

This wasn't the time for such questions, however. Ivan needed all his concentration just to stay on his feet as he half fell, half leaped down the steeply winding path.

When he ran into the clearing some minutes later the whole clan was in uproar.

'These are moon people!' Kharno shouted above the babble of raised voices. 'They do not understand our ways!'

And Lhien, who had moved to the centre of the group: 'Are you monkeys? Fit only to squabble and fight amongst yourselves? Do you care nothing for the lore of our forebears?'

'It is that lore I am invoking here,' Lheppo insisted, flourishing his spear in the direction of Josie.

'What! With a spear in your hand? Has that become a part of our wisdom now?'

'There's nothing unwise about defending myself,' Lheppo countered. 'She's the one who first reached for a weapon.'

'Yes, but only after you struck her.'

'Didn't I have reason to?' Lheppo shouted, tears of passion again spilling from his eyes. 'It was also the lore I was defending, remember that.'

'I don't care a damn about your precious lore!' Josie shouted back in English. Then, reverting to the language of the clan: 'I ... hunt ... too.'

'Never!' Lheppo broke out. 'No woman has ever hunted.'

'Well this one will!' she yelled, drowning him out, and for a moment Ivan thought she was going to hurl her spear. Instead, she scrambled in the dust for a stone and threw it as hard as she could, striking Lheppo a glancing blow on the forehead. 'Tit for tat, you dumb bastard!' she added grimly, a tight smile on her face.

He was clutching onto his spear in a desperate struggle to control himself, more tears spilling down. 'You see!' he cried hoarsely. 'This moon thing has no honour, no understanding.' He took a long sobbing breath and added as a final insult: 'She is not even a woman.'

'All the more reason for me to join the hunt,' Josie replied in English.

'Listen to her,' he jeered. 'To her gibberish. She is a moon monkey. She isn't fit to hunt amongst men. How could we trust ourselves to this thing? She would only put our lives in peril.'

'Like this, d'you mean?' Josie said, a dangerous edge to her voice, and this time she really did hurl the spear. Not straight at him, but deliberately low so the spear ploughed into the dust between his feet.

He stared at it in disbelief before raising his own spear. He held it quiveringly above his head for some seconds, his whole face working with suppressed emotion.

'Go on, do it!' Josie taunted him in English. Then in words he would understand: 'Show me how ... how a *man* hunts.'

'Think, my son, think!' Kharno growled.

With a broken cry Lheppo swung around and hurled his spear not at Josie, but at the cliff, where the flint head exploded into fragments.

'That is enough!' Lhien pronounced sharply, and shook her gourd rattle, bringing instant silence to the clearing. 'Now here is my judgment, so listen carefully. Both the moon woman and Lheppo have acted like fools. But this!' She pointed to Josie's spear still lodged in the ground. 'This endangers the life of another, which is more than just folly. It is tabu. By this action alone the moon woman has judged herself. She has shown that she is not fit to hunt with the people.'

'Then I hunt alone,' Josie answered no less decisively, and marched straight up to Lheppo as if daring him to hit her again. When he managed to restrain himself, the sweat glistening on his forehead, she laughed and wrenched the spear from the ground. 'Animal!' she hissed in his own tongue, the word meant only for him. And again, for good measure: '*Animal!*'

Lheppo responded to the insult by catching at her wrist, but she slipped free and reached for his forehead – a quick darting movement that caught him off guard, her fingers brushing lightly across the red mark where the stone had struck. It was a curious gesture, neither wholly aggressive nor truly gentle. Yet still he flinched at the moment of contact, as though there were fire in her fingertips.

'Keep off, moon woman,' he warned her, and took a slow step backwards.

'For the time being I will,' she replied, speaking now in a mixture of the two languages. 'But you watch your back, animal. Today you won't be the only hunter in the woods.'

Before Lheppo could answer, she sidled past him and off through the trees.

There was an exchange of embarrassed glances as the clan slowly resumed their places around the fire. Only Lheppo remained where he was.

'You, no-name,' he barked out, addressing Ivan. 'What did the moon woman say at the end? What did her words mean?'

'She said ... she said ... ' Ivan began uncertainly, and stuttered to a halt. Because he was no longer sure what her closing words had meant: whether they had been intended simply as a threat, or more as an obscure kind of promise.

11

At the moment of departure Aghri rested her forehead against Ivan's in the ritual farewell, and at the
same time pressed something furtively into his hand.

'May the bird spirit watch over you,' she whispered, and did what he knew to be a forbidden
thing – she brushed her lips lightly against his cheek.

He drew hastily away and glanced down into his
open palm. She had given him a tiny amulet of the
kind worn by the women of the clan. It showed a
bird in flight and had been carved from a tooth, with
the broad end of the tooth pierced and threaded by
a fine leather cord.

'This is a . . . a woman's sign,' he objected, hesitant
about whether to accept her gift.

'It makes no matter,' she explained, closing his fist
around it. 'This will keep you safe.'

Safe! That word, coupled with the amulet, was
hard to resist; and despite some misgivings he slipped
the cord over his head and tucked the tiny figure
inside his now ragged shirt.

'Go well, moon boy,' Aghri breathed, and would

have repeated the forbidden gesture if he hadn't turned and joined the other hunters.

On their standards they were heavily armed, with one or two spears apiece and a selection of knotted clubs, flint knives, and axes. In addition each man carried a small leather backpack which contained a sleeping rug and such things as fire-making equipment.

'Let there be no rancour in your hearts when you make the kill,' Lhien advised them in song, her feet adding a shuffling rhythm to her words. 'The beast awaits your coming, remember that. You are its fate. Your task is to lead its spirit home.'

'Our spears will bring peace to its soul,' Kharno assured her.

And with those words they set out, padding in single file along a path that slanted up the hillside towards the sparsely forested region around the base of the mountain.

The day was cool to begin with. The newly risen sun had yet to penetrate the canopy, and dew still glistened on the ferns and bushes that flanked the path; while all around them birds called through the freshness of the morning.

Ivan, who had never been this deep into the forest, was lost in wonder at it. The size of the trees! True forest giants, with moss-encrusted trunks and buttressed roots that stood higher than his waist. And the vines! Wherever he looked they looped and cascaded from the upper boughs, their broad leaves and waxy blossoms adding an exotic flavour to the forest's charm.

At one point, spotting a vine in full flower, he slowed and almost stopped.

'Keep up, no-name,' someone grunted.

That was Orhnu, one of the young hunters, urging him on; and for the moment he responded readily enough, easily matching his pace to the steady trot of the other hunters.

By mid morning, however, the mounting heat had begun to wear him down. The threads of sunlight that pierced the canopy were like fiery arrows which burned into his skin; and whenever they paused to drink beside some pool or stream, he found himself more and more unwilling to go on. His legs ached, his pack had begun to chafe his shoulders, and each footstep felt heavier than the one before.

'Can't we stop for a while?' he gasped, and received a stern look of reprimand from Kharno.

'The forest paths are our friends,' Arhik advised him softly. 'Do not fight them. Let them draw you on.'

From the way he and his brother loped tirelessly along, it looked almost as if they *were* being drawn on by some power outside themselves. Even Kharno, at least three times Ivan's age, continued to run without apparent effort. And shamed by their fitness and strength, Ivan forced himself to keep going for another hour or two.

It was early afternoon when they stopped for food. Totally worn out by then, Ivan felt almost too tired to eat; and while the others crouched in a circle, muttering together, he wallowed in a nearby pool, where a tiny stream had been dammed by sticks and leaves.

As he lay there dazed with fatigue, he heard Arhik mutter something about 'the folly of these moon people'.

'Leave him be,' Kharno whispered in reply. 'It is better for him to learn his lessons like a child.'

Then Lheppo, making no effort to lower his voice:

'What does he need to fear? No leech would feed upon a thing with milk for blood.'

It was the word 'leech' which roused him. He had heard it used once before, by Lhien, when young Tharek had been swimming in the shallows of the lake. What did it mean? he wondered ... and felt a sharp needle-like pain behind his knee. There was a similar stabbing sensation in one ankle; and another in his other leg.

What the ... !

He stood up in one swift movement, the water streaming down, and understood then what the hunters had been talking about – for the exposed skin of his legs, where his worn-out jeans had been cut away, was festooned with bloated shapes. Leeches! Huge creatures, their pulsating sides streaked with vivid slashes of scarlet and purple.

'Get them off!' he yelled, not daring to touch them himself, and leaped from the stream.

The others were immediately at his side, calming him as they drew him down onto the bank.

'Have patience, moon boy,' Orhnu said soothingly, his hands firm upon Ivan's trembling body. 'If we pull the leeches off while they're feeding, their poison will enter you.'

Kharno, meanwhile, rummaged in his pack for fire-making equipment, which consisted of several handfuls of tinder-dry grass and moss, and two iron-hard pieces of flint. Stripping lengths of bark from the nearest tree, he fashioned them into a neat wind-break, nestled some tinder within it, and began to strike the flints together, angling them downwards so the sparks flew into the nest of moss. In the brightness of the day it was impossible to see whether any of the sparks had caught, but after several tries a wisp of smoke rose from the tinder, and then a tongue of flame which Kharno fed with dry twigs.

'Soon now,' he promised, in answer to Ivan's silent appeal, and began warming a flint knife over the flames.

Not until the blade was too hot to touch did he apply it to the leeches, holding it against their squirming bodies until they shrivelled and fell away of their own accord. As the last one dropped off, Ivan wiped the sweat from his forehead and sat up. He was trembling still, but relieved, his skin unblemished except for some tiny punctures and a few smears of blood.

At the sight of the blood there were gasps from the onlookers.

'See, he is a man like us!' Arhik said in surprise, instinctively fingering the scar which disfigured one side of his face. 'He bleeds when the forest strikes at him.'

'Lhien's clay has done its work,' Orhnu agreed. 'It has transformed him.'

'Didn't I tell you he is a creature of the earth now?' Kharno chimed in.

But it was Lheppo who seemed most astonished, his heavy features pale with wonder, an almost faraway expression in his eyes.

'So she is mortal too!' he broke out hoarsely.

'She?'

'The other no-name, the female.'

Kharno clicked his tongue in exasperation. 'What has she to do with us today? She is no hunter. That has already been decided, and it is the hunt we must fix our minds upon.'

A faint shiver passed through Lheppo as he struggled to control his unruly thoughts, his eyes focussed on the bloody smears on Ivan's legs.

'This blood is a bad sign,' he said with sudden decision. 'We must abandon the hunt.'

'Why is that?'

'Because the beast will not recognise this scent. He wasn't marked with the no-name's blood, back in the cave, and it will arouse only fear and anger in him. He will fight as never before.'

'This is true,' Arhik muttered, and again fingered the heavy scar which lifted the corner of his mouth into a permanent half grin. 'I have faced such a beast in its fury.'

'You were a child then,' Kharno pointed out. 'Lost and alone in the heights. We are men. Hunters!' He clutched at his spear with pride as he spoke that word. 'We do not turn back once the rituals have been enacted. The painting in the cave is our pact with the forest, and we mustn't break that pact. Ever!'

'Not even when we carry the scent of death with us?' Lheppo objected.

Kharno pointed to the scabbed wound on Lheppo's shoulder, where he had deliberately cut himself in the cave. 'What about this scent? Does it count for nothing? The beast will sense that too. He will recognise your brotherhood and cast himself upon our spears, knowing we come without hatred in our hearts.'

'He will know it more surely if the no-name is not with us,' Lheppo growled. 'If we leave him behind, the beast will give himself to us in trust.'

Until then Ivan had remained watchful and silent, following the conversation as best he could; but now, at the mention of being abandoned deep in the forest, he leapt to his feet.

'You're not going to leave me here!' he burst out. 'Not on my own!'

'It's all right, moon boy, your place is with us,' Kharno said placatingly. Then to Lheppo: 'You forget that the beast recognised him last night, in the hunting dance. He expects the boy to be amongst us. We are all of us bound by the rituals, the boy included.'

Lheppo shook his head, but finally gave in. 'Very well,' he said, and tested the breeze – his face at that instant, with its widely flared nostrils and glint of teeth, almost more animal than human. 'But the no-name must keep to the rear and stay out of our way, for the end of the hunt is near now.'

'The breeze tells you this?' Orhnu asked excitedly, readying himself to leave.

'It speaks to me of the brotherhood,' Lheppo said with a nod, and again set off along the sun-speckled path.

To Ivan, bringing up the rear, it seemed unlikely that Lheppo had actually managed to scent their prey. Yet ten minutes later, when they descended into a shallow river valley, there in the moist earth bordering the stream were the v-shaped prints of a hoofed animal.

Kharno dropped to one knee beside the prints. 'The beast walks alone,' he advised them softly. 'It is an old bull near the end of its allotted days, just as Lhien's dream foretold; and it has come down from the high pastures to die. The signs tell me that it crossed our path not a hundred heartbeats ago.'

'See how carefully it moved,' Lheppo added. 'It must have heard us.'

'So is this the one?' Arhik asked, and peered intently through the screen of giant ferns that followed the line of the stream.

Lheppo raised one hand to the wound at his shoulder, feeling for the pulse of blood beneath the scab – testing his own heartbeat as he had earlier tested the breeze. 'It is the one,' he murmured. 'It awaits our coming.'

'Then we won't disappoint it,' Orhnu whispered, and with a broad grin that revealed his missing front teeth he slipped the pack from his shoulders.

The others all followed suit, discarding everything but their leather tunics and their chosen weapons. Only Ivan held back, stunned by the realisation that this was what he had been dreading for days: this final stage of the hunt when he must come face to face not just with a wild creature of the forest, but also with his own inherent fear.

I don't want to do this! he yearned to scream at his companions, except he lacked the courage even for that. The watchful presence of the trees, the unblinking sunlight, the barely audible murmur of the stream – all conspired against him, pressuring him to share their silence. To say nothing. To stifle his sense of foreboding and deliver himself up to the daunting process of the hunt. Trust us, the earth/the sky/the forest seemed to say; place yourself in our hands as you did on the night of the dance and all will be well.

But what if it wasn't? What if the dance had been wrong? (Lheppo hadn't believed in it, not for a moment.) And what if his status as a creature from another time proved to be no defence here in this savage world of the past? What then? He had already shown that he could bleed, back there by the stream. That may well have been a sign, an indication that he was as subject to injury and death as everything else here; that his own mortality, in the form of a shaggy beast, would surely rear up and confront him if he was foolhardy enough to venture further.

Arhik's hand settled lightly on his shoulder, making him start guiltily. 'Are you ready, moon boy?'

Again Ivan wanted to tell them that he would never be ready for this, but his lips refused to work, his mouth dryer than the tinder in Kharno's pack.

'The first hunt is always the hardest,' Orhnu assured him, and in a small revealing gesture he probed nervously with his tongue for the gap in his front teeth.

Ivan noticed then the fine speckle of sweat on Orhnu's jutting brow. So he was also scared! He, Ivan, wasn't totally alone in his terror. That helped to steady him, and somehow he managed to follow the others when they waded into the stream and began threading their way up the valley.

Tall ferns arched above him as he splashed along, their curved arms filtering out the sunlight. He might almost have been trapped within some green-tinged tunnel, the air warm and moist, an unnervingly stagnant quality about it. It was as if he had blundered into a place of death where nothing moved except for the flurry of water about his feet; where the wind had ceased to blow; where even the occasional birdsong seemed unnaturally far away, like a cry from another world.

I'm going to die down here! he thought desperately, and was about to turn back when he sensed something looking at him. Not one of his companions who had stopped a short distance ahead and were busy examining the muddy riverbank. He swung around, checking the shadowy spaces between the trunks of the ferns. Nothing! Or nothing that he could see. Yet the feeling of being watched persisted.

What's more, there was something brooding and secretive about this silent regard, as though the ferns had grown eyes and were waiting for him to lower his guard so they could coil their fronds about him and draw him to themselves.

'Kharno?' he called softly, an audible tremor in his voice.

'Hush!' Lheppo answered, his own voice reduced to a low rumble. 'The beast is near.'

The beast! Was that what he could sense? He lifted his head and flared his nostrils, just as Lheppo had done; but here in the shadow of the ferns there was no wind, the moist air like a close-fitting veil that made it difficult for him to breathe.

'The beast has backtracked,' he heard Kharno mutter. 'We must ...'

The rest was lost as something stirred in the greenish dark of the near bank; as a section of shadow seemed to detach itself from the surrounding foliage and lurch into life.

'Kharno!' he cried, bleating the name this time, because the shadow had taken form and shaped itself into a shaggy body smeared with half-dried mud; into a massive head weighed down by horns that skimmed the surface of the water as the creature charged. *At him*! Exactly as in the dance! Its bellowing cry like a roll of thunder in the close silence of the valley.

He tried to run, but couldn't, aware that he had no hope of escape. For he recognised the creature for what it was even in the two or three seconds that remained. He remembered, too, Lheppo's assertion at the end of the dance – how no man wrestles with the spirit of the buffalo and lives. Ivan could see why he had said that now; perceive the undeniable truth of Lheppo's claim in those heavily embossed horns that drew ever nearer, in the vast bulk of the body that churned its way across the stream towards him.

So he *was* destined to die in this place! In a sense Josie had been right all along: the ship would never return, not for him. And with that knowledge came a split-second of calm. Long enough for him to thrust out his spear in a feeble defensive gesture.

That alone would never have saved him. It was the other spear, flung by one of the hunters, which distracted the animal, glacing off its horns just before the moment of impact. Startled, it flung its head skyward, and instead of the horns, it was the creature's muzzle which slammed into Ivan and sent him spinning off to the side.

He landed flat on his back in thigh-deep water. Hastily he blundered to his feet, winded and with blood streaming from his nose. For a few panic-filled seconds he was too dazed to take in very much at all; then, as his vision cleared, he saw the buffalo whirl around near the opposite bank, its body all but lost in the arcs of muddy water kicked up by its hoofs.

Again it bellowed, and made a quick rush along the bank where it scattered the gathered hunters. Kharno was the only one who managed to launch a spear which merely grazed along the creature's back, further enraging it.

Red-eyed in the greenish gloom, its wet flanks steaming, it slewed around once more and faced back across the river. Ivan saw then that his own spear was lodged in the thick muscle of the animal's chest. Unwittingly he had injured it, as in the dance. Except that here in the real world he had inflicted only a flesh wound, for with an angry toss of the head the creature dislodged the weapon and sent it flying into a dense copse of ferns.

Something else flitted between the trunks, there amongst the ferns. Another buffalo? One of the hunters? Still stranded in the middle of the stream, Ivan was too unnerved to turn and look. *This* animal was already more than he could cope with. Although near-sighted, it had located him through scent alone; and now, with a raking stamp of the foot, it prepared for what Ivan sensed would be its third and final charge.

He knew he should turn and run, but again he couldn't, frozen to the spot as the animal snorted and lowered its head. This time, moreover, he was unarmed. Defenceless ... until someone stepped up to his side, a hulking figure who seemed to materialise from the surrounding shadows.

'Stand firm, moon thing!' a voice grated out, and he glanced up, startled, into the tattooed face of Lheppo. 'We will complete the dance together,' Lheppo added, and grounded the butt of his spear on the stream bed, its point angled upwards.

Lheppo's presence had broken the spell which bound Ivan, and he would have run then had Lheppo not held him there.

'Honour the beast!' he snarled, steadying the spear with his free hand. 'Meet it with courage in your heart.'

Those last words were roared above the snort and splash of the buffalo as it surged forward, straight across the stream towards them, with mud and gravel rising like an angry plume in its wake.

'I c-can't ... !' Ivan stuttered out, wrestling with Lheppo in his blind need to escape.

Lheppo's grip merely tightened, locking him there in mid-stream. Exposed. With nothing but a crude stone spearhead between him and the fury of the old buffalo.

Unable to break free, he gave up, watching with half-averted face as those lowered horns rapidly advanced. A few more strides, a few more greedy breaths, that was all there was time for. But then, when the animal was almost upon them, a stray shaft of sunlight seemed to arrow across the stream and disappear into the dark mass of the advancing body. And almost magically the charge was over. In mid-stride the buffalo faltered and buckled at the knees, its forward momentum carrying it to within a metre of where Ivan and Lheppo waited.

Still it was by no means vanquished. Its horned head swung dangerously, spraying them both with water. Next, with a grunting effort it lurched shakily to its feet and revealed the reason for its sudden weakness. A spear lay buried in its side just behind the shoulder.

Ivan spun around, bewildered, as someone sprang from amongst the ferns. Not one of the hunters – they had regrouped near the far bank – but Josie, her hair streaming out behind. She had retrieved Ivan's discarded spear, and with a wild scream she flung that as well, straight at the buffalo's quivering flank.

She might well have finished the hunt there and then, but the animal staggered slightly at the critical moment; and the jagged head of the spear, instead of finding its intended mark, did no more than slice across the muscled hump of its shoulder. Although not enough to bring the animal down again, this fresh wound made it roll its eyes and bellow in pain; and instants later, defeated, it blundered off along the stream bed, where to Ivan's relief it disappeared into the prevailing gloom of the valley.

Caught up in the fever of the hunt, Josie showed every sign of wanting to rush after it; but Kharno stepped into her path, and before she could dodge around him Lheppo had splashed over and grabbed her by the arm.

'Let go!' she yelled, punching at him. 'It's *my* kill! Mine!'

'Be still!' he cried, and hit her across the mouth, forcing her to her knees in the shallow water. 'You have desecrated the hunt.'

She wiped at her now bloody mouth and stared in outrage at the red stain on her open palm. 'Damn you!' she muttered angrily, and leaping to her feet she swung at him as hard as she could.

'No, Lheppo!' Ivan shouted, fully expecting him to fly into one of his rages.

But like the buffalo before him, Lheppo seemed suddenly to have lost all will to fight. He made no effort even to defend himself as she hit him again and again, his eyes fixed with a kind of greedy fascination on the smear of bright red blood on Josie's lower lip and chin.

'So it's true,' he whispered softly when Kharno dragged her off. 'You're of the earth now. You belong here amongst us.'

'Yes, worse luck,' she answered in English, and crouched sullenly in the shallows, her face turned away.

12

'The beast is wounded,' Lheppo said. 'We must track it down and deliver it from its pain. How else can we show it mercy?'

'There is no other way,' Orhnu grunted. 'But we cannot take the woman with us.'

'Why not?' Josie flashed out at him – and more hesitantly, in the dialect of the people: 'I ... wound ... it. I ... hunter.'

'No, you are not a hunter,' Kharno corrected her. 'As a woman, you have no role to play here.'

'Jesus!' Josie ran a hand through her tangled hair. Then, with a long-suffering look on her face: 'I ... wound ... beast. You ... dead if ... if ...'

'The hunt is still ours,' Kharno insisted. 'Lheppo and the boy must finish what they began in the cave. It is their business – *men's* business – not yours.'

'But ... the ... the ... ' Josie began, and gave up on the deep guttural sounds which she had yet to master. Turning to Ivan she said in English: 'Ask them about the spear, the one still buried in the buffalo's side. That's mine, isn't it? It belongs to me and I have a right to claim it.'

Ivan translated as best he could, aware of Lheppo following his every word – though still it was Josie he kept looking at.

'The boy speaks justly,' he interrupted before Ivan could finish. 'The spear is the woman's. It is hers to claim.'

'You mean you would let her come with us?' Kharno asked in astonishment.

'Only to retrieve what is hers,' Lheppo affirmed. 'From this point on she must carry no weapons, take no further part in the hunt. If she agrees to that, I say she should come.'

'So do I,' Arhik chimed in readily.

Kharno pulled thoughtfully at the fold of his cheek. 'This sounds fair to me,' he muttered at last, and turned to Josie. 'Do you agree to what Lheppo says? If so, I won't stand in your way.'

'Nor I,' Orhnu added.

Only Ivan remained silent – he, like Lheppo, looking at Josie for her reaction.

'I'm to stay unarmed, is that the deal?' she asked Ivan.

He nodded. 'You'll be an observer, that's all.'

He was prepared for her to refuse. He saw resentment flare up in her, only to give way to sly laughter as her mocking self briefly surfaced.

'Well, we don't want to upset their little boys' games, do we?' she said. 'I mean, it's a bit early on to start talking about equal rights. So yeah, tell them I'll tag along and be a good little girl if that's what they want.'

'She says ... ' Ivan reported, but was cut short by Lheppo.

'Let her speak for herself,' he said, and gazed

directly at Josie in silent challenge. 'Let her tell us her thoughts in the words of the people.'

She responded with another ripple of mocking laughter and answered him in a jumble of English and dialect. 'All right, you dumb creep, I ... no ... hunter. Not for a while anyway. I ... woman. Is that clear enough for you, or do you want me to ... to draw ... picture?'

'Your word is enough,' he answered, responding to the few phrases he had understood.

'It is decided then,' Kharno said. 'Now we must press on.' He pointed up past the overhanging ferns to where threads of sunlight angled down through the canopy. 'The day begins to wane and the beast must be relieved of his pain before the sun sets.'

While they busied themselves collecting their fallen weapons, Orhnu went off for their packs and other equipment. He was back within ten minutes, and again they set out along the deeply shaded valley, guided this time by a blood spoor and by the etched footprints of the fleeing buffalo.

The animal had kept to the cover of the valley to begin with, but after a kilometre or so it had clambered up towards a stony ridge where the forest thinned and the mountain loomed through the trees. Although there was less cover here, it was also harder to follow a trail on the rocky ground, which significantly slowed them down.

'The beast has a mind,' Kharno observed admiringly as the footprints disappeared altogether.

Reliant now solely on the blood spoor, they were forced to fan out across the ridge in search of bloody marks. Always they managed to find them, except for once, late in the afternoon, when the trail seemed to vanish completely.

By then Ivan felt almost too tired to think, least of all go on with the search, and while the others continued to quarter the ground he crept off down the hillside to where the shade was deeper and cooler. That was how he came upon the telltale splash of red, and another a little further on, where the buffalo had brushed against a broad-leafed vine.

In response to his halloo, the others came bounding down the hillside to join him.

'I don't understand it,' Kharno confessed, fingering the bloodied leaf to test the freshness of the trail. 'Why does the beast leave the ridge and choose this softer ground where he is easier to follow?'

'Perhaps his time is near,' Arhik suggested.

Kharno shook his head. 'No, this old bull is a fighter. He will resist us to the end. There must be another reason for this change of course.'

They came upon Kharno's 'reason' some half an hour later. It took the form of a very different kind of footprint, more widely splayed and many toed.

'What kind of animal made that?' Ivan asked, and was answered by a combined hiss of voices:

'Leopard!'

'We are not the only hunters now,' Kharno explained in hushed tones. 'Our age-old enemy has picked up the blood scent and goes before us.'

'What difference does that make?' Josie queried in English – and in dialect: 'We ... hunt leopard ... too.'

'The woman speaks like a fool,' Orhnu said derisively, and grounded his spear to show he had no intention of going on.

'No, not a fool,' Kharno explained. 'She lacks experience, that is all. She doesn't understand that we have to prepare ourselves to meet the leopard.'

'Prepare ourselves?' Josie repeated. 'You mean ... go back and ... and start again?' Then to Ivan: 'Is he saying we have to draw more pictures in that cave of theirs? Of the leopard this time?'

Ivan shrugged, only too willing to turn back. 'Must we ... paint leopard before we hunt it?' he asked Kharno hopefully.

The ageing hunter shook his head. 'We cannot control the soul of the leopard. He, is a hunter like us, but with greater strength and speed. Also greater cunning. That is why we need to prepare for the combat. We must make shields to protect ourselves from his teeth and claws, and have fire ready to hand.'

So saying, he led the way back up the ridge where they set up camp in a tumble of boulders. While Arhik lit a fire and Orhnu went off in search of small game, Kharno and Lheppo began stripping great sheets of bark from nearby trees in order to make crude shields.

By sunset the shields were all but complete, one for each of the hunters. Tall curved shapes more than half the height of a man, they consisted of an inner frame of green twigs onto which the bark was securely tied with twisted strings of grass or vine.

'The leopard will find these tougher than the hide of any bison,' Lheppo declared, hefting a shield above his head.

'And my spear sharper than the bison's horns,' Orhnu added from the dusky hillside.

A few moments later he stepped into the ring of firelight, his toothless grin tinged with pride as he tossed the body of a young porcupine onto the nearest boulder.

'You have done well,' Kharno murmured in

approval. 'We need to renew our strength if we're to face the old enemy.'

The gutting and skinning of the porcupine was completed within minutes, and soon their tiny hilltop fortress was filled with the smell of roasting meat. It was completely dark by then, and moonless, the stars so numerous and bright that in places they formed great frosted clusters that seemed to blur together in the blackness of the sky; and out beyond the reach of the firelight they cast ghostly shadows on the rocky sections of the hillside.

To Ivan, sitting slightly apart from the rest, it was as if the whole arch of the Milky Way had drawn closer; as if he had only to reach up in order to pluck star-diamonds from the deeps of space – blue-white spangles of light that could be cradled in his hands here on this new-found Earth. And lost in the beauty of the unspoiled night, he forgot his exhaustion and his torn and threadbare clothes, and sank back with a sigh of pure contentment. Somewhere in the back of his mind he knew still that none of this could last. Nor should it perhaps. Tomorrow the terrors of the hunt would begin anew; and some day soon the ship would return, to whisk him away for ever. Away from fear and ignorance and discomfort and all the other things he sometimes loathed about this place. Yet in spite of that he continued to relish the moment, grateful to be alive in this ancient time. This wasn't simply something he had read about in a book: he was *here* in person, an actual part of it all. This was truly how it felt to share the lives of cave people.

Josie was the one who fractured his mood, by shuffling round towards him with two hunks of roasted meat.

'You look as though you're off with the fairies,' she

said, and handed him his portion. 'Here, this should bring you back to earth.'

He took the meat and gestured towards the stars, vaguely embarrassed. 'I was thinking how beautiful it is, that's all.'

'And also how treacherous and uncaring, like everything else here,' she reminded him – except for once she sounded less than bitter, as though even she were affected by the grandeur of the night.

After that they ate in silence, tearing the meat from the bone with their teeth.

'You know something,' Ivan confessed, their meal over. 'I was a vegetarian back in ... in ...'

'The real world?' she suggested wryly.

'No, you can't call this unreal.' He cast a wary glance across his shoulder, out into the surrounding dark. 'I meant back in the future. I thought it was cruel then to kill other creatures for food.'

'Maybe it was ... *will* be,' she corrected herself.

He nodded. 'Yeah, but not here. It's sort of natural in a place like this.'

'And necessary,' she added quietly.

He thought about that for some moments. 'What about killing leopards?' he asked at last. 'Is that necessary too? They'll almost be wiped out in our time remember.'

'*This* is our time now,' she responded, her voice hard and neutral.

'Yeah, but you know what I mean.'

She shrugged, feigning indifference. 'I suppose it's natural to kill anything if you're in competition with it – if it's out to get you. It's a case of kill or be killed.'

That, too, took him a while to consider, the beauty of the starlit sky suddenly a little less appealing.

'About tomorrow,' he began hesitantly, 'd'you

reckon someone could get killed if we find the leopard? One of . . . of *us* maybe.'

'It's possible. Personally I don't give a damn. At least it'll be one way out of this rotten hole.'

He looked keenly at her face. In the uncertain firelight her expression seemed to change constantly, from indifference through to a brooding sense of despair.

'D'you really mean that?' he asked. 'About not caring if you die?'

'Why should I? In case you haven't noticed, this isn't exactly paradise. *Look* at how ragged and filthy we are!' She eyed her own blackened fingernails with distaste.

'So you aren't scared of dying?'

She tried to laugh aside the question. 'Hey, we're getting pretty heavy here. It's probably time to talk about the weather.'

'No, I need to know,' he insisted. 'Doesn't it spook you out when you think about tomorrow's hunt?'

She grew abruptly serious. 'It spooks you, doesn't it?'

'A bit.'

'I'd say a lot.'

'All right, a lot,' he admitted. 'I keep remembering that night the leopard was after us. The night we spent in the tree.'

'This'll be different,' she assured him. 'We'll be armed. You will anyway. And there'll be six of us. If you ask me, it's the leopard who'll need to be scared.'

'So you aren't?'

She very nearly evaded the question once again, but thought better of it. 'Part of me's scared,' she confessed, 'and part of me's really excited.'

'Excited how?'

She gestured towards the stars. 'The way you are by this sky maybe. Or by Lhien's songs. I've watched you when she's chanting those dumb stories or spells or whatever, and you get this look in your eyes. A *this is it* sort of look, as though your life depended on hearing her right through to the end. Well, that's how I feel when I'm caught up in the hunt. While it's going on, it's all that matters.'

'It doesn't feel like that to me,' he confessed. 'I just freeze up.'

She crouched closer to the fire, her matted hair shielding her face. 'It takes all sorts to make the world. That's what they say anyway.'

'Not in this world it doesn't,' he corrected her. 'If you're male and you can't hunt, you're no one. You might as well not exist.'

'It's no better if you're female and you *want* to hunt,' she pointed out.

'So it looks like we're a couple of misfits,' he said dismally.

She gave a hollow laugh and lifted her face, as though addressing her words to the sky. 'We step back tens of thousands of years and he calls us misfits! That must be the understatement of all time.'

'It's true just the same.'

'Only if you let it be. Me? I'm going to give this place a run for its money.'

On that note she curled up beside the fire and prepared to sleep.

The hunters were also looking decidedly sleepy, and one by one they bedded down in the cover of the rocks. When only Kharno remained he signalled to Ivan.

'You, moon boy, take the first watch. We must stand guard until dawn.'

And having scooped out a hollow for himself, he also lay down.

Alone in the insect-shrill silence of the night, Ivan collected his spear and perched on one of the boulders. But he soon felt too exposed up there – the surrounding dark too vast and threatening – and he took cover like the rest of his companions, down closer to the fire which he heaped with fresh sticks, some thick enough to burn for the next hour or more.

In an attempt to stay alert he spent the rest of his watch in a low crouch, which was a natural stance for the Neanderthal people but made his legs ache. Even so, fatigue overcame him eventually, and he fell into a light sleep and dreamed that he had returned to the future where he was again living with his aunt.

'Isn't this perfect?' she said, beaming at him, and in a way she was right, though in his heart he sensed that something was missing.

He was still wondering what it might be when someone shook him awake, and he found he was lying flat on his back, gazing up at the star-filled sky. Yes, he thought in those first instants of waking, this was what he had missed. This! But then Lheppo's savagely tattooed face loomed above him and he wasn't so sure.

'Do you have no ears, moon thing?' he demanded angrily. 'Does the night not speak to you?'

He listened hard, and the night *did* seem to speak, in an animal snarl that brought him scrambling to his feet.

'Where ... ?' he muttered, groping for his spear, and would have hurled it blindly into the night had Lheppo not restrained him.

'You will frighten only the shadows, no-name,' he said scornfully. 'At night, here in the forest, the leopard is master, remember that. He cares nothing for our spears and knives. Fire alone can keep him at bay.'

As if the word 'fire' had meaning to the forest at large, the leopard's coughing snarl again issued from the surrounding dark. Much louder this time, so that the other hunters also stirred.

'Rest, my brothers,' Lheppo murmured. 'Have no fear. The bird spirit watches over us as in times past.' And drawing a burning stick from the fire, he hurled it out over the hillside.

There was a scuffling noise from further down the slope; and as the stick landed – in the second or two before it fizzled out in the damp undergrowth – Ivan caught the briefest glimpse of silvered eyes, of a dappled body loping away into the sanctuary of the night.

'Has the fire demon done its work?' Kharno asked sleepily.

'Like always,' Lheppo assured him, and having rebuilt the fire he took up his spear and crouched on the nearest boulder. 'Sleep now, no-name,' he instructed Ivan, his jutting brow turned resolutely towards the dark.

Glad to be relieved as sentinel, Ivan settled down on the warm earth around the fire. Yet sleep did not come easily to him. As he sighed and turned, trying to make himself comfortable, he kept remembering the silvered flash of the leopard's eyes; and that in turn reminded him of the silvery starlight. Were they really one and the same? he wondered. Both of them beautiful but deadly? He stole a look at the heavens. Yes, the great swathe of the Milky Way was beautiful still. And also uncaring. As indifferent to his fate, perhaps, as the mind behind those silvered eyes.

With that less than reassuring thought he finally succumbed to sleep, where he again dreamed of the future: a treeless barren place whose ugliness filled him with the deepest despair.

'What are you doing here?' his aunt kept asking him. 'This isn't where you belong.'

And even in his dream he felt homeless and adrift. Lost in a vague limbo where the silver of stars merged into the flash of a leopard's eyes and the flickering presence of a time-ship.

What rescued him from all three was the homely image of Lhien, the bones and teeth in her long grey hair clinking softly together. She was dancing, her feet keeping time to the steady drum of his own heartbeat, her voice raised in song. The actual words meant nothing to him, but the melody seemed to convey a meaning of sorts, one he yearned to understand.

'Tell me,' he pleaded. 'Tell me now.'

But already she had begun to fade, her song giving way to Lheppo's grating voice.

'See, he is no ordinary man, this no-name. He twitches like one in a trance.'

He woke then with a rush, to a grey and comfortless dawn: the fire reduced to a heap of ash; the surrounding forest all but lost in thick mist which stood like a veil between him and the coming day.

13

Fine tendrils of mist still clung to the trees and lingered in the hollows when they struck camp and set out.

Slightly sickened in the stomach by the cold meat he had just eaten, Ivan trotted along at the rear. He felt exposed there and would have preferred to be further up the line, but Josie had pushed him aside in her eagerness to get underway.

They made their first stop in a misty glade more than a kilometre from the campsite. Disgruntled, his ragged clothes already sodden from the dew-heavy undergrowth, Ivan leaned on his spear as Kharno inspected a series of tracks in the soft earth.

'The leopard has returned to the hunt,' he announced. 'Look for yourselves, he and the buffalo follow the same path. He is challenging what is ours.'

'Then he'll answer to us, like in the old times,' Lheppo said.

'Yes,' Orhnu agreed, grinning his toothless grin, 'and with his belly full he'll make a ready target for our spears.'

'Once he claims the kill for himself,' Kharno cautioned them, 'he won't give it up easily.'

'He will when he smells this,' Arhik said, and held up a ball of damp clay in which he had parcelled the live coals from the previous night's fire.

Kharno nodded towards Josie. 'Give the fire to the girl. In the old story it was women who brought the fire demon back from the mountain. As keepers of the bird totem, it is theirs to carry.'

Having issued his instructions, he loped on, the others strung out behind as he followed the buffalo's meandering flight through the forest.

Ivan, stiff from the previous day's journey and hampered by the additional burden of a bark shield, found it harder than ever to keep going. Especially when the trail curved round and up towards the heights. The steady incline, with the forest thinning out on either hand, soon had him gasping for breath and in danger of being left behind. But worse even than the fatigue was his dread of what awaited them, and that also slowed his dragging footsteps.

'You have to slow down,' he complained during one of their brief stops. 'I need to rest.'

'There's no time for rest, no-name,' Lheppo said, rounding on him. 'The leopard is driving the wounded beast towards the mountain crags. If we don't catch them soon the trail will disappear.'

'Or be washed away,' Kharno added, pointing to a line of stormclouds on the far horizon.

As the morning wore on it was the gathering storm more than anything else which threatened their venture. By midday jagged tongues of lightning flickered above the forest behind them; and soon moist gusts of wind were ripping through what remained of the canopy.

'Not far to go now, the beast is sick at heart,' Kharno shouted above the wind, and was about to wave them on when, amidst repeated rolls of thunder, the rain swept down.

All they could do was huddle miserably together, shivering under the chill onslaught of the storm. Their shields offered some cover, but the rain, driven by the squally wind, battered at them from every direction, and within minutes they were soaked to the skin.

'We must keep the fire safe,' Lheppo whispered hoarsely, and despite Josie's protests he drew her close against him, protecting her and her precious parcel with his own body.

It took at least half an hour for the storm to pass. By then the hillside was crisscrossed by tiny streams and all signs of the trail had been washed away.

'The leopard has beaten us,' Arhik said in disgust, wringing the rain from his hair. 'He has stolen what is ours.'

'The spirit of the beast will think we have deserted it,' Orhnu complained. 'With no spirit body to run to, it will haunt these slopes for ever.'

Kharno let out a long sigh of resignation. 'Its sadness must be borne by the sky demons, not by us,' he said heavily. 'They have decreed we should go no further; and we are only men, we cannot question them.'

'This is true,' Lheppo began, but in the act of rising he stiffened and turned his head.

'What is it, my son?'

Without answering, Lheppo flared his nostrils as he had on the previous day, his tattooed brow furrowed with concentration.

'Cat,' he murmured at last, and straight away the

other hunters gathered into a tight knot, their shields raised to form a protective wall.

'How far?' Kharno whispered, his voice just audible above the tinkle of water cascading down the hillside.

'Near,' Lheppo answered simply.

'Then we must make fire, torches,' Arhik began, and was reaching for the clay ball when Kharno shook his head in denial.

'After such a storm where will you find dry wood? No, this time we must rely on our strength of arm and our courage.'

Their courage was put to the test almost immediately, for just above them, from somewhere behind a craggy outcrop of rock, there came a low growl.

'The leopard speaks to us,' Arhik breathed, a beaded line of sweat breaking out across his brow. 'He is warning us to stay clear.'

'Well, here is our answer,' Lheppo declared loudly, and snatching up a fist-sized hunk of rock, he hurled it over the lip of the crag where it clattered noisily against the hillside.

'You will only anger him like that,' Arhik said, unable to disguise his nervousness now.

'True,' Kharno agreed, 'but anger will obscure his cunning, like a cloud before the sun. It will make him less dangerous.'

They all threw rocks then, a barrage of them, and were met by a hissing snarl and a glimpse of a tawny head and shoulders, the lips crinkled back, the ears almost flattened to the skull.

It was that brief sighting of the animal which thoroughly unsettled Ivan. Up until then it had been a voice and a threatening image in his head – something he flinched from, but could more or less cope with. Now it was a physical reality, and much bigger than any modern leopard he had ever heard of; an outsized creature that only vaguely resembled his image of a leopard, with teeth and claws capable of ripping him apart.

I have to stand firm, he told himself despairingly, and dropped his shield to wipe a clammy hand across his forehead, aware that if he turned and ran he would be thoroughly shamed.

Seconds later the tawny head appeared once again, the yellowish fangs fully exposed, and immediately all thoughts of shame meant nothing to Ivan. He wanted to live, that was all; to survive until the ship could swoop down and carry him far from all this savagery.

But already Kharno was urging him to strip off his pack and prepare himself – Lheppo prodding at him with the butt-end of a spear when he just stood there, his shield propped uselessly at his feet.

'Don't fail us now, no-name,' he warned.

Trance-like, he managed to do as he was bid: to take a firm grip on his shield and spear and to step up beside the others. He even managed a few faltering steps when they moved forward in a solid line, Josie amongst them.

'Keep back, woman,' Kharno growled, but unlike Ivan she was too caught up in the hunt to obey – her cheeks aglow, her whole body trembling in anticipation.

Still holding the line, they clambered up to the lip of the crag and were about to scramble over it when the leopard attacked. Ivan, cowering behind his shield, was aware of a splayed body dropping towards them from an upper ledge; of two hunters to his right going down; of dappled limbs flashing out, one clawed foot almost tearing the shield from his grasp. A spear grated on stone, missing its mark – as did another. Then Kharno was buffeted aside, grunts of protest breaking from him as he tumbled back down the hillside. Lheppo, spearless, drove forward with his shield, but encountered only empty air. And now there was no one between Ivan and the leopard but Josie, those yellowish eyes gazing at him across her shoulder.

'Fight, no-name! Fight!' he heard Lheppo cry out.

But those yellowish eyes seemed to have taken possession of his soul. While behind those eyes the tawny body was bunching, tensing, preparing itself to ...

Ivan had ducked behind the shield, so he didn't see what happened next: how Josie flung the clay ball straight at the leopard's head; and how the clay broke apart, showering the animal with hot coals. There was a high-pitched yowl, a pungent smell of singed fur, a scampering of soft-pawed feet – and Ivan, his nerve completely gone, began running for his life.

Weaponless, shieldless, he half fell, half tumbled from the crag and down the hillside, his feet all but sliding from beneath him on the rain-sodden slope. Boulders, bushes, seemed to rise up in his path and he hurdled them recklessly. Then a tree stood in his way ...

A tree!

It was much smaller than the one he had climbed on that terror-filled night months earlier, but a tree all the same. And without slackening his pace he leapt for the lowest branch, heaved himself up, and climbed hand over hand until the trunk swayed dangerously beneath him.

He looked back then, at the scene far below. Josie,

having taken up Ivan's spear and shield, had joined the fight – or what was left of it. Kharno lay winded further down the slope; Arhik and Orhnu had only their shields, all their weapons shattered; and even Lheppo had been reduced to his flint axe. Yet somehow, between them, they had succeeded in driving the leopard back. Bleeding from several wounds, it was perched now on the dead body of the buffalo, clearly determined to defend its kill to the last.

Orhnu and Arhik led the final attack, by hurling jagged pieces of flint, several of which found their mark. Next, Lheppo closed with the animal. Axe in hand, and using his shield as a battering ram, he moved in. But despite its wounds the leopard was stronger than he had bargained for. Rearing up, it met his charge with two powerful swipes from its forepaws – one striking the axe from his hand, the other knocking him sideways. Instantly it was upon him, raking with its hind legs at the shield which was all that separated them. Shredded bark flew in all directions, Lheppo's muffled cries almost drowned out by the high screech of the leopard about to make another kill. Then, just as the shield gave beneath the onslaught, Josie tossed her own shield aside and ran forward, both hands steady on the spear which caught the leopard in the side and passed straight through.

It was the last and most telling blow of the fight; but even in its death throes the leopard continued to resist. With Josie clinging to the shaft of the spear, it dragged her across the ledge, each defiant twist of its body slamming her against the side wall. Bruised and grazed by the battering, she hung on almost to the end. One final convulsion broke her grip and sent her crashing to the ground. She tried to rise, but the wildly swinging shaft caught her across the side of the head and she went down again just as the leopard coughed up its life blood and died.

'Josie!' Ivan sang out from his vantage point in the tree, but she didn't move.

Nor did he for a while. Deeply shocked by the violence of it all, he waited for her to sit up, to wave reassuringly to him. When she continued to lie there senseless, he gave a choking cry and scrambled frantically back down the tree.

He reached the ledge a little ahead of Kharno. Lheppo had already disentangled himself from the shredded remains of his shield and knelt beside Josie.

'Moon woman,' he whispered, and shook her gently, his face hidden by the fall of his dark hair as he bent over her. 'Can you hear me?'

'Maybe her hunter spirit has chosen to follow the leopard into the glades of the everlasting forest,' Kharno suggested quietly.

'Never!' Lheppo said with passion, and rolled her over onto her back. 'See! She is with us still.'

It was true. Her breast rose and fell in a steady rhythm. Yet in spite of that there was a pallor about her – a bluish tint to her lips, a trace of unnatural shadow beneath her eyes – that made Ivan's own breath catch in his throat.

Almost against his will he recalled something she had said about death on the previous evening. *At least it'll be one way out of this rotten hole.* And it came to him then, as Lheppo groaned and his tears rained down upon her upturned face, that perhaps Kharno was right; perhaps that *one way* was the route she had chosen – her hunter soul, impetuous as ever, intent upon following the leopard even now.

14

By the light of the fire Ivan helped Orhnu and Arhik heap the last of the buffalo meat onto the sledge and then went over to a shallow pool in the rock to wash himself down.

The butchering and skinning process had appalled him. The sheer bloodiness of it! And the stench! He had nearly vomited once, but Kharno had been relentless.

'Blood is not to be shunned, moon boy,' he had said sternly. 'It brings life as well as death. That is something you must learn.'

Kharno was right of course. Still, it was good to wash the gore from his hands and arms, to feel clean again. Or as clean as he could ever hope to feel after the violence of the hunt and its bloody aftermath.

At least he was better off than Josie, he decided sadly, and he joined the others around the fire.

Josie was still unconscious, lying just outside the ring of firelight on a makeshift bed of bracken. Lheppo, who had taken no part in the butchering, was crouched beside her, his face turned away from the light. Every few minutes he sighed and murmured snatches of a song, then sighed again and withdrew into silence. Once he rose and began to shuffle his feet in a half-hearted kind of dance, but that too he abandoned with a sigh.

'What is he doing?' Ivan asked, puzzled.

'He wishes to sing her awake,' Kharno answered, and poked despondently at the meat sizzling on the fire. 'In his heart he would dance her back into being.'

'Why does he keep stopping?'

Arhik clicked his tongue, his scarred face heavy with disapproval as he spat into the flames. 'Even a child knows such things,' he grumbled.

Kharno silenced him with a quick sideways glance. 'Understand this, moon boy,' he said, careful not to let his voice carry as far as Lheppo. 'Only a true shaman – someone like Lhien – can lure the ailing spirit back from those shadow regions that separate us from the dead. We are mere hunters. We have no claim on the shaman's songs and dances, and no power to use them.'

'Then why ... ?'

'The heart wills many things,' Kharno broke in. 'Yours for instance. I have watched you, down by the lake. You would fly back to the moon if you could, but without the silver fish from the skies you are powerless. Well, that is how it is with Lheppo. Without Lhien he can do nothing but sit and watch, just like you beside the lake.'

'But Josie ... the moon woman, I mean ... she hates him. She ... '

Ivan was interrupted this time by a derisive grunt from Orhnu. 'This no-name is a senseless thing!' he said, and also spat into the fire to register his disgust.

'Enough talk,' Kharno added, and hooked a piece of meat from the fire. 'Here, take this to Lheppo,' he instructed Ivan. 'It will help to warm the cool space around his heart.'

Ivan did as he was instructed, carrying the meat on a slab of bark over to where Lheppo crouched; but when he handed it to him, Lheppo knocked it aside with an angry growl.

'Why do you send this Inhula to me?' he complained bitterly.

Ivan understood the term Inhula – it was a general word applied to all women.

'You dishonour the women of our clan by calling him that,' Kharno responded.

'What else must I call him?' Lheppo said, and turning from Josie he tore open Ivan's tattered shirt to reveal the bird charm Aghri had given him. 'Look at what he wears. The woman's sign! I saw it while he was sleeping last night. No wonder he cannot hunt.'

'Perhaps he has exchanged spirits with the moon woman,' Ornhu suggested.

'Who can tell with these moon things?' Arhik said, and quickly dipped his head in apology as Lheppo glared at him.

'Take care!' Lheppo growled, and returned to his vigil, sitting hunched and still over Josie's silent form.

'I still say he is not worthy of the word Inhula,' Kharno insisted, as though offering assurance to the surrounding night. 'The charm in itself proves little. He has the outward shape of a man and must answer for that shape.'

Ornhu made a point of ignoring Ivan as he again resumed his place at the fire. 'So what must we call him then, this man-thing with the woman's sign?'

'He is a no-name still.'

Arhik shook his head, his long hair swinging free. 'He is less than a no-name now. He is a nothing. A Dhena Tharoon.'

Translated literally, as Ivan was well aware, those two words together meant the-one-who-runs-away, or coward; and he shuffled closer to the fire, his eyes downcast, his cheeks aflame.

'Yes, a Dhena Tharoon,' Orhnu agreed, relishing the term. 'Or worse. A thing without soul. A rock, a clod of earth, a ... a ... ' He paused, searching for a word that would truly register the contempt he felt, and finally found one: ' ... a Jhali!' Which was the rough equivalent of a serf or slave.

'Hey, Jhali,' Arhik said, pouncing on the word. 'Hand us our meat. That is all you're good for now. That, and being a Dhena Tharoon.'

But as Ivan reached into the fire, Kharno pushed back his hand. 'We are not Jhali keepers,' he scolded his companions. 'I have heard of such people, in the lowlands far beyond the lake, but their ways are not ours.' Then to Ivan: 'Eat, no-name. Though remember that our meat is only a gift. It is not yours by right. Not any longer.'

'True,' Arhik said, and hooking his own meat from the fire he bit into it hungrily. 'A Dhena Tharoon has no rights amongst our people.'

'And a Jhali can possess nothing,' Orhnu commented between mouthfuls.

Soon afterwards, their stomachs full, they bedded down around the fire; and within minutes the only sound was the shrill cry of insects that rose from the forest.

Ivan, too dispirited to sleep, gazed up at the same sky that had so fascinated him the night before. Now, however, its beauty meant nothing to him; its black depths spoke only of emptiness. Of despair. Not just because of his shame, which stood like a second self at his shoulder; but also because of Josie, her body only a few paces from where he lay, her spirit wandering in some dark and mysterious forest of the mind that he could barely imagine.

Another gusty sigh from beyond the firelight reminded Ivan that he wasn't the only wakeful one. He shared the night with Lheppo who had not left Josie's side since the end of the hunt. A few murmured words of one of Lhien's songs followed a sigh – a sad and lonely sound that seemed to drift up into the emptiness and lose itself amongst the stars. And moved as much by Lheppo's plight as by Josie's, Ivan rose from his sleeping hollow and crawled over to where Lheppo crouched brooding and sad-eyed in the shadows.

He hadn't expected the hunter to acknowledge his presence, and was surprised by the breathy grunt that broke from those full lips – not exactly a greeting, but not a rejection either.

'Can this Jhali sit with you?' he asked, purposely humbling himself before the other's obvious show of grief.

That in turn surprised Lheppo whose deep-set eyes caught the firelight as he glanced round at him.

'You are her moon cousin,' he said with resignation, and shuffled a little to one side, making room. 'It is right that you should grieve for her.'

For a while they watched together, searching in vain for signs of animation in the waxen pallor of Josie's face. When none appeared – the minutes stretching into an hour, her body as still as the night itself – it was Lheppo who broke the silence.

'Tell me, no-name, has her spirit taken flight? Has she journeyed back to her home in the moon?'

Ivan answered without hesitation, the guttural tongue of the people coming more easily to him than ever before. 'Her home is here now. She told me so. If she has left her body, she is wandering in the spirit glades of the everlasting forest, just as Kharno said.'

'So Kharno was right?' The hint of a sob in his voice. 'We have lost her?'

Ivan shook his head, remembering his and Josie's first meeting: the way she had stood beneath the ship and questioned his courage. 'No, she is a ... a fighter,' he said. 'She won't give up her body without a struggle.'

Lheppo paused long enough to stoop towards a tiny rock pool, sip up a little water, and dribble it slowly between Josie's parted lips.

'This struggle,' he said at last, 'it continues inside her?'

'I think so. See, she swallowed the water. She is still in there. The body alone couldn't do that.'

He tried to sound confident, for Lheppo's sake, though in fact he wasn't sure whether the swallowing mechanism meant anything at all – whether it involved the mind or was just a simple reflex.

'Aah,' Lheppo breathed, partly satisfied. 'She lives.' Then, with an almost shy gesture towards the amulet at Ivan's throat, 'Does the bird totem tell you these things?'

'Yes,' he lied. 'Lhien's voice speaks to me ... through the bird spirit.'

'What else does her voice tell you?'

Ivan raised the amulet to his ear, pretending to listen. 'She tells me that ... that ... No, the voice is too faint,' he finished lamely, unsure of how to go on.

'That is because of your man-shape,' Lheppo said with a nod. 'The bird totem speaks clearly only to a true Inhula.'

Again they retreated into silence, except that now Ivan was doing more than just watch over Josie: he was thinking about the way she had swallowed the water. True, it may not have been a vital sign, but surely there were others he could look for. Such as whether she was responsive to heat and cold. Or ... or ... her eyes! They could tell him something, couldn't they?

On impulse he reached down and raised one of her eyelids. The pupil, cool and grey, didn't so much as flicker.

'Are you searching for her soul, no-name?' Lheppo asked wonderingly. 'Does it stir in there?'

Stir! That one word triggered a memory in Ivan: of himself as a child at the doctor's surgery, having his eyes examined. And in response to that memory he scurried over to the fire for a burning twig and held it close to Josie's face.

This time when he raised her lid, the iris immediately drew into a tight circle and Josie herself moaned and turned her face away.

There was a gasp from Lheppo. 'Lhien is here,' he whispered in awe. 'She has spoken through the bird sign and hailed the moon woman back from the spirit glades.'

'Yes, she'll return to us soon,' Ivan said with relief, and listened again to the rhythm of Josie's breaths, recognising it now as the rhythm of sleep. 'We must let her rest. She'll be well by morning.'

'By morning?' Lheppo queried, anxious again, and clutched at Ivan as he was about to turn away. 'But the morning is far off. What if her moon home should call to her?'

'I don't think it will ... ' Ivan began, but was interrupted by Lheppo, a new urgency in his voice.

'Look!' He pointed to where the merest sliver of moon had risen above the mountain. 'It has come to lure her home! To take her from us!' And ignoring Ivan's muted protests, he drew the silver droplet from inside his tunic – the same droplet he and Josie had fought over many days earlier.

Like Aghri's amulet it had been pierced and threaded onto a fine leather thong which Lheppo slipped gently around Josie's throat.

'Our brothers in the mountains call these moon tears,' he explained, hastily knotting the loose ends of the thong. 'Too heavy for the skies, they fall to earth never to return. This will hold her here amongst us. While she wears it, her heart, like this fallen tear, will be bound to the earth.'

Ivan wasn't so sure about that, but he said nothing, leaving Lheppo to see out the night-long vigil while he, Ivan, returned to his place beside the fire.

In the previous hour or more nothing about his own situation had really changed. His sense of shame remained, despite his talk with Lheppo. But at least Josie was safe. She wasn't destined to die here – not yet anyway. Perhaps not ever. Which was a relief in itself, but also meant that for the time being he wasn't utterly alone. With that to console him, he fell asleep.

Many hours later he swam up through the dark into the greyest of grey mornings. The forest lay submerged in shadow further down the slope; and the surrounding crags, with their sparse covering of bushes and stunted trees, showed hazily through a dense cover of mist.

148

It was the mist which confused him, deadening sounds so that they seemed to come from a great distance. The voices especially sounded tinny and far off, and he thought for a minute that he might still be asleep. Then he spotted the blurred outline of two figures facing each other on the upper ledge – one broad-shouldered and brutish, his dark hair tied into a knot on top of his head; the other so pale and slight that there was something almost ghostly about her.

As the fug of sleep cleared from his mind, he recognised the pale figure as Josie, still weak and shaken by her ordeal. She was tugging feebly at something around her neck, trying in vain to pull it free.

'I don't want your damned moon tear!' Ivan heard her say in English. 'You can shove it!'

'Why do you wake in anger?' Lheppo asked, bewildered by her tone, and he reached out to calm her.

She smacked his arm away. 'Keep your filthy hands off me!'

It was typical of their morning confrontations, except that for once Lheppo accepted her reprimand without protest.

'I cannot fight with one who has stood between me and death,' he said simply, and bowed his head.

'Why not?' she demanded, reverting to words he would understand.

'Because you have a claim upon me. Like a painter in the cave, you have taken possession of my spirit. From now on my life is yours. We are bound to each other.'

'Crap!' Josie said angrily, and then in dialect: 'You ... speak ... lies.'

It was Kharno who answered her, his voice floating out of the mist towards them.

'No, he speaks true.'

15

The cave was brighter than before. A whole series of flares had been speared into the dusty earth, their smoky light illuminating the paintings. It was also hot in there, partly from the flares, and partly because of the press of people – the entire clan assembled solemnly around the far wall which held the painting of a leopard.

Of all the animals shown, the leopard was the only one surrounded by images of Neanderthal hunters. These weren't painted realistically like the animals; rather, they were stick-thin figures drawn in black, with the outline of a hand superimposed on each of them.

Now, as someone beat a drum and Lhien danced, her feather cloak rustling, Josie accepted a root-brush from Kharno and attempted to add another stick figure to those already there.

To Ivan, looking on, her painstaking effort appeared crude in the extreme, and he wondered for a moment whether she had decided to make fun of the whole process. But no, she seemed serious enough, a look of genuine concentration on her face. And with good reason. This ceremony was an important step for her, and for the clan too, which was about to defy its own traditions and accept her as a fully fledged hunter.

With two quick strokes of the brush, she added pointy breasts to her figure and stepped back, the painting complete. Or very nearly so. Guided by Lhien, she filled her mouth with a reddish ochre, placed one outspread hand palm downwards on her painting, and blew out the ochre in a single breathy gust.

Her own hand, when she drew it away, might almost have been stained with blood. As were her lips. Not so the outlined hand on the wall. That appeared curiously unblemished, like the innocent hand of a child, or the imprint left by her unsullied spirit self.

'She has set her hand upon the leopard and quelled him,' Lhien sang, and shook her rattle in the painted leopard face. 'This hunter amongst hunters has brought him to submission.'

'Name her,' the people sang in response, stamping out the tempo. 'Name her in defiance of him.'

The drum stopped, and Lhien shuffled closer to Josie. In the smoky silence her brilliantly painted face and wild bush of hair made her look like some masked figure that had stepped from the surrounding walls. Dipping her fingers into the reddish ochre, she drew two bloody stripes down Josie's cheeks.

'With this sign of his life-blood, I name you,' she chanted. 'From this day forward you are Utha, leopard slayer. This is your spirit name and you will answer to none other.'

'Utha,' the people sang. 'Leopard slayer.'

And amidst laughter and the wail of frightened children, the ceremony was over, the clan slowly filing from the cave, out into a day of full summer sunlight.

Already the fire had burned down to an even bed of coals, the cooking stones so hot that they sizzled fiercely when Kharno spat on them.

'It is time for the feast,' he declared, and led the way into the smallest of the caves.

This was the only one with an outlet up above – a long chimney-like opening that enabled air to circulate freely through the whole space; and it was in here that the catch from the lake was stored in readiness for the cold months ahead; and here too that the buffalo meat, laboriously dragged back through the forest by the hunting party, had been hung to dry.

As always when he entered this cave, Ivan had to resist the urge to stop in his tracks, the strong odour of the fish like a wall that he had to step through. By holding his breath he managed to stay in there long enough for Kharno to hand him a great hunk of meat, and then thankfully he was back in the light and air, able to breathe freely again.

Before he could accustom his eyes to the brightness, someone muttered, 'Give it here, Jhali,' and the meat was snatched from his hands and borne away. Not by one of the hunters, as he had supposed, but by the childlike figure of Tharek.

That depressed Ivan more than any of the slights he had endured since their return that morning, and he went and sat apart from the rest of the clan who had gathered about the fire in excited anticipation of the feast to come.

While they waited – the smell of roasting meat wafting enticingly across the clearing – Aghri emerged from the nearest cave, her hair greased and plaited for the occasion, her face decorated with bluish clay. She stopped beside the fire and cast a regretful glance in Ivan's direction, as if apologising for what must happen next. Then, with her feet beating time, she launched into a song of the hunt.

It was an old song – Ivan could tell that from its clever rhymes and complex rhythms – and it told an ageless story of struggle and endeavour. Aghri changed it only to the extent of inserting the names of the present hunters, Josie's new-found name of Utha prominent amongst them. Of Ivan himself there was no mention, and he was grateful to her for that. Though equally he realised that the role of the coward, or even of the Jhali, had no place in such songs of celebration.

She finished to a roar of approval, and straight away the feast began, the people plucking pieces of cooked meat from the stones.

Ivan would have liked nothing better than to join them, drawn as much by their air of happiness as by the mouth-watering smell that drifted from the fires. And although he knew he wasn't really welcome, he rose, intending to saunter over. What stopped him were two muttered words – 'Dhena Tharoon' – spoken just loud enough to carry to where he stood. They were followed by careless laughter that may or may not have been directed at him, but either way it made no difference; and with his cheeks burning he turned his back on the feast and headed for the lake.

Seated glumly on the narrow spit of sand, all but surrounded by a glitter of water and light, he reviewed his situation. It could hardly have been worse. The only hopeful thing about the general disaster of the past few days was the fact that he had survived. And against the odds. Which added some weight to his lingering half-belief that he wasn't meant to die here; that his ultimate fate lay elsewhere, in another time and amongst people more like himself.

With the sun burning down on his unprotected head, he clung to that possibility as never before. One day the ship would return. He would *make* it reappear if he had to.

But how?

The answer came to him from an unexpected source. What was it Kharno had said of Lheppo up there on the crags? *In his heart he would dance her back into being.* So why not do the same with the ship?

No! It was absurd. Ridiculous. The kind of thing that might impress a primitive mind, but not someone like him. Not someone civilised and rational.

Even so, he couldn't resist a quick glance across his shoulder, to make sure no one was watching. After all, a few shuffling steps in the sand didn't really matter. Now, how was it that Lhien began her dances?

He could see her clearly in his mind's eye; and in obedience to that image he bent both arms and drew them up, winglike, level with his shoulders. Her feathered cape he simply imagined; as he did the soft clink of bones and teeth in her hair – his own hair already long enough to fall like a veil before his face and shut out the reasoned brightness of the day.

He felt awkward to begin with, his limbs stiff and ungainly. As his confidence grew, he entered more into the spirit of the dance, his mind fixed all the while on the image of the ship, until soon he had forgotten his immediate surroundings. He might easily have been out there on the lake, with nothing but the sky above and the water below. Like the ship itself, he moved gracefully across the sand and slewed around, as if searching for some place to rest. Ankle-deep in the water now, he gathered himself and sped through the shallows, leaving a glittering arc of spray in his wake; and as that settled so did he – sinking down and down until . . .

He wasn't sure what alerted him to her presence, but all at once the illusion of the dance no longer held him. Flicking back his hair he saw her. Aghri. Watching curiously from amongst the trees just up from the shore.

She picked her way delicately down to where he stood.

'You wish for it to come?' she asked, gesturing towards the wide spaces of the lake.

He pretended not to understand. 'It? How do you mean?'

'The silver fish from the skies,' she answered simply. 'What you call the . . . the *ship*.' She had to struggle with the foreignness of the word, and as she forced it out she gave a small laugh that enlivened her heavy features.

He looked at her wonderingly. 'How did you know what I was doing?'

Again she laughed, but more at his folly now. 'It was a good dance. It told me the story of the ship's coming more clearly than words. That is how a dance should be, like a story for everyone.'

'Yeah, a story,' he agreed with sudden bitterness, reverting to English, and slumped back onto the sand. 'That's about all it'll ever be. Never the real thing.'

155

She sat beside him and reached for his hand. 'What are these moon sounds you make? I hear only unhappiness in them, and after such a dance you should be glad.'

'Glad about what?' he asked in words she could understand. 'I don't see any ship. I keep thinking it will come, but it never does.'

She tipped back her head, laughing at him again. 'Oh, it will come. Sometimes we have to wait more than a year, sometimes only a moon or two; but always in the end it comes. If you look carefully in the cave of the spirits you will see it painted on the wall.'

'The hunters painted it?' he asked, surprised. 'Why?'

'For the same reason that they paint the buffalo and the antelope. And see, it worked. The ... the *ship* was humbled. It offered you as a gift to us.'

'As a gift? Is that how you see me?'

'It is how Lhien sees you. And I too,' she added shyly. 'Lhien thinks you will always be with us, but sometimes at night I dream you are gone.' She paused and sighed, much as Lheppo had sighed that night up on the crags. 'These dreams of mine,' she continued hesitantly, 'are they true? Will you leave us one day?'

'Jo ... I mean Utha, she wants to go,' he said, evading her question.

'No.' She shook her head emphatically. 'Utha has been named. Her destiny is here now. The moon and its people will fade from her memory. You will see.'

'What about *my* destiny?' he replied, his voice again tinged with bitterness. 'I have also been named. They call me Inhula, Dhena Tharoon, Jhali. Does that mean I have to stay too?'

'These are not names,' she said. 'They are insults.'

'Yeah, tell me about it,' he agreed in English.

She frowned, puzzled by his tone. 'So my dreams are false?' she asked hopefully, and pressed his hand against her body. 'You will live the story of your life amongst us?'

He could feel the fullness of her breast through the thin leather tunic, and he snatched his hand away, astonished to find himself aroused by her. For a second or two all he could think of were Josie's jeering remarks about how ugly and primitive Aghri looked. And yet here he was ... here ... !

Turning towards her, he forced himself to look critically at her heavy brow ridge with its delicate filigree of tattoo; at her greased and plaited hair; at the broad boniness of her features; at the sturdiness of her limbs and body. But he could sense that already he had dwelt in the past too long. No matter how hard he tried, he couldn't see her as ugly, or even plain. Not any more. He suspected that if someone had confronted him with a picture of himself at that moment, it was his own slight frame and narrow features he would have found unsightly.

Hastily he tried to hide the astonishment he felt, but it was too late for that, his face giving him away.

Pressing her forehead to his she lisped, 'Then you will walk again through my dreams?' And when he failed to answer, a note of promise in her voice now: 'Trust me. You will find a name in the end. A true name. One to be proud of.'

'But there's no place for me here,' he groaned. 'The ship is my only hope.'

'No. There is a name waiting for you somewhere. At the Great Hunt maybe. I know it.'

The Great Hunt? He registered the words, but

again she had placed his hand on her breast, and for the present that was all he could think of. That and the terrible emptiness of the lake behind him.

'You'll see,' she whispered as he leaned against her. 'The bird totem will protect us, the way it has always protected our people. Only believe, and one day it will grant you a name you can live by.'

Part 3

THE GATHERING

16

The cave smelt close and musty when Ivan woke for the second time.

Earlier he had been disturbed by Josie's familiar hiss of 'Get away!', and he had raised his head and seen Lheppo's shadow pass across the wall as he returned sheepishly to his own sleeping hollow. There had been nothing unusual about that. It was something that happened on most nights, and Ivan had soon drifted back to sleep.

This present waking was different, however. No voice had disturbed him; no alarming sounds had issued from the forest. So why should he be so wakeful?

He remembered then what lay ahead – the journey, the gathering of the clans, everything – and with all thought of sleep gone, he picked his way between the resting bodies and crawled under the leather door-flap, out into the clearing.

The night was all but over. The stars had begun to fade, the eastern sky already streaked with pale spokes of grey. Only in the forest was it still pitchy dark, and to hold that dark at bay he stirred up the coals in the central fire and added sticks until he had a small blaze going.

As he crouched above it, warming himself, the leather doorflap again swished aside and Lhien also emerged. With a yawn that revealed her near perfect teeth, she settled sleepily beside him.

'The late summer days are long,' she muttered thickly, and yawned again. 'Why do you make them longer by rising before dawn?'

When he continued to stare moodily into the fire, she nudged him gently with her bare shoulder, as if urging him back to the cave.

'You should be resting, moon boy. The path to the heights is steep. It will test us all.'

'It's not the journey I'm worried about,' he admitted in a whisper.

She ran one hand through her tangled hair and sighed. 'Ah yes, I see what it is that troubles you. And you're right. It will be hard for you amongst the clans.'

'It can be hard down here sometimes,' he pointed out.

'You mean because of Arhik and Orhnu?'

'Who else?'

'They are young,' she explained. 'They act as they do partly because they have no parents to guide them.'

'What happened to their parents?'

She added more wood to the fire before answering. 'Their father was a man of courage. He died heroically in the Great Hunt.'

'And their mother?'

'She died of grief. When they brought back the body of her husband, she set her face against the sun and waited for the snow.'

'You mean she froze to death up ... up there?'

'Her sons were young,' Lhien answered with a nod. 'For two years they were lost in the heights; for two years, before we found them and brought them to our caves, they had to fend for themselves. Such a life made them hard and unyielding. It is why they cannot easily forgive your ... your ...'

'My weakness?'

'I cannot call it otherwise,' she agreed softly.

'And you?' he pressed her. 'Do you forgive my weakness?'

She gazed directly at him, the burgeoning dawn light reflected in her eyes. 'For me it is not a question of forgiveness,' she said carefully. 'When I look at you, I see someone as lost as those two small boys up there in the snow. Perhaps you will find your way, perhaps not. Who knows? Until the fates decide, you are welcome in our caves, you are free to share our food. There will always be a place for you around this fire. But as for the child of my blood ... she is another matter.'

'You mean Aghri?'

Lhien nodded. 'I cannot grant her to you, moon boy. Not while you wander the world like a man with no guiding spirit. I must reserve her for another. That is one more reason why you will find it hard amongst the clans. For I tell you now, many hunters will be eager to win her.'

'They can have her if they want,' he said sullenly.

'Your words and your face speak different truths,' she replied with a sad smile. 'So listen to the advice of your heart and stay behind while we are gone. It will be too painful for you amongst the clans; there will be too many rivals, too many voices raised against you. Here, alone, with the lake near by, you will be at peace. If the fates are minded to, they may bring the silver fish from the skies to carry you away.'

The thought of being close at hand should the ship return was what nearly swayed him. He raised his head and gazed at the surrounding forest, its canopy now brushed with silver by the dawn light. Surely he would be all right here alone. It looked so beautiful, so peaceful. Or at least it seemed so until he allowed his eyes to sink towards the unlit depths beneath the canopy where the night still lingered. Then straight away he changed his mind. By day, perhaps, he might be able to survive with no other living soul for company; but the nights would be a different matter. To have to sit here in this island clearing, enclosed by a sea of unbroken dark! No, it was out of the question. Anything would be preferable, even the ridicule and rejection that awaited him elsewhere.

'Well, moon boy?' Lhien asked. 'Will you be guided by me?'

He shook his head. 'I'm sorry, but I'd die if I was left here on my own. I know it.'

'In spirit you will be no less alone amongst the clans,' she reminded him. 'Aghri will not be at your side. She has already agreed to stifle the love in her heart, and not only because I have asked her to. There are also her unborn children to be considered. If they are to live free from fear they will need a brave hunter as a father.'

'Well, that rules me out,' he said in English, and gave an unhappy laugh.

'Do these words contain moon wisdom or moon folly?' she asked.

'They just speak the truth,' he said soberly, and stood up as Gunjhi and Ilkha crawled from the cave and shuffled over to the fire.

'The Jhali has done his work well this morning,' Ilkha said in the same sneering tone as her husband, and stretched her hands out to the fire.

Gunjhi was about to nod in agreement when Lhien turned on them.

'What nonsense is this?' she said angrily, and was still chastising them when Ivan slunk from the clearing.

Within the forest it was quite dark at ground level, and under other circumstances he would have turned back; but as on the first morning of the hunt he didn't have any time to spare. The whole clan would be on the move soon after sunrise, and there was one thing he had to do. On the off chance that the ship arrived while they were away, he had to leave behind some kind of message, some clue to the fact that he and Josie had been marooned in this particular time zone.

The question that plagued him as he hurried down through the shadowy undergrowth was what form that message should take. It had to be something large and unmistakable and easily constructed. Like a wooden cross, for instance, that was a common enough symbol; though for all he knew the cross sign might be aeons old.

What then?

As he neared the shore and spied the sand spit between the trees, pale against the dark grey waters of the lake, one thing at least became clear: that must be the site of his message. Anyone approaching from above couldn't help but spot it. Yet still there was the question of what to place there. The simplest option was to scratch a written message in the sand, but of course it would be washed away by the first rain. He needed something considerably more permanent.

The answer came to him as he bent aside two saplings in order to step down onto the shore. He fingered the smooth bark of the young trees. Yes, these were what he needed. And taking out his knife, which he usually kept hidden, he cut a number of the thinner saplings, trimmed off their leaves and side branches, and carried them out onto the spit.

At the point where it was broadest and the sand whitest, he threw down his load and cut the separate sticks into shorter pieces. These he pressed into the sand, joining them end-to-end until they formed three distinct letters. S O S. A modern and at the same time universal symbol which any pilot would recognise instantly.

The first pale strands of sunlight were staining the spit as he added the finishing touches and headed for the caves. There was barely enough time now to assess his own handiwork. Briefly he paused on the upward path and glanced back. Seen through the trees the letters looked rough but legible, which was what counted most; and he had embedded them deep enough to resist the pressure of the wind, but not so deep that they could be covered over by sand. Not for a while anyway. With luck they might last weeks, months maybe. Better than any bonfire, they would stand as a clear beacon to searching eyes from the future.

That was always supposing, of course, that his and Josie's future still existed, that their impact upon this ancient world hadn't already changed the whole history of mankind. Yet if history had really been deflected, why hadn't they also been changed? Why hadn't they ceased to exist when their own future vanished?

As always such problems were too complex and

bewildering for him to solve. Especially on this particular morning, when he had other, more pressing worries. Such as whether he had lingered too long beside the lake. The day had well and truly dawned by then, long strands of dusty sunlight streaming down through the trees; and Kharno *had* announced on the previous evening that the sunrise would witness the clan's departure.

Ivan paused again, listening for sounds of activity from the camp up ahead; but there was nothing, and he ran on, his footfalls only slightly slower than his rapidly beating heart. Probably he was worrying needlessly – or so he hoped as he laboured up the last and steepest section of the path. The clan might not value him as they did Josie, but they would never abandon him altogether; never pack up and depart without so much as a shouted warning.

And yet the ship had done precisely that! His own people had dumped him here unceremoniously and then disappeared. So why should he expect primitives like the Neanderthals to act any better? People who owed him nothing. To whom he was an unwanted burden.

He half guessed then what awaited him, even before he burst from the forest and slumped to his knees in the dust – the central fire heaped with earth; the cave mouths blocked by underbrush and lengths of timber; the clearing empty.

17

The first few moments were the worst. It was like being abandoned by the ship all over again, and he experienced the same bewildering mixture of horror and disbelief.

How could people go on doing this to him? It seemed incredible that anyone – but these people especially – could be so cruel and uncaring. Because the fact was, in his heart of hearts he *had* expected more of the Neanderthals: more care, more compassion, more humanity. Above all more humanity, never mind how rough and savage they might look; never mind how much he may have disappointed them. Hadn't Aghri made it plain that his disgrace didn't alter the way she felt? Hadn't Lhien, only that morning, assured him of the clan's continued protection?

You are welcome, she had said, *you are free to share our food. There will always be a place for you.*

What's more he had believed her. And in spite of all, they had done this to him! They had quietly packed up their few possessions, collected their children, and left.

He took a long sobbing breath and was about to give way to tears when he sensed that something about the surrounding scene was wrong. The barricaded cave mouths for a start. If Kharno had genuinely intended leaving him here, why block off the caves like this? It was the same with the central fire. Why bother to douse it with earth? That was only necessary, surely, when there was no one to tend it, no one to prevent its breaking free and rampaging through the forest.

Fully alert now, he noticed something else: a loose leather bag nestled securely in the shadow of the caves. Attached to it was a light framework of green branches, designed to make it easier to carry; and inside the bag, when he ran over and pulled it open, he found his warm cloak.

So! For the first time since leaving the lake he breathed easily. The clan hadn't abandoned him as he had feared. Unlike his own people, they hadn't regarded him as dispensable. They had simply set out at sunrise, according to plan, and left this pack as a sign that he should follow. Considering how at ease they were in the forest, it probably hadn't occurred to them that he might feel left out. Any adult, after all, could catch up with a whole clan on the move, burdened as they were by young children.

Eagerly he slipped on his pack and looked about the clearing, sure now that they would have left other signs for him to read. Like that fresh blaze on the tree over there, to show which path they had taken. And hitching his pack a little higher, he set off in pursuit.

In the next half an hour or so he came across other axe marks in the trees, and always they told him the same thing: that in the eyes of the clan he might be a Jhali or a Dhena Tharoon, but for all that he was still one of them. In spite of his peculiar looks (he had learned long ago that in Neanderthal terms he was less than handsome), in spite of his non-existent survival skills, they had made a place for him. A lowly one it was true, but a place all the same; and for the first time since his arrival, he felt a rush of real gratitude towards these people who had taken him in.

So much so, that he no longer cared about the sneering attitude of the young hunters and their wives; and when he spied Arhik through a gap in the trees, he hailed him like a lost brother.

'The Jhali is with us again,' Arhik sang out to those ahead, and flourished one of the two spears he carried. Then to Ivan: 'What kept you? Did you fear to walk through the sunlit forest on your own?'

'Yes, I felt like a child lost in the snow,' Ivan answered deliberately, and saw the deep scar on Arhik's face darken.

'What do you know of the snow regions, moon boy?' he demanded, and there was fear in his eyes as on the day of the hunt. 'It's not like this soft country around the lake, where the leopard shuns the sunlight. There the mammoth and the bear rule the land by day as well as by night. To walk there is to be in constant peril.'

'Is that how you ... ?' Ivan began hesitantly, and indicated Arhik's badly scarred face.

He shrugged. 'It was a bear,' he said, motioning Ivan past him on the narrow path.

'So how did you survive?'

'I was lucky. The bear took me for dead and returned to its kill. But he left me this,' he added with a faint grin, and indicated the splintered fragment of bear claw attached to a string around his neck. 'Lhien says that while I wear it I need never fear the great bear again.'

'You mean you'd face a bear if you had to?'

A sombre note crept into Arhik's voice. 'We must all do what we have to, moon boy. Even you when the time comes.'

Ivan half turned on the narrow path. 'When do you think that time will be?'

'I am only a hunter. I cannot tell you these things. The bird spirit controls all our destinies. When it speaks, you must listen, that's all I know. Now save your breath for the climb ahead.'

He fell silent after that, his bare feet padding softly on the trodden path at Ivan's back. A little further along the path his wife Gunjhi trotted tirelessly between the towering trees, their baby daughter fast asleep in her pack; and further along still, whenever the path straightened, Ivan could see the rest of the clan strung out in a long line, all of them wearing the same framed packs – the men also burdened by spears and axes.

At mid morning they stopped to rest in a clearing crossed by a shallow stream. By then the lush lowland forest had given way to much scrubbier growth – the trees not nearly so tall and much craggier, their trunks and branches free of vines or creepers. Here, far more light penetrated to the forest floor which was dense with low ferns and bushes; and only a few birds called from the sparse canopy, their echoing voices replaced by the constant buzz of cicadas.

As the members of the clan shucked off their packs and squatted in the long grass, Josie wandered over to Ivan. 'You took your time catching up,' she remarked, and sank down beside him, spear in hand. 'What were you up to? Ship spotting again?'

'Not really. I left a message down by the lake, that's all.'

She raised her eyebrows, a half-amused smile on her lips. 'What kind of message?'

'An SOS, in case the ship comes while we're away.'

'You're hopeful.' Laughing outright at him now.

'I have to be.'

'Why's that?'

'Because I want my old life back, same as you.'

'No, not the same as me,' she corrected him. 'I've given the ship away, you know that. I've accepted the fact that wanting something won't make it happen.'

'Well I haven't.'

She clicked her tongue in a manner that reminded him of the other hunters. 'Maybe that's the difference between us – why I've become a hunter and you're still a hanger-on.'

'So what am I supposed to do?' he said impatiently. 'Forget about where I came from?'

She stared moodily at a line of birds winging above the trees. 'You might as well. All that memory stuff makes everything worse than it already is.'

'Okay, so I try and forget,' he conceded. 'What then?'

'Then you pin your faith on this,' she said. She patted the shaft of her spear. 'These are the only things that talk around here.'

'Not for me they aren't.'

'Well as I say,' she told him, straightening up, 'maybe that's why you're the hanger-on. Like old Charlie Darwin once said, either you adapt or you die.'

'And you think I'm going to die?'

She looked away, as if to spare his feelings, but he was insistent.

'Well, do you?'

'More or less,' she said with a sigh. 'Look at you. You're a Jhali, a nothing. You don't even have the status of one of those babies over there. Is that all you want from life?'

'You know it isn't.'

'Then what *do* you want? And don't talk to me about the bloody ship. I've finished with that.'

'I ... I ... ' he began, and couldn't go on, unsure of what it was he really yearned for. Escape, yes, but beyond that ... what? Not the life of a hunter – he lacked the nerve or the killer instinct or whatever it was a hunter needed. No, for him there had to be another way. Though what it might be, and whether such a way existed, he had no idea.

'You see,' Josie said, breaking in upon his troubled thoughts, 'you haven't a clue, have you? You're the same good little student who stepped onto the ship all those months ago. Well, writing essays and doing as you're told may have won you a free trip back then, but not any more. There are no free rides in this place. Here you have to earn your keep the hard way. In case you haven't noticed, it's a matter of kill or be killed – the survival of the fittest.' Again she patted her spear, almost lovingly this time.

'I don't believe killing's all you care about,' he said quietly.

'You don't?' She gave him a wide-eyed knowing look. 'Personally I'm not so sure. If we don't kill, we don't eat; and if we don't eat, we die. Sounds pretty simple to me.'

'There are other things worth caring about,' he insisted.

'Like what?'

He glanced across at Lhien, as though seeking

173

inspiration from her; but all he could think of were the dances she performed around the fire – plus the dance he himself had created near the lake's edge – and it seemed absurd to set them against Josie's notion of the hunt.

'There's the ... the clan,' he stammered out instead. 'You care about people like Kharno. And ... and Lheppo.'

At the mention of Lheppo she burst out laughing. 'What, him? That gorilla? He's useful, that's all, someone worth having at your side in a tight spot.'

'That isn't how he thinks about you.'

'Yeah, well Lheppo can dream on as far as I'm concerned. He's strictly a hunting partner, nothing else. So don't go getting any ideas about us.'

Shouldering her spear, she sauntered off to join the rest of the clan who were ready to resume their journey. As was his habit now, Lheppo made way for her and followed dutifully at her heels; and she, as usual, spared him hardly a glance, treating his constant devotion as nothing more than her due.

Still troubled by his conversation with Josie, Ivan grabbed a quick drink from the stream and also joined the line, though not this time at the rear. As an alternative to Josie's harsh view of things, he fell in beside Aghri, wanting the reassurance of her gentler manner.

But for once she had no comfort for him.

'I'm sorry, moon boy,' she murmured, and turned her face away. 'I cannot walk with you. Not today, not ever.'

'Not ever?' he echoed her, surprised at the unpleasant jolt those words gave him; and he reached for her hand, but that too she snatched away.

'It cannot be,' she whispered sadly, signs of real

174

distress on her face. 'Our life paths must part here. I have given my word.'

'To Lhien?'

She nodded. 'And to the children I have yet to bear. To them especially.'

'Why? Because I'm not a hunter? Because I can't provide the clan with food like Lheppo?'

'Food is important, moon boy. Without it we die.'

'What about other things? Your ... your dances and songs? Don't they count too?'

He could see they did, but still she held out against him.

'When the winter comes you will understand,' she said in a choked whisper, her eyes brimming with tears.

It was her tears more than her actual words which deterred him. Miserably, he drifted back through the line, until he was again positioned just ahead of Arhik.

'Don't be sad, no-name,' Arhik muttered from behind, a note of genuine sympathy replacing his usual sneering tone. 'I knew as a child what it meant to walk alone. It is a hard road for those who must take it, but that is the way of things in the great lands, and we cannot change the making of the world, you and I.'

From then on the journey was sheer slog: up through the thinning forest to the rocky alpine country where nothing grew above knee height; and on towards the mountain pass, a great V carved between two peaks.

Footsore and weary they reached the pass just on nightfall and took shelter in one of the shallow caves that lined the cliff walls. Hardly more than an over-hang, it served to keep out the wind that roared across the pass at night, and there Lhien cracked open her precious ball of hot coals and made a small fire from the kindling they had carried with them.

The kindling lasted only long enough for them to cook a simple meal of roast meat and tuber-like roots which they baked in the coals. Then, their hunger satisfied – too tired even for one of Lhien's songs – they curled up together in the dark and slept, with a single sentinel to guard them during the long wind-swept hours.

The dawn brought with it a warmer wind from the south-west, which blew at their backs as though urging them on. After eating leftovers from the night before, they moistened the clay ball with water from their skin bottles, packed it full of glowing coals, and tramped on through the pearly mountain light. On either hand the snow-capped peaks soared above them, the sky like a flawless blue-white dome, so free of cloud that it seemed to have been scoured clean by the freshening wind.

They cleared the pass at mid morning. The boulder-strewn ground fell steeply away, and before them lay a huge grassland plain, bleached yellow by the late summer sun and surrounded by an unbroken ring of snow-covered mountains. The furthest peaks were almost too distant to see, floating in the early morning haze like faint mirages.

'This land has been won by the people,' Kharno explained to Josie and Ivan, nodding towards the plain. 'But in the foothills of these mountains, that is where the great bear and the mammoth roam. It is their land, and the hunter must tread those slopes with caution.' He turned briefly to the two young hunters at his back. 'Arhik and Orhnu will tell you of the ways of the bear.'

'That we will,' Arhik agreed nervously, fingering his bear-claw necklace.

'And Lheppo,' Kharno went on proudly, 'he will tell you of the mammoth. For it is his task to lead the Great Hunt this season.'

'When the mammoth feels the ground tremble and fail beneath its weight,' Lheppo announced with a grin, 'it will know the people have arrived.'

'That must come later,' Kharno advised them. 'Here in the uplands it is already autumn and the grains are ripe. Before the winter wind strips the grass stalks bare, we must join the other clans for the harvest. If the weather holds we will have more than dried meat and fish to eat in the cold time.'

It was then that he pointed out across the plain, and Ivan, shielding his eyes from the glare, saw in the far distance a wisp of blue-grey smoke. Beneath it, dark against the pale yellow grasslands, he could just make out what looked like a cluster of dwellings.

'The gathering place,' Lhien murmured in Ivan's ear.

There was an edge of warning to her voice which brought back to him her advice on the morning of their departure – how he would find it hard amongst the clans – and with those words echoing ominously in his mind he joined the others as they descended slowly towards the plain.

18

———————•———————

Ivan wasn't really prepared for what he found at the camp.

For one thing there were the dwellings: not crude lean-tos as he had imagined, but sturdy huts not unlike the houses of poor farming people in his own century. Circular in shape, and built of mud and straw, with thatched roofs, they were clearly capable of keeping out the most violent weather. And the decorations on their walls! Around every door were painted the stick-figure ancestors of each family, placed there to hold at bay the brooding shapes of mammoth and bear. These animals, which Kharno had spoken of with such awe, were shown in all their might. Painted in rich earth colours, and so realistic that they seemed caught in the act of lumbering forward, they gave to the otherwise lowly dwellings some of their own wild beauty.

Then, too, there were the many people who now inhabited the camp. Far more than Ivan had expected. Seven clans in all – including Kharno's people – and numbering over a hundred men, women, and children. Moreover, like the camp itself they in no way resembled his mental picture of them, some clans quite different in appearance from others.

The mountain people, for instance, were shorter and broader and far hairier than everyone else, even the bodies of the women cloaked in a fine down. Other clans had truly massive brow ridges which made them look nearly as savage as the painted shapes on the huts. Others again wore large nose-rings and earrings made from ivory; or were heavily tattooed, their faces and arms and sometimes their whole bodies covered with interlocking patterns; or they had chosen to file their teeth and fashion their hair into weird shapes, or decorate themselves with cuts in the skin that had healed to form crescent-shaped scars.

'My God!' Josie muttered as they paused at the outer ring of huts. 'Anyone'd think the circus had come to town.'

Yet if she and Ivan were astonished at how different all these people looked, that was nothing compared with the astonishment *they* aroused when they walked into camp. Children whimpered and ran to their parents in terror; men and women clutched at each other and cast nervous glances at the sky; while a number of female shamans, decked out in the likeness of their totems, danced across the newcomers' path in an attempt to ward off these spirit-demons from the skies.

Lhien was the one who stepped forward and restored calm.

'The moon people will do you no harm,' she announced. 'They have left their moon homes and come to dwell amongst us. They are of the earth now, mortal creatures.'

'Do they bleed, these moon things?' a man asked – a deep-chested young fellow with a shaven head and a long spike of ivory through his nose.

'I have seen it with my own eyes,' Kharno answered him.

A shaman spoke up then, an old woman draped in an otter-skin cloak. 'Sometimes the sky demons make us see what isn't there. Perhaps the blood was an illusion.'

There were furtive whispers between Lheppo and Josie – Lheppo holding tightly onto her arm – but she shook him off and walked straight up to the young man with the nose-spike.

'Here, see for yourself,' she said, and handing him a flint knife, she bared her left shouder.

A sigh rose from the onlookers at the pallor of her skin, and someone hissed: 'Treat her with care, Thalhu. Remember that the moon folk walk in madness.'

'Yes, I have heard about their wailings when the moon is full,' Thalhu agreed, holding back.

'Do I look mad?' Josie challenged him, gazing straight into his eyes.

With a sheepish grin he took the knife from her, hesitated a moment, and finally nicked her shoulder with the scalloped edge. A mere fleck of red appeared in the tiny cut, but that was enough to produce a ripple of relieved laughter from the assembled clans.

'It's true!' Thalhu cried in delight, and smeared the blood with his thumb – an action that brought a warning growl from Lheppo. 'She is a creature of the earth now, one of the people.'

The old woman in the otter cloak, however, was still not satisfied.

'If this moon woman is of the people,' she said

testily, 'why does she carry weapons like a man? Has she no womb? Has she no love in her heart for the gentle paths of womanhood?'

'The ways of the moon people are sometimes strange,' Lhien answered on Josie's behalf.

And Lheppo, his voice hoarse with indignation: 'She will bear great hunters one day, you will see!'

But it was Josie herself who silenced the rising murmur of criticism.

'My name is Utha, leopard slayer,' she said simply, and straight away there was silence.

'Is this also true?' Thalhu asked, and when Lhien and Kharno nodded together, he bowed his shaven head as a sign of respect. 'Then she has earned the right to walk the paths of men. I for one will hunt with her on the great day.'

'And I,' the gathered hunters declared.

One of them – a little older than Thalhu, his cheeks and chest shiny with decorative scars, his raven-black hair caught up in an ivory comb – pushed his way through the throng.

'I am called Ancharn,' he declared proudly, 'of the horse clan. I too accept this moon warrior and agree to hunt at her side. But what of her companion? This other moon creature? He seems to be a man, but he carries no knife or spear. Is this also the way of the sky people?'

Ivan was suddenly conscious of everyone's attention switching to him, and his cheeks reddened under the pressure of their gaze.

'He hasn't yet won a name,' Kharno explained.

'So he is still to try his skills in the hunt?'

'No, he has tried his skills and found them wanting.'

'You mean he is a Dhena Tharoon?' Ancharn

181

demanded, and edged away as if fearing contamination. 'A person without courage?'

When no one else answered – Ivan himself tongue-tied with shame – Lhien spoke up for him as she had for Josie.

'He is a lost thing,' she said gently. 'Like a child who awaits his true calling. Until the spirit of his earthly self beckons and gives him guidance, we of the bird clan are his protectors.'

The old otter-clad shaman, her curiosity aroused, shuffled over and gazed deep into his face.

'It is as you say,' she agreed, nodding her head vigorously. 'I see no one there in his eyes. He is empty. A being without a soul.'

'A Jhali?' Thalhu took her up, and also edged away – the whole crowd drawing back slightly now. 'I have heard of such beings, but never seen one before. Will he stay like this, a lost soul all his life?'

'That is for the bird spirit to decide,' Lhien admitted.

The conversation might well have ended there had Thalhu not suddenly leaned forward and jabbed at Ivan with the knife, the point slicing across his cheek. It wasn't a particularly aggressive gesture. Intrigued by this moon creature he did not understand, Thalhu wanted merely to see whether he would also bleed – the moon woman, after all, had not objected to being cut.

Yet to Ivan, one hand clamped to his bleeding cheek, this was the final indignity. It was no good objecting. There were too many ranged against him for that. Nor was there any point in retaliating. Even had he wanted to hit back, he would have stood no chance with someone as hulking and strong as Thalhu. The inescapable truth was that Lhien had been right all along: he was hopelessly out of place here amongst the clans; someone who lacked all standing as a human being. And feeling utterly defeated, he hunkered down on the dusty earth, hot tears of humiliation spilling from his eyes.

'Yes, a true Jhali,' Ancharn grunted, and with that the impromptu meeting broke up.

It was Lhien who came to his rescue, not Aghri as he might have hoped.

'Come,' she said softly, and led him to the far edge of the camp where a hut had been set aside for the clan's use.

It was dark and musty inside, lit only by a few stray threads of sunlight that somehow found their way beneath the thatch; but after the bright glare of public attention Ivan was glad enough of the refuge. His face pressed to the rough earth wall, he wished himself anywhere but here in the high country. So that when he fell into a light sleep an hour or more later, not surprisingly he dreamt of the ship.

It was hovering just above the ground out amongst the huts, and all the people had fled in fear. All except him. He was the one the ship had come for, he was sure of that, because a hand had appeared at the open port, beckoning him over. 'Come,' it seemed to say, just as Lhien had said earlier, but with none of her gentleness. And although he tried to respond – although he yearned to leave this desolate plain ringed in by snowy peaks – he found he couldn't, his feet unaccountably rooted to the earth. 'Don't leave me here,' he pleaded. 'Not here.' But with a whoosh the ship was gone, drawing the day after it; and with a groan he awoke, clammy with sweat, to find himself in pitchy darkness.

For a few panic-stricken moments he thought he

had slipped through a hole in time itself; that he was lost in a way someone like Lhien could never conceive of. Then, as the dream receded and he felt the solid ground beneath him, he realised that night had fallen.

'Aghri?' he called softly. 'Lhien?'

No one answered, and he groped his way around the wall to the low doorway.

There was a keen autumnal edge to the air when he stepped outside; and if he had been impressed by the night sky down in the forest, up here it was breathtaking: a glittering drift of stars that stretched from horizon to horizon, the great sweep of the galaxy arrayed in the blackness above him.

Faced with such vastness and mystery, it was easy to believe in the time routes – invisible pathways connecting the various episodes of the Earth's seemingly endless existence – and easier still to realise how difficult it must be for a ship to find its way back to this one tiny portion of time and space. How insignificant he and Josie seemed compared with all of this. How puny and unimportant. Scarcely more than two fleeting shadows marooned within an eternal shimmer of starlight.

Feeling dwarfed by the majesty of it all, he was about to duck back into the hut when he was attracted by the sound of someone singing. It had very little in common with the kinds of singing he had grown up with. Like Lhien's nightly performances it was hoarse and guttural, with a tonal quality all its own. He felt drawn by it just the same – by its insistent rhythm and its weird underlying melody – and half against his will he was tempted away from the hut and through the camp to where a peat fire illuminated the dark.

All the people had gathered here, clustered around the fire in a rough circle, and the first thing that struck Ivan was their air of celebration. *They* gave no sign of feeling dwarfed by the vastness of the night. Their eagerly raised faces, made ruddy by the firelight, suggested that they felt at home beneath the stars; that for them the night had become a time of wonder, not of fear.

They were intent on the old woman in the otterskin cloak. Bedecked in a matching skin cap, and with long whiskery shapes painted across her cheeks, she was busy enacting the story of her people in a mixture of song and dance.

Ivan was unable to follow much of it, which she rendered in either a regional dialect or some older tongue; still he understood enough to realise that the story described how the otter spirit had saved her people from extinction. Not just by teaching them how to fish, but also by revealing to them the secret of play. Like the otter itself, and in spite of her years, she twisted and turned in the bright pool of firelight, as though chasing some phantom fish; and when she had it in her grasp she laughed and twirled around until she was giddy with happiness.

For a few precious minutes, it seemed to Ivan, she became the otter; she made its life and its joy her own.

Then she sank out of sight and another shaman took her place. This was a younger woman, her head weighed down by horns, her face painted into the crude likeness of a bison's snout.

Again an ancient story was enacted; again Ivan followed just enough to catch the gist of the song. But above all it was the dance he responded to: something ageless about the practised movements which channelled the truths of the story directly to him.

One shaman followed another, their various stories merging into one. But not their dances. They remained separate, distinct, giving to each performer a remembered identity. This one was the horse dancer, that one the snake, that the buffalo or the deer. It was as if each of the dancers succeeded in drawing a little of the outside world into the life of the clan. So that with the completion of each dance Ivan felt less threatened by the night sky and the surrounding dark; more at ease here on this gloomy plain. In some obscure way this tiny camp in the middle of nowhere became the centre of everything – a place of warmth and safety and belonging.

He fell asleep before the performance was over. Not because he was bored by it. Quite the reverse. Many of the children and the older folk had long since curled up in the dust, lulled by the familiar stories and the hypnotic rhythm of the dancers; and like them, though still outside the magic ring of firelight, Ivan lay down beneath the open sky and slept.

Later he retained only a hazy memory of being woken; of Lhien ushering him back to their hut which received him like a newly returned ship – which, in his fuddled state, he almost mistook for the ship itself. A haven, there to protect him from any as yet untold mysteries of the night.

19

In some respects that first night of story and dance gave to Ivan a false sense of security, by making him feel more at home than he really was. For in the days that followed he was left in little doubt that here amongst the clans he remained a total outsider – someone with no clear purpose in life, no calling, and therefore no soul. In short, he remained a Jhali, which was how most people addressed him.

Not that they were needlessly cruel. He didn't count, that was all. They treated him as a non-person who just happened to be caught up in the great harvest, which was what occupied the clans for the first weeks.

Day after day they set out at dawn, in search of the ripest patches of barley-like grass which grew in profusion all over the plain. Working in teams, they cut the barley with stone knives, threshed it there and then, on stamped areas of bare earth, and carried the grain back to camp in shoulder packs.

It was back-breaking labour most of the time, offering them little opportunity to stop and socialise.

As Ivan and Josie were both aware, the clans were caught up in a race against the seasonal clock, striving to harvest as much grain as they could before the weather turned against them. Even so, in those mellow autumn days, buoyed up by an abundance of food and company, the people were in high spirits and often laughed and talked together in the course of their work.

Whether cutting or threshing, Ivan couldn't help but notice how much attention Aghri received from the young unmarried men. Ancharn and Thalhu, in particular, made a point of complimenting her at every opportunity; and as the days wore on they began vying with each other to win her favour. On one occasion, for instance, Ancharn took the ivory comb from his hair and placed it humbly at her feet. To which Thalhu responded by offering her the ivory spike from his nose.

They seemed strange gifts to Ivan, and also to Josie, but Aghri was clearly impressed by them. And that, more than anything else, left Ivan with a hollow feeling around his heart, as though something had been drained out of him.

'What is it, moon boy?' Lhien asked that evening, sensing a shift in his mood.

He told her then about the gifts, and she explained what made them precious: how each scrap of ivory had to be dearly bought during the Great Hunt; and how an article like a comb would have taken Ancharn many days to carve.

'Such gifts are not given lightly,' she went on. 'They contain within them all the hunter's courage and devotion. They are a gift from the deepest self. Can you understand this, moon boy?'

He understood all too well, and that only

188

depressed him further. It also bewildered him. Why should he care about this budding love amongst a group of primitive hunters? He was a mere onlooker. A being from another time, with altogether different ideas about love and beauty. As Josie had said of Aghri at the outset, she was anything but attractive, on the standards of their own time anyway. So what did it matter if she was carried off by some hunter from another clan?

Yet the fact was that it did. The thought of her disappearing for ever made his life feel far emptier than it was already. Pointless even. And telling himself that he would soon be out of there – that his real future awaited him further along the time route – didn't help at all. It was the here and now that he cared most about; this immediate and troublesome jealousy which he could neither fully understand nor control.

At night, lying sleepless on a bed of barley stalks, he passed the time by thinking up extravagant ways of outbidding his rivals. He would promise to take Aghri with him on the ship; or vow to excel in the Great Hunt; or ... No, they were all absurd fantasies – in his heart he knew that. Of course he could always match his rivals' ivory gifts with a gift of his own, by offering her his steel knife. Yet that, he sensed, would be a dangerous game. Once he or Josie started introducing future technology into these primitive times, there was no saying where it would end. The greater future of mankind might well be put at risk.

As he lay there debating these things with himself, he heard Lheppo pad softly across to where Josie lay, followed moments later by her hiss of rejection. It was a nightly ritual Ivan had grown used to, yet for

189

once he felt almost sorry for Lheppo. What would happen, Ivan wondered, if he paid a similar visit to Aghri? There in the warm darkness, with everyone else asleep, would she find it possible to reject him as she did by day?

Probably not.

But then what? He would still be a nobody here amongst the clans; still a nameless thing. Nothing would really be changed. And it was that consideration which kept him where he was, fretting on his lonely bed until sleep eventually claimed him.

As an alternative to appealing to her in the dead of night, he did the next best thing. The following morning when the harvest resumed, he went out of his way to work close beside her, even jostling others if they tried to step between them.

After an hour or more of having him dog her heels, Aghri was forced to take notice.

'Leave me in peace, moon boy,' she pleaded. 'Our destinies are no longer twined, you know that.'

'What makes you so sure?' he answered, aware as he spoke that to an extent he was arguing against himself.

'Lhien has explained it to me,' she said, and he could see that she was close to tears. 'There is no place for you here. Your fate lies elsewhere. One day the silver fish from the skies will come for you, and we will know you no more.'

She had voiced his own secret belief; yet it wasn't that which prompted him to drift away and leave her to the other suitors. It was her tears, which eased the pain around his heart, but left him feeling wretched in another way altogether. Guilty somehow, as if, by claiming her for himself, he was merely offering her a share of his own loneliness and uncertainty.

For the rest of the day he worked as far from her as he could get, so as not to witness Thalhu and Ancharn's patient courtship. Similarly, at night he made a bed up for himself on the opposite side of the hut, close to the door. It was there, in the small hours, lying sleepless and fretful, that he heard the first distant rumble of thunder.

Leaving his bed he stole outside. The sky was heavily overcast, the night bereft of stars. For some moments he could see nothing, the camp and the surrounding plain sunk in darkness. Then a stab of lightning lit the distant mountains, followed by another and another, with more thunder rumbling in their wake. As the thunder died, in the brief lull before the next vivid flash, the first cool gust of wind wafted between the huts, bringing with it the musty odour of damp earth.

There was a rustle of movement in the nearby doorway, and Lhien appeared at his side, her ageing face caught in a burst of lightning.

'This is the end of the harvest, moon boy,' she murmured. 'The sky demons are telling us to stop. The rest of the seed is for the earth, not for us.'

She was proved right. During the next three days the rain lashed down, flattening the barley, pounding the sodden ears of grain into the mud where they would nestle through the long winter, in readiness for the spring.

While the stormclouds rolled overhead, the clans could do nothing, forced to shelter in their huts; old and young alike frustrated by this time of inactivity. Of them all, Ivan was the only one who felt secretly glad to be done with the harvest, because it also meant he no longer had to witness the daily courtship of Aghri. For three whole days she was safe within her own clan – averting her face whenever he drew near.

Only once did he try talking to her, but seeing the tears again start from her eyes he soon left her in peace – or such peace as either of them could find in the close confines of the hut, with the rain whispering constantly against the thatch, and the sad murmur of wind beneath the eaves.

The fourth day dawned fine and clear, and there was a new sharpness in the air which heralded a coming change in the seasons.

'Now is the time for the painting,' Kharno told Ivan, and flared his nostrils. 'But this year we must be quick. The wind tells me that the sky demons are impatient.'

That was a view shared by most of the shamans who performed a hasty ceremony for a group of young adolescent boys – smearing their faces with mud before sending them off as an advance party.

'This is their first step towards manhood,' Kharno explained. 'Their task is to locate the mammoth herds and prepare the pits by covering them with fresh grass and branches.'

'Pits?' Ivan queried. 'I don't understand.'

'The combined might of the clans is no match for a mammoth on the open hillside,' Lheppo put in. 'To prevail against this greatest of beasts, we first have to trap one in a deep hole; and such is their strength that even then the outcome of the hunt is never certain.'

Kharno moved his arm through a broad half circle, indicating the surrounding foothills. 'In ages past our forefathers dug deep pits close to all the mammoth feeding grounds. Without their labours there would be no Great Hunt.'

'And without the ritual of the painting there would be no chosen beast to receive your spears,' Lhien added quietly.

It was a timely reminder, and together with the other clans they gathered around one of the oldest huts in the camp.

Like most of the other dwellings its walls had once been covered in paintings from past hunts; but over the years the rain and frost had worn away the pigments and left the mud walls bare again.

'Let the painting begin,' the old woman from the otter clan announced, and Lheppo, as that year's leader of the hunt, stepped forward and made the first brushstroke: a long looping trail of black which outlined the great shoulders and steeply sloping back of a fully grown mammoth.

One by one the hunters followed him, each adding a leg, or the slack part of the belly, or perhaps the vast flaring shape of trunk or tusk. It was a slow painstaking process, interrupted by constant comment and discussion. Even disagreement. Sometimes, when enough people felt it to be wrong, a whole section of the painting was scrubbed away.

'This is how it must be,' an old hunter would say, and redraw the trunk or subtly change the attitude of the head.

'No, I have seen it with my own eyes,' someone else would insist, wresting the root-brush from him. 'It must be like ... so.'

Slowly then, and amidst an endless stream of lively talk and argument, the painting advanced. By midday the final outline of the animal had been agreed upon; and by late in the afternoon it was all but complete, with a shaggy coat of brownish fur, gleaming tusks, and a wildly staring eye.

As the light began to fail and the hunters stepped back from their work, there was a general air of consternation. It was plain to all that the painting didn't live, it didn't capture the living soul of a wild mammoth. It remained a painted shape, nothing more; a stiff unconvincing thing, lacking some vital spark.

'There is no power in it,' Lheppo said gloomily. 'The beast itself will baulk at this spirit likeness.'

'It will not give itself up to us readily, that is certain,' Arhik agreed nervously. 'Some of us will die, I fear.'

Others disagreed, Josie foremost amongst them.

'What the hell are they playing at?' she muttered to Ivan in English. 'The damned painting has already cost us a day. Who cares what it looks like? Not the animals, that's for sure. I say we get on with the hunt.'

Unwittingly Ancharn echoed her feelings. 'The mammoth does not see as the people see,' he declared, the shiny scar tissue on his cheeks and chest catching the last of the sunlight. 'In the eyes of the beast this will be a fine spirit self.'

'I hunger for more ivory,' Thalhu joined in, and fingered the makeshift twig in his nose, which produced a round of laughter. 'I say we place our trust in the work of our hands today.'

'If it's ivory you want, I have something here that might interest you,' an old woman cried, adding to the laughter as she opened her mouth to reveal her one remaining tooth. 'This will be a lot easier to harvest than those tusks.'

'It's the tusks that will do the harvesting if you trust your lives to this,' a grey-haired hunter said, and spat on the ground at the base of the painting.

In the end, however, it wasn't this discussion which resolved the issue. Just as the sun dropped from sight, a gust of icy cold wind blew across the plain from the mountains, bringing instant silence. Everyone but Ivan and Josie understood what such a wind meant, for there was no more argument after that.

'The earth aches for the coming frost,' Lhien said softly.

'The sky demons are heavy with their burden of snow,' another of the shamans went on.

While from another: 'I have never known the season change so soon. The winter will be upon us if we delay.'

'Yes, we don't have thick furs to protect us like the bear people,' an old man growled. 'If the winter catches us up here, the cold will kill more than any mammoth.'

'It's agreed then,' Kharno said, summing up the overall feeling, and turned to Lheppo. 'The painting must serve as it is. We have no time to make it live and breathe.'

All eyes were now upon Lheppo who scrubbed uncertainly at his tattooed brow and gave a reluctant nod. 'We hunt tomorrow,' he said, an ominous ring to his voice. 'May our totem spirits go with us and keep us safe.'

There was a murmur of approval, and people began heaping dry blocks of peat on the newly lit fire. As the flames licked up around them, the shamans painted their faces and donned their cloaks.

Night had fallen by the time the ceremony began – essentially the same ceremony Ivan had witnessed in the sacred cave weeks earlier. By the light of the leaping flames, and in time to the stamping of feet and the staccato beat of rattles, the painting was consecrated.

'This is the likeness we grant to you,' the shamans sang, offering the painted animal to the larger world of the mammoth. 'This is our gift, proffered from the heart.'

Next, each of the hunters was enjoined to put his mark upon the beast and claim it as a brother; and starting with Lheppo they made small cuts in their upper arms and, one after another, placed a dab of blood on the painting in the region of the heart.

'It is done,' the shamans sang, and were answered by the assembled people. 'The chosen beast is bound to us.'

The briefest of blessings closed the ceremony; and straight away – whether to escape the cold wind or the consequences of what they had just done – they went off to their separate huts in order to sleep and prepare for the upcoming hunt.

Ivan was amongst the few to linger on. Throughout the ceremony his eyes had rarely left the painting; and now, by the dying light of the fire, he saw what was wrong with it. The front legs of the animal were too stiff, too straight. *They* were what gave it its wooden, unconvincing look.

As a child he had been fascinated by pictures of mammoths in his aunt's encyclopaedia. One of those pictures came to mind – an artist's recreation of a mammoth at bay, surrounded by a ragged band of Neanderthal hunters. He closed his eyes to visualise it more clearly, and knew at once what needed to be done to the painting. Quite a small change really. Half an hour or so was all he would need.

He very nearly stooped for one of the root brushes there and then. What made him pause was a sense of someone watching him from the shadows. He thought it might be Lhien, but when he shaded his eyes from the fire he saw it was Aghri, her normally open face pinched with concern.

'Don't do it, moon boy,' she whispered. 'If you touch the painting the hunt will claim you.'

'What does that matter?' he answered, trying to act out a carelessness he didn't feel.

'It will matter to me if you die out there. And you might. Your mind is not fashioned for the spear, like Utha's. You aren't meant to be a hunter.'

'Then what am I meant to be?'

She had no answer to that.

'Leave it, moon boy,' she whispered, renewing her plea, and she reached for his hand – the softness of her touch enticing him away, back through the silent camp to their own hut.

That night he slept fitfully, his dreams all about being trapped in cul-de-sacs and blind alleyways and valleys surrounded by sheer cliffs. He woke shortly before dawn, troubled by just such a dream, and lay in the dark listening to the wind.

Whichever way he turned, it seemed, he was as trapped as he had been in his muddle of dreams. If he joined the hunters he would fail – he knew that as surely as he knew the sensation of hunger or thirst. On the other hand to stay here with the women and young children was to consign himself to limbo; to continue as a non-person leading a non-life. In which case he might as well be dead, confined to a shadow existence at the edge of Neanderthal society.

The only other alternative was to wait, to bide his time in the ever waning hope that the ship would rescue him from his dilemma. There was nothing else he was good for; nothing he could turn his hand to.

He took a long searching breath. No, that wasn't entirely true. He could paint. He had proved that in the sacred cave. So why not go out now and add the final touches to the painting? Why not put it right where it was wrong? Not in order to impress the hunters, nor for the sake of the hunt; but in secret, and for his own sake, in order to regain some sense of his own worth.

The idea had no sooner occurred to him than he saw how foolish he had been to listen to Aghri the night before. He had responded to the lilt of her voice, to the touch of her hand in his, to the fleeting comfort of her presence; whereas all along it was the painting he should have listened to. In its silent appeal to be made whole, it at least offered him something he could *do*. The possibility of action. By means of the painting he could, like Josie, make his mark here, no matter how small and insignificant that mark might be; never mind that nobody but himself would know about it. Because finally it was himself he had to live with day by day – perhaps *only* himself if the ship failed to come and he stayed on as an outcast.

His mind made up, he rose stealthily and crept out into a wind so cold that it took his breath away. The dawn was still some way off, the stars just beginning to fade over to the east where the snow-topped mountain peaks showed as a faint bluish-white; and drawing his skin cloak warmly about him he stole silently through the camp to the fire.

He needed only a few minutes to coax a flame from the glowing coals and a few minutes more to remove the crust of ice from the paints in their stone pots. Then, working from his childhood memory of the painted mammoths in the encyclopaedia, he set to work.

He could not have said where his memory left off and his inner sense of a living animal took over; but at some point it was as if he had discovered the very essence of this wild creature taking shape beneath his hands. As he changed the angle of the legs and added details to the uplifted trunk and staring eye, he lost touch with his surroundings – and even with his sense of self – and entered into the spirit of this thing he was remaking. For half an hour or more he was like Lhien in her dances, indistinguishable from the animal that inspired him.

The last brushstroke brought with it not just release, but also a vague feeling of surprise. He hadn't realised how late it was, the stars gone, the eastern sky awash with pale sunlight. And the flickering light from the fire – that too seemed brighter than he remembered. Dreamily (for a part of him was still caught up in the painting) he looked around ... and became fully alert then, as he took in the silent circle of people watching him from the far side of the fire.

'There is magic in his hands,' someone breathed – the old shaman from the otter clan, who hobbled forward and peered into his face as she had before. 'Yes, he is a wanderer this one. It shows in his eyes. While the rest of us slept, he has been up in the mountains where the herds dwell. He has *seen* the beast we seek and brought its spirit likeness back here with him.'

'What a man paints he must answer for,' someone else said, and Ivan made out the shaven head of Thalhu. 'Let him add his blood to ours.'

'That is not his way.' It was Kharno, speaking up for him. 'Haven't I said before that he is no hunter? He merely dreams amongst us. His spirit self still dwells in its moon home. He will return there one day, you will see.'

'Whether he returns or not,' Thalhu insisted, 'he has given breath to the life of the painting. When we face the chosen animal in the heat of the hunt, it will look for him. If he is not there, the betrayal will be ours as well as his, and we will all answer to the spirit's anger.'

'And if he *is* there,' Lhien came in, 'he will be the one to answer.'

'Only if he fails to claim blood brotherhood with the beast,' the otter woman shrilled in reply.

'How can he?' Now it was Lheppo speaking on his behalf. 'He is a shrinking thing. Blood repels him. His gorge rises at the sight of it. Even his meat must be cooked to the dryness of a burnt stick.'

Thalhu thumped his spear angrily into the dirt. 'I still say he is endangering us all. If he refuses to give one small drop of his blood here in the camp, it will be our blood that will stain the mountain slopes. I for one will make him answer for that. A life for a life, I say.'

'Yes, a life for a life,' others agreed, their voices drowning out any further protest.

All at once the crowd pressed forward, their bodies hedging Ivan in. Still crouched before the painting, he felt the sharp point of Thalhu's spear against his neck.

'What is it to be, moon boy?' he demanded. 'Your blood or ours?'

'You cannot raise your hand against another,' Kharno called above the throng, but was shushed by Ancharn.

'The moon boy is not of the clans,' he grunted, and added his spear to Thalhu's. 'He cannot be protected by clan law. So let him answer for his actions here and now. For if he refuses us, I can promise him that my spear will bear the scent of his blood to the beast.'

The pressure of the spears against Ivan's neck increased, the cold touch of the stone points paralysing him.

'You are denying us?' Thalhu cried, taking his silence for refusal, and was about to thrust forward when the rhythmic sound of a ceremonial rattle was heard, and Lhien pushed her way through the crowd.

She was decked out in all her finery, her face painted, a flint knife in her free hand. Shuffling her feet in time to the rattle, she held the knife up for everyone to see.

'Put your mark upon the beast,' she intoned, her eyes willing Ivan to look at her. 'Stain it with your life-blood.' When he didn't move, staring back at her in fright, she folded his hand around the knife. 'Do it,' she sang, her face so close to his that he could smell the night-staleness of her breath. 'Do it while this song lasts.'

He could feel the combined will of the people pressuring him now – their common desire, at that moment, almost as real as the spears at his throat. He looked at the knife Lhien had given him, at its jagged edge; and although he wanted to use it, he knew with startling clarity that he couldn't. It simply wasn't in him to slice into his own skin, his hands and arms refusing to obey.

'Do it,' Lhien sang again, but plaintively now, as he looked up past the people to the dawn brightness of the sky.

This is the last time ... he thought wonderingly, all fear gone from him. The very last time I shall ever ...

Yet he was wrong, his whole body flinching sideways as one of the spears punctured the skin of his neck and drew back.

'Aah,' the people sighed, intent upon the dribble of blood which ran down his neck.

And still he couldn't move, aware of what must happen next, of what he must now commit himself to.

But like the letting of his blood, that too was a decision he had no direct say in. For already Lhien had grasped him by the wrist and dabbled his fingers in the tiny pool of blood gathered in the hollow of his collar bone. Before he could think about snatching his hand away, she had pressed his fingertips to the painting where they left behind a bright red mark.

'It is done,' she sang.

'He is bound to the beast,' the people answered.

20

Ivan made his decision long before the hunting party reached the mountains. At the first opportunity he would wander off on his own and wait for the clan in the narrow pass that led down to the forest. He didn't relish the thought of spending nights out here alone; but it was preferable to another humiliation. He had found it hard enough having his own small clan think badly of him. He still smarted from the memory of those days following the buffalo hunt, with even Lhien looking at him askance. How much worse it would be to have *all* the clans treating him like a pariah.

As he trudged along behind Kharno, surrounded by heavily armed hunters, he had a vivid image of himself being pursued through the camp by a band of jeering children, Tharek amongst them; while Aghri, flanked by her two suitors, turned her face away.

No, that he could never endure, and involuntarily he slowed his pace, as if drawing back from his imagined shame – only to feel the prod of a spear between his shoulder blades.

'Stay with us, moon boy,' Thalhu muttered from behind, and prodded at him again. 'You are a part of the Great Hunt now. We must all move and act as one.'

'You heard the man,' Josie added, grinning back at him. 'We're one big happy family here. All for one and one for all. You know the score. God, it's like being home in the dear old future. My mother was always full of that stuff.'

Her tone was as mocking as ever; yet her flushed cheeks and the brightness of her eyes belied her actual words. Clearly she was in a state of high excitement at what awaited them in the foothills.

Well, good for her, Ivan thought, his inner voice matching her tone. As for himself, he had very different plans. Though to satisfy Thalhu he quickened his pace and tightened his grip on the spear, acting out the part of someone who had every intention of seeing the hunt through to its end.

They reached the western edge of the plain at about mid morning. The mountains had taken on a pale lilac hue, the whitened peaks rising halfway up the sky. A washed-out sickle moon showed just above them, its lower point tilted downwards.

'A bad sign,' Kharno grumbled. 'When the moon tips its face to the earth, the snow will fall.'

'Yes, but soon we will have fresh meat to warm us,' Ancharn said by way of encouragement.

'And ivory to make us rich,' Thalhu added with a laugh.

'And the thick fur of our mammoth brother to protect the children from the cold,' Orhnu joined in.

They were trudging up one of the lower slopes by then, their bare legs swishing through the knee-high mountain grass.

'Hush,' Lheppo cautioned them. 'These are the feeding grounds of the mammoth and the bear. We must move with care from here on.'

Stealthily, fanned out across the slope, they topped a rise and began a steeper climb. Here, too, the grass grew thickly, but dotted amongst it were stunted bushes, some laden with blood-red rose hips, others with purple or yellow berries which the hunters picked and ate as they continued their advance.

The sun was directly overhead now, the deep creases in the mountains up ahead almost purple. The air had taken on a crystal clarity, brittle and chill despite the piercing brightness of the sunlight. And every sound – the hunters' muted footsteps, a distant birdsong – seemed to ring across the slopes for all to hear.

Again they topped a rise and were about to follow the curving path of a fold in the hills when Ivan spotted a huge grey shape immediately above them. With a startled cry he ducked and turned to run, but blundered straight into Thalhu's burly chest.

'Hey, Jhali!' he said, and shook Ivan roughly by the shoulder. 'Do you have so little heart that you flee from rocks now?'

Rocks? Ivan turned back and saw that what he had taken to be a mammoth, skulking in the grass, was just an outcrop of stone.

There were murmurs of amusement from all sides, nearly as muted as the hunters' footsteps, but unmistakable; and Ivan resolved that he would make his escape that night. Not a moment later. While they all slept he would creep off into the dark. The natural slope would lead him to the plain, and after that he would be away and free.

What he was about to discover, however, was that

here in open country the hunt advanced far more swiftly than down in the forest. It was unusual, in fact, for a hunting party to camp before a conflict, mainly because the mammoth herds felt little need to skulk or hide. With no natural predators apart from the Neanderthals, they roamed the slopes at will and openly defied any who barred their way. For a hunt to begin, all the hunters had to do was make contact with a herd – or in this case with their advance party of adolescent boys, which they did within the hour, thanks to the tracking skills of Kharno and some of the older men.

As the hunting party laboured up yet another hill there was a stirring in the grass immediately ahead, and a group of young faces peered out at them, small brown hands motioning for them to duck down.

'Are the beasts near?' Lheppo asked the boys in a whisper, and received a series of vigorous nods.

'What about the pits? Are they ready?'

It was Tharek who answered him. 'Come,' he said, and led the way up a steep rise to a point where the hillside bulged and then dipped into a natural hollow. At least it appeared to be natural, as did several thick clusters of bushes within it.

'See, the pits have been cunningly prepared,' Lheppo whispered in response to Josie's questioning glance.

'Where?'

He pointed to the clusters of bushes. 'There are deep holes beneath them. Some have been staked. And look!' He pointed further up the slope. 'There is the herd we seek.'

Following the line of his arm, Ivan made out what he took to be brown boulders or bushes scattered across an upper hillside. Only when one of them

206

moved did he realise that this was indeed the herd. Much to his relief it didn't look particularly daunting – not at this distance anyway – and he made no effort to hang back when the hunters moved off.

Changing direction, they skirted the hollow, so as to leave no scent there, and made for a point well to the south of the herd. Ivan soon saw the sense in this. For one thing the breeze was from the north. For another their route took them up a deep crease in the slope, which meant they were completely shielded from the herd by a swell of land to their right.

It was mid afternoon, the lower edge of the sun already tipping the peaks, when they reached the lower crags. From there they could look down to where the herd continued to graze; and immediately the hunters began their preparations for the coming assault.

Shrugging off their packs, some produced clay balls of hot coals, others long strips of peat. Placing a heap of coals on each of the strips, they bound the peat to short sticks in such a way that the coals were trapped inside, with just a tiny air vent at the top. All each man then had to do was blow in this vent until the heat from the coals spread through the peat, producing a kind of smouldering torch.

Torches and spears in hand, and keeping to the cover of the crags, the hunters moved off to the north, until they were directly above the herd which still showed as small brown dots on the hillside. The animals had yet to scent any danger, but as the hunters slowly descended they grew restive and wary.

For a while both hunters and prey were unsighted, protected from each other by an outcrop of rock. On hands and knees, using the cover of the long grass, the hunting party emerged from behind this rock, and for the first time Ivan was given a clear view of a mammoth.

It was a lone bull, a hundred metres or so away, and huge. Far bigger than anything he had been prepared for. With a shaggy coat that drooped beneath its belly in long curls; a nobbly head which looked as if it were made of solid bone; and vast tusks that curved and twisted to form the fiercest weapons he had ever seen. Everything about the animal exuded power. The massive shoulders especially: coupled with the slope of the back and the stocky hindquarters, they gave to the animal almost the appearance of a battering ram. Nothing, it seemed to Ivan, could stand in its way and survive; and he began to edge back behind the rocks.

Yet once again Thalhu was there to block his escape route, prodding him on with his spear, and Ivan had no choice but to advance with the rest. To within eighty metres of the herd ... fifty metres ... forty or perhaps less ... the nearest bull now towering above them as they wormed their way between the coarse clumps of grass, their bodies flattened against the earth.

Up until then their torches had given off only faint wisps of smoke which carried away to the south; but all that was to change within moments. At a signal from Lheppo the whole party sprang to its feet and the torchbearers whirled their torches above their heads, the rush of air causing the peat to glow, and smoke to issue from the vents in long plumes.

Those plumes, more than their wild yells and the brandishing of their weapons, were what protected them. With trumpeting cries several of the mammoths came thundering up the slope, intent on trampling these puny intruders. One – the nearest of the bulls – ventured to within a few paces of the hunters. So close that the ground throbbed beneath their feet. Only at the very last did it catch a whiff of smoke and shy away, as did the others. And the hunting party, using their advantage, swept forward.

What followed were a few terrifying seconds of uncertainty during which the conflict could have gone either way. Had just one of the bulls held its ground the hunters would have been forced to retreat; but the mammoths' primal fear of fire was too strong. For all their bulk and power, they were the ones to break, the whole herd lumbering off down the hillside with the hunters in hot pursuit.

That first mad rush carried Ivan along with it. He was given no time to think or even to be scared. Yelling and screaming like everyone else, he rushed down the slope, jostled on either side by bodies and limbs far burlier than his own. For a few unthinking minutes he was as much a hunter as anyone else, a bloodlust he didn't know he possessed welling up inside him. The time routes, the ship, the distant future, all those things from his other life might never have existed. As he screamed and ran and brandished his spear, he was no less primitive, no less of a killer, than any of his companions.

'Kill ... ! Kill them!' he heard someone cry, and was unaware that it was himself. For in a very real sense he *was* a Neanderthal while the onward charge lasted. So natural did the hunt seem at that moment that he might easily have been born to this land, this wild existence, these people.

Then all at once the mad downhill pursuit was over. As the herd thundered into the dip below, a lead animal crashed through the flimsy covering of bushes, down into one of the pits. It lurched out

209

instantly, a long stake trailing from a bloody wound in its underside, and turned at bay just as another of the mammoths toppled into an adjoining pit. This second animal trumpeted and reared, but was too badly staked to escape, its cries of distress causing the whole herd to wheel.

Once again there was a period of nerve-racking uncertainty, in which either the herd or the hunters might have held sway. What tipped the balance was Lheppo's war cry. Snatching a torch from the nearest hand, he ran straight at the assembled herd which wavered and broke as they had earlier. Though not before a bull – the first of the wounded animals – had swung its tusks in a great raking pass that caught Lheppo a glancing blow and felled him.

He rose unsteadily to his knees, blood streaming from his thigh, and hurled his spear straight at the animal's throat, bringing it down. Now the two of them were on their knees, only a few paces apart, the rest of the herd having fled; most of the other hunters already swarming around the second mammoth still trapped in its pit.

Josie had also joined the fray. Together with Kharno and two other hunters, she hurled her spear past Lheppo into the bulky body of the fallen bull. Still it refused to give in. Coughing blood, it struggled up from its knees and stood shakily on all four feet. Too weak to charge, it was still strong enough to lash out with its trunk which fanned past Lheppo's dazed eyes and knocked one of the other hunters senseless.

'Help him!' Josie cried, appealing to Ivan who had lost all forward impetus and was standing there helpless in the face of so much carnage. 'D'you hear me?' she screamed, and threw her second spear which glanced off the smooth curve of a tusk and sailed away into space.

Kharno and his remaining companion had begun searching around them, desperate for fresh weapons, for the bull had taken one shaky step forward, and another, its tusks almost within reach of where Lheppo knelt.

'Don't just stand and watch!' Josie yelled at Ivan. 'Do something, damn it!'

When he failed to respond, too shocked to move, she grabbed him by the shirt and dragged him forward. Right into the mammoth's path.

It towered directly above him now, a mountainous thing which was coughing up its life-blood, great gouts of red that splattered down upon his face and chest like rank drops of rain. He could feel blood running through his hair; smell it; taste it on his lips; see nothing but a fine spray of red in the air all around him. The same rich scarlet seemed to saturate the whole hillside, and he thought frantically: What am I doing here? What ...?

This was not the world he had visualised, aeons ago now, when in his other life he had written an essay about Neanderthal people. Not this world of conflict and gore. He had had in mind a less testing place. Of wildness and adventure, yes, but nothing as basic and barbarous as this. Where life was to death as the hand is to the glove, the two fitting together intimately. Where endless and bloody conflict – or so he mistakenly believed at that instant – defined the whole of existence.

Someone was screaming at him again, shaking him, but he didn't care any more. Didn't care when a red-streaked tusk brushed feebly against him, or when the spear was wrenched from his grasp.

There was an 'ouf!' from close at hand as someone – Josie? – drove in between the bloodied tusks; followed by a breathy sigh that could as easily have come from animal as from human lips. And he looked up into an eye more soulful than any he had ever seen before.

He cared then, even before the mountainous shape collapsed into the grass before him. He cared so much that he turned and ran, driven not by fear – not this time – but by a desire to distance himself from something he was powerless to change. He especially. A Jhali. A non-person. One who had no real role, no say, in the violent working out of these ancient rituals.

He was well up the hillside before he could bring himself to stop. He looked back and was surprised to see how insignificant it all appeared from above. Two brownish shapes surrounded by a swarm of much smaller creatures, and that was all. Yet he wasn't in any way fooled by the softening effects of distance. The memory of all that blood – and the smell! – was too fresh; actual drops of it still coated his face, his hands, his arms.

Using clumps of grass, he cleaned himself up as best he could and ran on. Not blindly. He had a clear plan in mind. One that took him up to the crags first of all, where he collected his pack, plus a small parcel of pre-cooked grain and one of the remaining clay balls, warm from the coals within.

Cries of triumph sounded faintly from below, but they no longer interested him. His sole concern was to set a course while the light lasted. Already the sun had dropped behind the peaks, and long shadows reached halfway across the plain. How long till full night? An hour, or maybe a little more. If he hurried, that would be just long enough for him to reach the plain and take a sighting on the pass, far to the south.

With no time to lose he set off at a steady run – following the line of the crags to begin with, and then, when he was well clear of the hunting party, plunging down along a meandering fold that led to the plain.

Each spring, that fold was filled with a roaring torrent of water, fed by the melting snows. As a result it was boulder strewn, which sometimes made the going hard, its upper slopes thick with bushes. Hurrying along in the cover of these bushes, Ivan detected a movement immediately to his left, and before he could duck for cover a huge brown bear trundled into view. Ivan was so close he could see the purple berry-juice staining its snout, hear the rasp of its claws on the stony ground, and he froze exactly where he was, taking refuge in stillness.

The bear seemed to realise it wasn't alone because it growled a warning and swung its head warily. Its small near-sighted eyes probed the dim light for signs of movement; its nostrils flexed as it tested the breeze. But fortunately for Ivan the faint breeze blew directly into the animal's face; and letting out another irritable growl, it turned and ambled back into the bushes.

Still trembling from this fresh encounter with the natural world, Ivan hurried on – his close call conjuring images of Arhik's scarred face and the way the young hunter broke into a nervous sweat just before a hunt. Those images made more sense to him now that he had seen the size of the bear's claws and gauged the power in those mighty forelimbs. He even felt a new respect for Arhik, aware of what he must have endured up here as a child. All that terror and loneliness. At least he, Ivan, was no longer a child; and nor, in the strictest sense, was he lost. A short period of being alone, that was all he had to endure; and after that he would be back with the clan again. *His* clan, which there in the eerie silence of the gully – with the light failing and the formidable images of mammoth and bear dogging his heels – felt more like a family to him; a loving, squabbling family of the kind he had never known.

With that thought to egg him on, he quickened his pace and reached the plain as night was falling. Just enough light remained for him to pick out the pass – a v-shaped break in the mountains far away to the south – and to memorise the faint pattern of stars which had already appeared immediately above it. Then, in the deepening chill of evening, with the wind at his back, he mentally prepared himself for what he knew would be a long and testing night.

It seemed to him later that every detail of that journey lay recorded in his memory. The constant glitter of starlight; his own faint shadow always there at his feet; the sliver of moon which peered across his shoulder; and most memorable of all, the unutterable feeling of isolation. Never in his whole life had he been so alone. Always, in the past, there had been other people near by; people he could reach out to, rely on. Now there was no one, not a soul. Just himself, the earth, and the sky. Nothing else as he trudged on through the brittle cold, the frosted grass crackling beneath his even tread.

He wasn't conscious of the cloud until it was immediately overhead: a great dark wall which blew in from the north and blotted out the stars as it advanced. With it came a smell of something more than cold; and despite his weariness he quickened his pace. On his own calculation the dawn was only an hour or two off, and so was the pass, which meant that the cloud in itself posed no threat. With or without the aid of the stars he would reach his destination. He felt sure of that, though still something about the dark shadow high above made him shiver and break into a stumbling run.

Almost without realising it he treated that last portion of the night as a kind of race, between him and the cloud. His self-allotted task was to reach the pass before the cloud closed off the far horizon; and to that end he put out all his remaining strength, as if here at last was a challenge he could meet. He *could* prove himself equal to this primeval world; he *could* demonstrate to the earth and sky, if not to the people, that he was worthy. A creature of courage and endurance, like everything that flourished here.

With his eyes fixed on the few remaining stars he plodded on. Gradually, one by one, the stars disappeared; but just as surely the eastern sky grew lighter. All around him the world had begun to materialise, as though being born anew. The mountains emerged once more from the gloom; pale formations of birds crossed the plain, their cries welcoming the dawn. And with only minutes to spare – less than a hand's breadth of clear sky still showing above the horizon – he reached the northern extremity of the pass.

He had done it! Unaided and alone! He had shown what he was capable of.

Suddenly, as he walked on between the sheer cliffs of the pass, he felt less tired, his footsteps lighter, his whole inner self buoyed up by a sense of exultation. He felt he could overcome anything. Closing his eyes, he raised his face to the clouds ... and immediately shivered and shrank back as something soft and icy cold brushed past his lips.

He knew what it was even before he opened his eyes and turned to face the wind. The first snow of winter. A flurry of dancing flakes that settled upon his upturned cheeks.

Part 4
THE NAMING

21

Ivan awoke in the early evening, roused by the constant patter of rain on his skin cloak. Easing aside a flap of sodden leather he peered out onto a dreary rain-soaked hillside, bare except for a few stunted trees and bushes. The real forest lay far below, the pass a kilometre or two behind him.

He retained only a dim memory of the last phase of his journey – of the slog through the pass in the deepening snow; and how, numb with weariness, he had made his way down here, to these softer climes, where the snow fell merely as rain.

Stiff and sore – partly from lying still for so long, partly from the cold – he crawled out from beneath the cloak and rummaged in his pack. The ball of clay, thank goodness, was still hot to touch; and quickly, before he lost too much body heat in the chill evening air, he hunted around for fuel.

All the sticks he found were sodden, but he managed to collect enough dry moss and lichen from the trunks of the trees to start a tiny blaze. By adding twigs and then smallish sticks he gradually built it up, and by nightfall he had a real fire going.

Huddled beneath his cloak once again, he let the heat from the flames soak into him. All he lacked now, apart from human company, was some means of heating the pre-cooked grain, but that couldn't be helped and he ate a portion of it cold. The rest he saved for later, conscious that it might be a day or so yet before the clan arrived.

His hunger more or less satisfied, he looked around. Oddly, now that he had the comfort of a fire, he felt more threatened by the dark than he had the night before, when he had walked alone beneath the stars. Maybe it was because of the gnarled trees and bushes which seemed to flicker and stir out there in the shadows. Or perhaps it was the distant hoot of owls that spooked him, their cries rising feebly from the denser forest below. Whatever the reason, he edged closer to the flames and imagined what it would be like to spend all his nights like this, huddled before a lonely fire with no company other than his own.

Abruptly he shut the thought off, as too terrible to consider. No, the clan would arrive eventually. They *had* to. It stood to reason.

On the other hand what did reason have to do with anything here? Cause and effect, that was the only law which prevailed in these primitive times. It was still raining, after all, hissing in the fire and pattering steadily against his cloak; which meant that the snow continued to fall up there on the plain. The pass by now would be choked with snow – cause and effect! – waist-high drifts banked against the cliff walls. And by this time tomorrow night? If it went on snowing, how deep would it be then? Or the night after? Each day adding to the difficulty of the clan's journey, making it harder and harder for them to get through.

Throwing off his cloak he stood up in the chill and rain and listened; listened past the forlorn hoot of owls in the valley, past the soft trickle of water on the surrounding hillside, straining for the least sound of footfalls. There was none, those upper slopes so empty and still that he might have been the only person left alive; the sole human survivor on a planet swept by snow and rain.

He huddled down again, fighting off panic. What to do? That was the question. Think! Think! Yet for some minutes his brain refused to work, the outer dark threatening to invade him completely.

Taking long deep breaths he managed to bring his panic under control. The most pressing thing, surely, was to find shelter. To get away from this exposed hillside. In the morning, perhaps, he should make his way down to the lake. He would be safer in the caves. More comfortable. With enough food to last him for months if necessary.

Months!

There, he was back with that same terrible question. What if the clan never reappeared? What if the snow claimed them?

He came to a decision then, silently and grudgingly, knowing it would be better to perish in the snow, better to share the clan's uncertain fate, than to lead a life of desolation down here. And with that decided, he banked the fire with damp logs, wrapped his cloak about him, and set himself to wait out the dark hours.

For much of the night he dozed rather than actually slept. Periodically he roused himself to collect more wood and rebuild the fire, for he knew that if it went out he would be in real trouble, an easy prey for whatever might be stalking the darkened hillside. More than once, as he lay down again to rest, he felt for the small figurine which still hung from a cord at his throat, clutching onto it partly for comfort, but also in a kind of silent homage to the fabled bird spirit, bringer of fire.

The last time he woke, the dawn was near. Rags of mist swirled about him, clammy against his bare skin, and there was a definite greyness in the air. The rain, unfortunately, continued to fall, a steady drift of it which swept down from the heights and obscured the lower regions of the forest.

A few mouthfuls of grain were all he allowed himself. Then, as the dawn broke grey and dismal, he ignored the rain and descended the slope in search of good-sized trees.

Here there was fuel in plenty, and he collected together a great heap of sticks, as many as he could carry, which he tied into a bundle with lengths of vine. Next he took out his knife and cut swathes of bark from a suitable tree, stuffing some beneath his shirt, for extra warmth, and more again between his shirt and cloak. The longer pieces he tied around his calves and ankles, as crude leggings. There was nothing much he could do about the dilapidated state of his shoes, but at least he could insulate them, which he did by tucking dry threads of lichen in around his feet.

At last he was ready, or as ready as he could ever be under the circumstances; and after returning to the campsite where he filled the clay ball with fresh coals, he bound the bundle of sticks to his pack and hefted them both onto his shoulders.

Laden with almost more than he could carry, he

made slow progress up through the crags. Before he had covered half the distance the rain had turned to sleet; and when he glimpsed the pass high above him, feathery flakes of snow were already blowing into his face. A few paces more and a thin crust of snow crunched beneath his feet. It grew deeper with each step, and reached nearly to his knees by the time he emerged into the pass.

Here the wind was fearsome, a wild unbridled thing that whistled between the cliffs and drove a powdery wave of snow before it. Head lowered, taking short sipping breaths in an effort to keep out the cold, he blundered on. Step by slow step, sometimes sinking thigh deep into newly formed drifts, he forged a path for himself – keeping to the open pass in those places where the wind's fury had exposed ledges of bare rocks and staying close to the cliffs if they offered him shelter. More than once he was forced to rest in one of the many cave-like overhangs, crouched there for a few minutes while he gathered his strength for the next onslaught.

He was very nearly spent when he spotted what he was after – a dark opening in the cliff over to his left. Compared with other caves he had passed so far, this one had a double advantage: it was situated at the far end of the pass, close to where the land descended abruptly towards the plain; and because it was set high in the cliff, it offered a commanding view of the surrounding country.

Lugging his pack behind him, he laboured towards it, climbing slowly from ledge to ledge. At last, gasping for breath, he crawled into a cavern that burrowed deep into the hillside.

It was eerily quiet within the entrance, the shriek of the wind reduced to a low moan. Also, for the first few minutes at least, it felt almost warm in there. He knew that was only an illusion, however; and quickly he scanned the plain below, hoping for some glimpse of movement, some suggestion of human activity, dark against the prevailing field of white.

As he had feared there was nothing. Just a blur of flying snow that reduced visibility to less than a hundred metres. And he shrugged off his pack and load of wood, slapped the powdery snow from his hair and cloak, and set about lighting a small fire to keep the chill at bay.

Hunched over the tiny flame, he waited out the day. Every half an hour or so he crawled to the entrance and checked the plain; but the snow continued to fly, and no struggling figures emerged from it.

By mid afternoon, in desperation, he tried shrieking back at the wind, calling out the names of his lost companions, as though the magic of their names alone would conjure them.

'Lhien! Aghri! Kharno! Utha ... !'

The words were merely torn from his lips and whisked away to the south. Lost. Like him. Like them. Even Josie's new name proved powerless up here in the stark and lifeless world of ice.

'Arhik!' he tried last of all, recalling how Arhik and Orhnu, as children, had survived for two years high in the mountains, in a place more lonely and desolate than this.

That too did nothing to still the wind or to ease the growing anxiety which gnawed at him as the afternoon advanced.

With less than an hour of daylight left, he gave up. Although there was still plenty of fuel, he couldn't face a night alone in the cave; and shouldering his pack he fled back through the pass to his sodden hillside where he spent another uneasy night.

Once again the dawn brought no respite from the driving rain; and growing hunger only added to his misery. Lean-cheeked and hollow-eyed, he loaded himself with wood as before, and returned to the wind-tormented pass.

This time the snow was significantly deeper. Some of the drifts reached higher than his chest and forced him to back-track; and even on the wind-blown ledges he had to struggle through a thick powdery layer of snow that dragged at his feet and slowed him to a crawl. His periods of rest in the shallow over-hangs grew steadily longer, and in the end all that drove him on was a sense that he would freeze if he didn't keep moving.

He was seriously chilled by the time he made the short climb up to the cave. Slipping off his load, he felt tempted to lie down on the icy rock and sleep; but he knew how dangerous that would be, and he made himself relight the fire, forming a nest of lichen with half-frozen hands and blowing on the coals until they spurted into life.

The warmth soon cleared the dullness from his mind, and again he scanned the plain, though with the same result. Nothing. Only a whirling screen of white overhung by louring grey skies.

Where were they? Kharno, more than any of them, would understand how hazardous it was to delay their return. With each passing day the snow grew deeper, the weather colder, the chances of survival on the open plain less likely. Knowing all of that, they would surely have set off for home at the first oppor-tunity. And it was nearly three days since the hunt now. Plenty of time for them to have packed up and left; for them to have cleared the pass and be well on their way down to the lake.

A sudden hopeful thought struck him as he again gazed out from the cave. Could they perhaps have passed him on that first day, while he slept exhausted on the hillside? Could they already be waiting in the caves below?

He did a quick calculation: there was the time needed to slaughter and apportion the mammoth carcasses; several hours for the journey back to the camp; more time to divide up the harvest; and then the crossing of the plain. No, all in all they could never have set out on that first day. That was asking too much. But the second day – that was a different matter.

So what was keeping them? They could hardly have wandered off in the storm: the wind was at their backs, and all they had to do was walk before it to reach the pass. What could have held them up, then? Unless of course it was the cold; unless they had succumbed to the relentless chill of the wind. They were lowland people, after all, not used to these upland climes.

He had a sudden image of the two babies turning blue with cold; of the clan digging snow caves in an effort to save them, hazarding their own safety for the sake of the next generation. He glimpsed them camped somewhere on the plain, growing ever colder, their limbs too stiff and chill to go on.

Was that really how it was for them? Perhaps. And in an agony of unease he nearly left the warmth of the fire and blundered out into the storm.

What brought him to his senses was the first blast of freezing air at the cave entrance. In these conditions he could do nothing to help. Because of his slight build and softer background, he would probably succumb more quickly than they. Like it or not, he was far more useful here, with his store of wood and life-giving fire. For if they did make it this far, fire might well be the key to their continued survival.

Determined to see out the remainder of that day, and perhaps the next if he had to, he returned to the fire and ate the last remaining mouthfuls of grain. They warmed him almost as much as the tiny flame, and for a while he took heart. Kharno and his people were tough, he reminded himself, far tougher than he would ever be. They *would* get through, come what may. The whole clan wasn't likely to perish through a single mischance.

As the day wore on, however, the wind told him otherwise. Like a wild beast moaning at the cave entrance, it whispered to him of disaster. Here, I am the arbiter of life and death, it seemed to say, I decide the fates of those who brave this high country. And by late in the afternoon he had almost come to believe it.

Feeling utterly despondent he shouldered his pack for what he suspected might be the last time. All his earlier resolve had vanished, worn away by the unflagging energy of the storm, and he could see little point in prolonging his vigil into the future. For once he didn't even bother to trample out the fire. Taking advantage of an unexpected lull in the wind, he stepped into the grey of early evening, meaning to hurry back along the pass. A quick glance across the plain was all he allowed himself – a plain far more visible while the wind held off. A vast expanse of white, unrelieved by any suggestion of colour. Just a tiny speck of black over there by . . .

He drew a long icy breath that made him shudder. Could it be ... ?

Too scared to hope, he rubbed his eyes and looked again. This time there was no mistake. He *could* make out something in the near distance. Not a rock or a bare patch of earth, for it was moving. Slowly, almost imperceptibly, but making progress all the same. In the direction of the pass!

'Aghri!' he sang out, his voice hoarse from lack of use. 'Lhien! Kharno!'

So overjoyed for the moment that, without consciously realising it, he passed across an invisible threshold; took a first faltering step along a strange and wondrous path from which there would be no turning back.

22

Ivan met the clan just below the pass in the dying minutes of the day, and he saw at a glance that they were close to exhaustion. He thought at first it was because of the sleds – crude affairs made from mammoth bones and piled high with supplies – which they dragged in their wake. Then, in the dusky light, he noticed that Josie and Orhnu were supporting Lheppo between them, and the reason for the long delay became clear. The wound Lheppo had received in the hunt – that was what had slowed them down.

'Welcome!' Lhien cried, and floundering towards Ivan she hugged him tightly, her cheek icy cold against his own, her hair and eyelashes thick with frost. 'We thought we had lost you to the winter demons.'

The others added their welcome to hers, and despite their exhaustion they seemed genuinely delighted to find him alive – Aghri especially, who had stayed with the clan, much to Ivan's relief.

'The bird spirit has blessed us this day,' she said,

and frozen tears, like bright crystals of light, appeared on her cheeks.

Even Gunjhi and Ilkha were glad to see him, their babies warmly cocooned in backpacks made from mammoth fur.

Josie was the only one who didn't greet him as he would have liked, her face haggard with fatigue.

'Is that you? Ivan?' she asked uncertainly, and dashed some of the frost crystals from around her eyes. 'Why'd you run out on us? The hunt was over.'

With no ready answer, he moved forward as if to take her place at Lheppo's side, but she pushed him away.

'No, I'll manage,' she said, a hint of possessiveness in her voice.

Lheppo in turn seemed unwilling to let her go. 'We have come far together, moon boy,' he said through cracked lips, and with Josie's help he limped on, the rest trailing along behind.

The wind increased as they entered the pass, lifting the surface snow into fierce eddies which stung their faces.

'Up there!' Ivan shouted above the wind, and pointed through the whirling snowflakes to the mouth of the cave.

It was almost dark by then, the cave entrance a pale oval illuminated by the tiny fire within.

'No, moon boy,' Lheppo said, holding back. 'I cannot climb to your nest in the sky. Not with this leg.'

'I know all these caves,' Arhik broke in, shouting past the shriek of the wind. 'There is a bigger one further along that can house us all.'

'Make it close, Arhik,' Josie said by way of warning, and Ivan could see from the strained looks on their faces that she spoke for everyone.

'Just a little further,' Arhik explained, and led the way to the far side of the pass, the surrounding snow faintly luminous in the gloom.

Buffeted by the ever-rising wind, and aware that there was no chance now of reaching the forest, they followed him to what looked like a mere crack in the cliff. Only when they came close did they see the actual opening: a gaping black hole festooned with icicles and shielded from the pass by a fallen sheet of rock which blocked out both wind and snow.

Had one of the able-bodied hunters entered first, what happened next might well have turned out differently; but in deference to Lheppo's wounded state, they stood aside for him and Josie.

As Ivan was to realise afterwards, it was another of those critical turning points. A moment in which his life (and Josie's) might have branched off into any one of three or four alternate routes – future pathways that suddenly blinked out and ceased to exist. For as Lheppo and Josie limped through the broad entrance to the cave, there was a deep roar, and something shaggy and monstrous reared up in their path.

Because of his encounter with the bear in the foothills, Ivan knew instantly what it was that confronted them: a fully grown mountain bear, enraged at being disturbed at the start of its long hibernation period. It roared again, and with cries of alarm they all fell back – all, that is, except for Lheppo and Josie. Hindered by his wound, Lheppo staggered and nearly fell. He managed to keep his feet, but by then the bear was upon them; and with no weapon to hand Lheppo's only recourse was to protect Josie by flinging himself in its path.

Ivan didn't see the actual blow, but he heard it: a loud thwack that sent Lheppo and Josie spinning from the cave. He thought for a minute that they had both been struck, but it was only Lheppo who fell – Josie letting out a low moan as she dropped to her knees beside him. Then in a jangle of shattered icicles the bear cleared the entrance and came at the rest of the clan.

Kharno and the two young hunters were the ones who held their ground. Scrambling for the nearest sled, they retrieved their spears and surrounded the bear as it lumbered out into the storm. Half blinded by the flying snow, it was still a formidable enemy, swatting aside Kharno's spear which whirled off into the night, and parrying Orhnu's tentative thrust with a blow that snapped the shaft in two.

Josie, directly in the animal's path, screamed up at it in defiance, refusing to budge from Lheppo's side; and the bear, bewildered by this pale thing crouched in the snow, faltered slightly.

That was when Arhik acted. With his spear couched beneath his arm to keep it steady, and his free hand clutching onto the bear claw at his throat, he cried out, 'Forgive me, brother bear!' and drove in.

As with Orhnu, the shaft of his spear was snapped in two by a single blow, but he continued his charge, the splintered shaft catching the bear in the shoulder and lodging in the joint.

It was far from a crippling wound. Under other circumstances an animal as powerful as the bear would have fought on; but together with its sleepy state and this alien winter world it had so recently retreated from, the sharp pain in its shoulder was enought to see it off. And bowling Arhik head-over-heels in the snow, it broke and ran, the 'Uh! Uh!' of

232

its retreating breaths soon drowned out by the wind.

One by one the clan members gathered around Lheppo's still form. In the stormy dark it was impossible to assess the extent of his injuries. He continued to breathe, that was all they were sure of. To examine him more carefully they needed light, warmth – in a word, fire – and out there in the snow and ice, with no access to wood or peat, fire was the one thing they lacked.

Lhien had already begun to keen, convinced that her son was lost to her, when Ivan scurried off across the pass. Minutes later he returned with a load of wood. By then the clan had carried Lheppo into the cave, and Kharno was bent over a crudely made lamp – a stone container of fat in which a wick had been embedded. As the smoky flame illuminated the cave's icy interior, Ivan threw down his load with a clatter.

'There's more on the other side of the pass,' he explained briefly, and this time Arhik and Orhnu accompanied him.

Between them they brought back all the remaining wood, plus the smouldering coals which Orhnu carried in a makeshift leather sling.

While the two young hunters helped Kharno set the fire, Ivan joined the circle of women gathered around Lheppo. Ivan had expected him to look deathly pale, but there was an unnatural flush to his face, his forehead hot to the touch.

'I fear the bear has killed my son,' Lhien complained softly.

To Ivan, however, it didn't seem nearly as straightforward as that. The bear's attack was one thing, accounting for Lheppo's state of unconsciousness. His high temperature was something else altogether.

The reason for the fever became apparent when they tried moving him closer to the fire. In an effort to help, Gunjhi took hold of a leg, and under the pressure of her grip Lheppo moaned and rolled his head in distress.

'Here, let me see,' Ivan said, and folding back Lheppo's leather leggings, worn to guard against the cold, he revealed the wound from the recent hunt.

It was obviously infected, the surrounding skin swollen and inflamed, with traces of yellow pus oozing between the scabs.

'My God!' Josie breathed. 'No wonder he was in pain.'

Ivan looked across at Lhien, her face drained of colour in the flickering firelight. 'Can you cure this?'

She shrugged uncertainly. 'There are herbs in the forest for such things, but they need to be applied before ... '

'We'll get them,' he interrupted.

'I think not, moon boy,' Kharno said quietly, and nodded towards the cave entrance. 'Listen to the wind. Another storm is upon us. I scented its coming out there on the plain. If we try to reach the forest, we will all die.'

There was no doubt that a note of fury had crept into the shriek of the wind.

'One man then,' Ivan suggested, 'to get down to the forest and back.'

Kharno shook his head. 'Would you risk your life in such a venture, moon boy?' And when Ivan failed to answer. 'With the storm at your back, you might get as far as the forest, but against this wind the return journey would destroy you.'

'You might be right,' Josie said, 'but I'd be willing to give it a try.'

'You?' Ivan asked in surprise. 'For Lheppo?'

'Why not? We can't just let him lie here and die like ... like an animal.'

'But you said before, all those other times, that he ... '

'Never mind what I said before,' she answered in English, and Ivan saw with amazement that there were tears in her eyes. 'This is different. I'm Utha now, and this is all I have – the clan and ... and Lheppo. Without him I'd have been dead back there when the bear came at us. That's why I have to get to the forest. He needs my help.'

Sensing her intention, Kharno reached out and took her by the wrist.

'Nobody doubts your courage,' he said gently. 'It is as constant as the skies. But what are these herbs you will gather? Where are they to be found? These are mysteries known only to Lhien.'

'Then I'll take her with me,' Josie replied.

'That I cannot allow,' Kharno said with another shake of the head. 'She is the soul of the clan. If we lost her, we would be a people adrift in the seasons, with no one to bind us to our mother earth. And look at her, Utha, look at us both with the eyes of truth. We are no longer young, Lhien and I, and we have already walked to the limits of our strength. Out there we will perish. If we allow our love to drive us into the storm, the sky demons will consume more than just one life this night.'

There was nothing Josie could say to that, and scrubbing the tears from her eyes she resumed her place at Lheppo's side.

'So you think he may not last the night?' she asked after some minutes, harking back to the last thing said.

Kharno sighed and glanced across at Lhien, leaving her to answer for him.

'If my son's heart is strong,' she said, and touched a finger to Lheppo's chest, 'he will survive. But the poison is strong in him too. Who can say what the outcome will be? All we can do is place our trust in the bird spirit and wait.'

Lhien's method of waiting was to strip off her outer garments and don her feather cloak. Rattle in hand, and in spite of her fatigue, she began to dance, singing all the while of legendary struggles with the demon death.

While she performed her rituals and Josie continued her vigil at Lheppo's side, the rest of the clan ate a simple meal and lay down around the fire to sleep. It wasn't a big fire. Because of their limited stock of wood, all they could afford was a smouldering bed of coals to take the edge off the cave's icy chill.

Having satisfied his hunger for the first time in days, Ivan slept soundly for a few hours. He was disturbed by a dream in which he wandered through a blizzard, buffeted by winds that whispered to him of loss; and with a start, his heart racing, he awoke to the storm-racked night and the ongoing drone of Lhien's voice.

Outside, the wind moaned its dreary way along the passes, while within the close confines of the cave the lamp swirled and flickered, throwing grotesque shadows on the walls.

Josie still hadn't moved from Lheppo's side, her head slightly bowed with fatigue, and Ivan crawled over and sat beside her.

'How is he?' he asked.

'Burning up,' Josie answered shortly.

Ivan looked at Lheppo's parched lips. 'We should

236

probably be giving him plenty of fluids.'

'I've tried, but it does no good. Here, I'll show you.' She left the cave for a few moments and brought back a handful of snow which she melted in her mouth and dribbled onto Lheppo's slightly parted lips.

His immediate reaction was to choke and cough, the veins standing out on his forehead as he gasped and fought for breath.

'You see,' Josie said when he had again settled into a state of restless delirium. 'It's no good.'

'So what can we do now?'

Some of Josie's old self showed through for a second or two. 'Nothing, unless you want to join Lhien for a bit of a song and a dance.'

'I would if it would help,' Ivan admitted.

'So would I.'

Turning his back on Lhien, Ivan eased aside Lheppo's legging and took another look at the wound. He had never seen anything quite so angry before – or so ugly – the thigh swollen to twice its normal size and horribly discoloured.

'This is the trouble,' he murmured. 'Put this right and he'd be fine.'

'Yeah, but how do you go about fixing something that bad?'

'I know what they'd do in our own time.'

'Which is?'

'For a start they'd lance the wound and let all the poison out.'

Josie turned towards him, her voice suddenly different, more hopeful. 'Why can't *we* do that?'

'Because there's no point. We have no disinfectant, no antibiotics. We'd make him suffer for nothing.'

'What about before?' Josie insisted, refusing to give up on the idea.

'Before when?'

'Our own time. The eighteenth and nineteenth centuries, for instance. Did they have disinfectant and antibiotics and stuff in those days?'

'Not antibiotics.'

'Disinfectant then?'

'Maybe not.'

'So what did they do? Surely they didn't sit around like this and watch people die. They must have had some kind of treatment. What was it?'

'I'm not really sure,' he confessed, 'but at a guess I'd say they cauterised infected wounds.'

'Cauterised? What the hell's that?'

'They would have used heat ... fire, to burn them clean.'

Josie was already on her feet, some of the anxiety and fatigue lifting from her face. 'What are we waiting for? We have fire right here.'

'Yeah, but not all the other things.'

'Such as?'

'A clean surgical instrument for lancing the wound.'

'There's your knife.'

'I said a *clean* instrument, as in sterile. You go sticking germ-laden blades inside him and you'll finish him off.'

'The blade doesn't have to be germ-laden,' she pointed out. 'You can sterilise that in the fire, too.'

He couldn't really argue with that, but still he held back.

'Well?' she said impatiently. 'Why not do it?'

He felt in his pocket for the knife. 'Because it doesn't seem right.'

'Seem?' She looked at him incredulously. 'What are you talking about?'

'It's just that ... ' He hesitated and had to start

again. 'It wouldn't feel right using the knife.'

'Damn your feelings!' she said explosively, and the sleeping clan stirred and mumbled in their sleep.

Lhien, on the far side of the cavern, turned to watch them without pausing in her song.

'But the manufacture of steel is still thousands of years away,' Ivan objected feebly. 'If we start messing around with modern technology we might ... '

'Might get stuck here, d'you mean?' she broke in. 'Kind of.'

She dragged her hair back from her forehead and brought her face close up to his, her gaze burningly intense in the uneven glow of the lamp.

'Hasn't the penny dropped for you yet?' she hissed. 'We *are* stuck here. This is all there is. All there'll ever be. For you, for me, but for Lheppo especially. You let him die, and he'll be gone for good. There'll be no ships dropping from the skies to whisk him away; no fairy godmothers to rescue him in the nick of time. We're the only hope he's got. Us and that knife. So use it before it's too late!'

Ivan took the knife from his pocket and offered it to her. 'Here, you try.'

He was ready for her to snatch it from him, but instead she shook her head, both hands raised defensively.

'No, I couldn't,' she said with a shiver. 'I could cut myself. You've seen me do it. But not him. If I were to cut Lheppo and he ... and he ... ' She shivered again. 'You're the one who's read all about this medical stuff, not me. I didn't even know what cauterised meant. He'd stand a better chance with you. You know he would.'

'But you're the hunter,' he responded desperately. 'I can't even ... '

'You can!' she came back at him. 'And this is the only time I'll ever ask anything of you. I promise. If you do this for me . . . for *us*, I'll never expect another favour as long as I live. You have my word on that. And I'll stick up for you. So will Lheppo.'

Half won over by the sheer passion in her voice, he opened the main blade of the knife and stared at it, wondering if he had the nerve to see the process through.

'Lheppo believes in you,' she whispered, 'because of the way you stood your ground in the hunt. You're not a born hunter. He knows that. But you didn't run away either, not until the hunt was over. That impressed him, and the others too. They said so afterwards. Lhien even did one of her dances to keep you safe. You'll be letting them all down if you don't go through with this.'

It was her final point that he couldn't resist. Even so, making up his mind was like crossing another of those invisible thresholds; or like turning his back on a future he called his own and choosing to become someone else. Someone he had only the haziest notion of.

Momentarily daunted, he glanced once more at Lheppo's flushed and silent face, as if seeking guidance there. Apart from its feverish appearance it was ordinary enough, similar to all the other Neanderthal faces he had grown used to over the months. The only surprising thing about it was its youth. Here in the gentle lamplight, it was clearly the face of a man-boy, of a person newly embarked on the long road of adult life. It might almost have been himself lying so straight and still; *his* lips twitching and muttering incoherently; his own precious life about to be sucked into the unredeeming dark.

He closed his eyes, trying to visualise what it would be like to find himself in Lheppo's position – and hastily he opened them again, thankful even for the sanctuary of the cave. For a split second, as he saw it anew, it ceased to look stark and unlovely. Compared with the everlasting dark beyond the doorway, this lamplit interior with its warm family circle was a place of glittering promise. A mini-world of life, endeavour, hope. Something worth striving for, both now and always.

While his vision of it held, he turned, knife in hand, towards the fire.

23

With a piece of leather to protect his hand from the heat, Ivan held the blade amongst the coals until the clear steel discoloured and took on rainbowed hues. The hot metal smoked slightly in the cold air as he picked his way amongst the sleeping forms, back to where Lheppo lay.

Lhien, aware that something was afoot, had abandoned her song and shuffled nearer, her feet still keeping to the rhythms of the dance; and Kharno, disturbed by the unusual activity, stirred awake and rose from his sleeping hollow.

As Ivan knelt at Lheppo's side, the knife poised above the wound, Kharno's voice rang out sharp and clear.

'What is in your mind, moon boy?'

Lhien sounded a low warning of her own. 'The laws of the clan are plain. We are not free to offer a life to the spirit demons. They must take it for themselves.'

'They think I want to kill him,' Ivan muttered to Josie in English.

'Never mind what they think,' she said, and reached surreptitiously for her spear. 'Just do it.'

In spite of the cave's chill he had begun to sweat, his hand trembling as he brought the knife down. Concentrate! he told himself, and focussed hard upon the bloated wound, until everything else – all other sights and sounds – were pushed into the background. Faintly, he could hear voices raised in protest; yet none of that counted here in this silent space which he shared only with Lheppo and the knife. Even Josie's cry of, 'For God's sake get on with it!' had little effect on him.

He was thinking rather of something Lheppo had said weeks or months earlier, just before he had cut himself in the sacred cave: *Only blood is strong enough to bind the spirit world to us.*

Only blood!

And with those words clear in his mind Ivan plunged the knife into the wound. Plunged it in so deep that hot poisonous matter welled up over his hand.

There was a groan from Lheppo and a shrill cry of anguish from Lhien, but it was only Josie's response that mattered.

'Keep back!' she growled to the encircling clan, feinting at them with the spear. Then to Ivan, in English: 'I can't hold them for ever. Finish what you started!'

The wound was bleeding freely now. He made no attempt to staunch the flow, but went instead to the fire. Covered all the way by Josie, he reheated the knife blade, holding it in the coals until it glowed, so that this time when he pressed it to the open wound, the exposed flesh hissed and sizzled, and as Lheppo moaned the stench of cooked meat filled the cavern.

Even Josie was taken aback. 'Jesus! You sure you know what you're doing?' While the rest of the clan wailed in anguish.

He turned towards them, wanting to explain, and understood instantly that he couldn't. The word 'cauterise' had meant nothing to Josie, so how could he explain it to these people from another culture? There wasn't even a word for it in their language. Yet clearly he had to do or say something, and quickly. They were looking at him in horror – Aghri on her knees in tears; Lhien tearing the tiny bones and feathers from her hair.

'What kind of being are you?' she demanded in a fearful whisper.

'Are you the fire spirit fallen from the sky?' Kharno added hoarsely.

Ivan realised then that he had to appeal to them in a way they would understand. This was their world after all.

'No, I'm not the fire spirit,' he answered, 'but I have invoked its healing power. I have called upon it to burn up the poison in Lheppo's leg.'

They continued to eye him doubtfully, and he did something else then: he spoke in the only other language at his disposal. The language of dance.

His movements were clumsy to begin with, for he had no idea how a fire dance should be performed. Mentally he pictured the dancing flames in the central fire back at the caves, and he tried to copy those. Or not simply to copy them, but to let them flow through him. To become one with those flames; to let them consume his inner self much as the heat from the fire had consumed the poison in Lheppo's body. And gradually, under the influence of the fire image, he felt himself being transformed. Each turn of the hand mirrored the flickering glow from the fire's heart; each step, each turn of the body, enacted the leaping-falling motion of a flame. His hair, as he twirled and spun, seemed filled with sparks, his eyes with the gleaming lustre of the coals at his feet.

He *was* the fire now, whirling around Lheppo's prostrate body; entwining it in flame; enclosing it in a purified circle which he marked out with the rhythmic pattern of his footsteps. His panting breaths had become the wind that drove him on; the humming song that burst from his lips was dull and low, like the distant roar of flames through the forest canopy. In his dervish dance of heat and light, he lost contact with the cave that contained him, his encircling feet carrying him out into the far-off world of sunlight. Where he knew what it was to burn and consume, and also to nourish and heal; his inner face more radiant than the sun, his spirit self quick-tongued and fierce, like some ancient god of the hearth that recognised no power beyond its own.

He was on his knees, gasping for breath, when he finally came to himself. All about him there was utter silence, and he looked up into eyes less than an arm's length from his own – older, more knowing eyes than he would ever possess. They were framed by long grey hair in which a single flame-coloured feather caught and held the lamplight, and they spoke to him of understanding. Now the grey hair swished and swung as Lhien nodded to those around her – more faces, more eyes telling him they knew him at last. Knew who he was – who he *really* was – and why he had fallen from the skies, down into the timeless circle of their lives.

'See!' Lhien murmured. 'The fire spirit has left him.'

'Yes, but it has done its work,' Kharno said, and pointed to the pink edges of Lheppo's otherwise blackened wound. 'It has danced within his flesh and left him whole.'

Aghri's face appeared beside Lhien's, equally trusting. 'Will this dance of fire truly save him?'

Ivan wanted to tell her – to tell them all – Yes! Yes, your brother/son/friend will sleep and then wake like his old self. He will be whole again. Except it was too early to be sure about that. A glance at Lheppo's flushed face confirmed that the fever still raged through his body. Only time would tell whether he was healed or not.

'The spirit will decide Lheppo's fate now,' Ivan said, and struggled to rise, puzzled at how stiff and tired he felt; unaware that the dance had lasted well over an hour, and not just a few minutes as he believed.

Lhien and Aghri helped him up, Aghri clinging to his hand as he stood dazed and unsteady between them.

'This is the first welcoming,' Aghri said in a solemn voice, which also puzzled him.

And Lhien, cupping her hand lovingly around his face as though he were a second son: 'Whether Lheppo lives or dies, we are a fortunate people. For we have been doubly blessed by our sister moon.'

But it was what Josie had to say which stayed with him ever after.

She had resumed her place at Lheppo's side, his head now cradled in her arms. 'You had me fooled for a while there, Ive,' she admitted, and gave him one of her wry smiles. 'I really thought this place was too much for you, and I was wrong. You're a bloody wonder, d'you know that?'

24

The storm and Lheppo's fever subsided together.

Outside, in the breaking day, the note of the wind changed, shifting down a tone or two; and when Ivan reached past Josie's sleeping form and felt Lheppo's forehead, it was noticeably cooler. A few hours later fat flakes of snow floated gently from an overcast sky, the storm having run its course; while inside the cavern Lheppo slept peacefully, no longer racked by nightmarish dreams.

The rest of the clan also slumbered on, worn out by their ordeal; and it was only when Ivan again checked Lheppo's temperature, brushing Josie's arm as he did so, that she stirred and woke.

'Wha'?' She blinked sleepily, a hint of anxiety in her voice still. 'Is he all right?'

'He's fine. Go back to sleep.'

But fully awake now, she crawled over to the door, came back with a mouthful of snow, and moistened Lheppo's lips with her own.

It was an action she had performed a score of times since the lancing of the wound, and Ivan couldn't help but notice how lovingly she did it.

'Is he the one then, this *animal*?' he asked quietly, and smiled the kind of mocking smile she would understand.

She accepted the implied criticism without protest. 'It'll have to be someone, I suppose. So why not him?'

'That isn't what I asked,' he pointed out.

'I know.'

'Well, is he the one or not?'

She shrugged and wiped a hand across her mouth. 'Yeah, I reckon he is.'

'Really?'

'I know it must sound crazy, but that's the way things are. He's right for me. He's ... ' She paused, hesitant. 'How can I put it? Everything's different here. I *feel* different. Kind of half Utha and half Josie. Or maybe less than half – of Josie I mean. Sometimes at night I even dream of myself as a Neanderthal, and that really scares me.'

'Why should it?'

She turned and met his gaze. 'Because it's a lie.'

'How d'you mean?'

'A bit of me's still up there in the ship.'

'Yes, but like you told me before, the ship's a thing of the past,' he said, and laughed at his own feeble joke. 'This is where we belong from here on.'

'So you feel like that too?'

'After last night I do.'

'What about Aghri? Is *she* the one?'

'Maybe.'

Now it was her turn to adopt a mocking smile. 'God, you're cagey. I never know what's going on in that head of yours. Like the dancing. I had no idea you were into all that.'

'Nor did I. Not till it happened.'

'Oh come on! You're not going to tell me you haven't been practising. It was like watching a forest fire or something. You're as good as any of those shamans at the gathering.'

'I wish.'

'You are, honest. The rest of the clan think so too. I saw it in their faces while you were whirling around. As far as they're concerned you're a genuine shaman. The real thing.'

He gazed at her in disbelief. 'How can I be? That's for women only.'

'The same as hunting's for men,' she retorted, and patted her spear. 'We're moon people, remember. We can break the rules and get away with it.'

'For a while anyway.'

She gave him a quizzical look. 'I don't follow.'

'You're a hunter now,' he explained, 'and if you're right, I'm on my way to becoming a shaman. Well, those aren't just jobs or professions, like they would be in the future. Here a hunter or a shaman is what we *are*, and once we accept those identities we're as bound by the rules as everyone else. In a way your dreams are right. We've become Neanderthals. There's no going back.'

'Never?'

'Never's a long time,' he admitted.

She reached for a piece of dried meat and tore off a shred with her teeth. 'So if the ship came down here in the pass, this very minute, would you leave or not?'

'I can't say for certain, not any more,' he answered honestly. 'But I'm sure of one thing. If I did choose to leave, it would be a betrayal.'

She gestured towards the sleeping people. 'Of yourself or them?'

'Of them partly. They took us in, saved us, taught us things. We owe them a lot.'

'Yeah, but what about you? Would you feel betrayed too?'

'I suppose so. You said just now that a bit of you is still up in the ship, and I agree. It'll always be like that probably. But that means there's also a bit of me down here. A pretty big bit I'd say, which would be left behind if we headed out.'

She nodded. 'That's close to how I feel. I didn't mean for any of this to happen, but somehow I've got myself all tangled up in this place. It's like those big vines you see in the forest, that burrow right into the heart of a tree. Lheppo told me once that if you chop one of them down – the tree or the vine, it doesn't matter which – the other one dies. Although they start out different, and separate, they end up dependent on each other. As if they really belong together ... as if that was how things were meant to be.'

'*Meant* to be?' he echoed her doubtfully. 'Is that the way you see what's happened to us? As our fate?'

'Why not?'

'Surely we had some choice in the matter.'

'Not that I can see. We didn't choose for an animal to crash into the ship; or for the ship to take off before we could scramble back on board. It all just happened.'

'Okay, so it was an accident. That's still a hell of a lot different from saying it was meant to be. Listening to you, anyone would think there's a purpose in our being here.'

She smoothed Lheppo's bulging brow with the tips of her fingers, her nails stained and broken like everyone else's in the clan.

'Maybe there is a purpose behind it all,' she said

thoughtfully. 'Who knows? Maybe we're the ... the seeds of the future.'

Ivan moved around to Lheppo's other side, to see her better. 'You can't be serious.'

'Why not? We're here, aren't we? And we'll probably have children like everyone else.'

'Hey, hang on a minute,' he said, taken aback. 'That's a pretty big step.'

'Big step or not, it'll probably happen. What's the point of it all if we don't have kids?'

He needed a few minutes to digest that.

'So you're saying that the real purpose of our being here is to add to the gene pool,' he said at last, 'to *dilute* the Neanderthal strain and make way for the people of the future. People like us. Is that about right?'

She gave him a sheepish smile. 'That's roughly the idea.'

'Well, it's weird. What you're suggesting is that we're caught up in a time loop. Think about it: for us to travel back to the past, we first have to exist in the future; and for there to be a future like ours, we have to live on here in the past. It's a closed circle, don't you see? Going round and round for ever.'

'So what's wrong with time loops?' she queried defiantly.

'Just about everything I can think of. They don't make sense for one thing.'

'They do to me.'

'And for another,' he went on doggedly, 'everyone agrees that they make nonsense of our notions of time.'

'Who's everyone?' she challenged him.

He waved his hands airily. 'The ... the scientists, the people who worked out the theory of the time routes. According to them time is like a two-way shuttle. There're no loops along the way.'

'Big deal!' she said contemptuously. 'The trouble is, those clever scientists of yours didn't get trapped here, did they? If you dropped them out of a time-ship somewhere and forgot to go back, they might change their tune. They might start thinking about time in terms of circles or loops, instead of as a – what did you call it? – a two-way shuttle.'

'I doubt if you'd change their minds that easily.'

She laughed and indicated the icy chamber in which they crouched.

'You call this easy?'

'You know what I mean. Having to live in the past doesn't change what's right and true.'

'Try telling that to future generations,' she countered, 'generations who number us amongst their ancestors.'

'But none of this makes any sense!' he broke out, bewildered by the direction their conversation had taken. 'People can't breed here in the past so as to give rise to themselves in the future. It's a contradiction in terms.'

'I'm not convinced about that,' she began, and was interrupted as the rest of the clan showed signs of waking.

Rousing themselves, they gathered in a circle about Lheppo's sleeping form.

'Lheppo will stay with us now,' Kharno grunted, and patted Ivan affectionately on the shoulder.

'Yes, the fire in the knife has driven out the fire in his body,' Arhik commented. 'This is a mystery that only the spirit itself can explain.'

Orhnu gave Ivan a toothless smile and shuffled sleepily into the circle. 'Show us the knife again,' he pleaded, 'the moon weapon that can resist the heat of the flame.'

Reluctantly Ivan drew it from his pocket and opened the main blade. That simple action produced gasps of amazement from all sides.

'It is indeed a wondrous thing,' Kharno observed. 'Are there many like it in the lands of the moon?'

'No, this is the only one of its kind,' Ivan lied.

'With magic as powerful as this,' Lhien advised him, 'you will be a great shaman. The knife and the dance together will make the fire spirit your familiar.'

Aghri sidled up beside him, her shoulder fitting warmly against his.

'When the clans gather again in the high country,' she said, and there was a ring of pride in her voice now, 'we will tell them of the healing powers of this spirit knife. With it you will help the old and cure the sick. The clans will know you after that.'

The others murmured in agreement, and Ivan looked around at their eager faces and then down at the knife in his hand. He had intended burying it somewhere deep in the cave, where it could play no further part in the history of these ancient people; but seeing the trust in their eyes – sensing their new-born faith in him – he changed his mind. The damage, if any, was already done: the knife had worked its magic on Lheppo hours earlier, tempting him back from the brink of death. What did it matter if he, Ivan, used it again, on similar occasions? Whether it saved one life or many, still the fact remained that he had allowed the future to change the course of the past.

Though perhaps that didn't matter either. Perhaps Josie was right after all, and time moved in endless loops or cycles, with the past and future dependent upon each other in ways he would never fully understand.

'Yes, this knife is a wondrous thing,' Kharno sighed for the second time, and reached out to feel the keenness of the blade.

Lhien, however, clicked her tongue in disagreement. 'The knife on its own – even a knife as beautiful as this – is fit only for cutting,' she said disparagingly. 'Without the dance it is nothing – a thing of destruction. The dance, that is where the true power lies; that is how the spirit is summoned. For the knife to heal, the fire spirit must dance along its cutting edge.'

As if to illustrate the truth of her words, there was a restless moan from Lheppo who stirred and came to.

'I dreamed of . . . of fire,' he muttered faintly. 'It had a face and it stalked me through the forest.'

'You see, he has witnessed the face of the fire spirit,' Lhien cried, her voice rising above the laughter and general show of relief.

Old and young alike, they were overcome with happiness at having Lheppo back amongst them. Yet Josie was the one Ivan watched most keenly – the way she raised Lheppo's head and pressed it against her. There was a tenderness about that simple action which made him realise once and for all that regardless of who was right about the nature of time, she at least was now caught up in a time loop of sorts.

And himself? Was he perhaps a part of that same loop, with his head bound to one place and his heart to another? He looked around at Aghri, at the broad lines of her face now wreathed in smiles, and realised that he was.

25

For a full week the clan remained holed up in the cave, unwilling to leave until Lheppo was strong enough to travel.

Because of the grain and meat loaded on the sleds, they ate well. Similarly, they remained warm and snug in their cave shelter, for now that the storm had passed, one or other of the hunters made a daily trip through the snow-choked pass for fresh supplies of wood.

Each morning Lheppo woke a little stronger; and on the eighth day, with the edges of his wound firmly knit together, the clan set off for home.

Clearing the pass was the hardest part of their journey. The sleds kept lodging in the deep drifts, and Lheppo had to stop frequently to rest. That long slog through the powdery snow – the crust often so brittle that they crashed through and had to be hauled out by willing hands – fatigued them all; and when they reached the treeline in the early afternoon they were glad enough to stop for the day. Glad also to be clear of the cold and able to bask in the late autumn sunlight.

On the following day the going proved much easier, though still they didn't push themselves, mindful of Lheppo's lingering weakness. As they meandered down through the forest, they constantly strayed from the main path in order to feast on the last of the season's berries; and once, hearing a steady drone of bees overhead, they stopped long enough for Orhnu and Arhik to raid the hive for honey – dark gooey stuff, streaked with wax, which to Ivan and Josie, sugarless for many months now, tasted delicious.

Here at these lower altitudes it was still very much autumn, the trees alive with colour as their leaves flared and fell, carpeting the ground with rich yellows and purples and reds. To Ivan's eyes, these were the self-same colours used on the walls of the sacred cave, in the many paintings which bound the clan to the natural world. Which would bind him too – he knew that much in advance – once this journey was over.

Well, let it come, let it happen, he thought contentedly as he walked on through the drifting leaves, so enraptured by his surroundings that he no longer felt inclined to struggle against what Josie referred to as their fate or their destiny. He, too, was now prepared to accept this new existence on its own terms.

It was late on the third day, the light just about to fail, when they straggled into camp. While Kharno and Aghri hurried down through the dusk for fresh water, the others cleared the mouths of the caves and relit the central fire. So that by the time the stars appeared, it was as if the clan had never been away. Meat sizzled on the cooking stones; a breadlike aroma wafted up from the small barley-cakes nestled in the ashes; and the people had resumed their appointed places in the bright circle of firelight.

For Ivan that was the most carefree evening of his life. Pressed by Lhien and Aghri, he danced out the story of the time he had spent alone in the high country. And then, drowsy and content, he watched as the hunters, one after the other, enacted the drama of the mammoth hunt. Even Josie was persuaded to add to the dance, her clumsy movements bringing peals of good-natured laughter from the rest.

Last of all, Lhien gave thanks to the bird spirit who had again brought them safely home. In a low throbbing song which drew on an old language Ivan could barely follow, she told of how the winged spirit had helped to make the world; and when she came to the part about the creation of fire, she motioned Ivan to her side, the two of them slowly dancing in unison.

Later that night, when they all retired to the cave, Aghri abandoned her former sleeping-hollow in order to lie close to Ivan; and in the course of the night, when he turned and half woke, he heard no harsh words of rejection from where Josie and Lheppo lay together – only the murmur of soft voices, and the even softer murmur of the wind from the outer dark.

The dawn, as he had known it must, brought with it the trial of the sacred cave.

It was a cold, raw morning, and with the autumn mist swirling across the clearing, the clan gathered sleepily around the lingering coals of the fire. Thalek, hungry after the long night, reached for a scrap of meat left on one of the cooking stones, and was reprimanded so sternly by Ilkha that the baby on her back burst into tears.

'We must fast before the making of a shaman,' Gunjhi explained in gentler tones, and drew Thalek into the shelter of her cloak.

The rest of the adults busied themselves by fashioning reed torches which they lit from the coals. Then led by Lhien, who was decked out in all her finery, her face painted to the likeness of a mask, they entered the sacred cave.

Ivan's initial task was to paint a ritual version of himself. Pressing a root brush into his hand, Lhien pointed to a row of stick figures set high on the wall. There were no animals near these figures which formed a frieze above the ongoing drama of the other paintings. Also, there was a strange stillness about them, as though they stood outside the turbulent action of the hunt.

'This is the line of our shaman ancestors,' Lhien explained to him in song, and indicated with a shake of her rattle that he should add to it.

Grinning nervously, Lheppo shuffled forward and offered them a stone pot filled with black paint which she and Ivan both spat in – the froth of their saliva quickly subsiding into the pigment.

'Thus you are bound to the line,' Lhien sang as Ivan dipped in his brush and, with a few sure strokes, produced another of the stick figures.

This one was similar to the rest, but not identical. Unlike all those that had come before, it had no breasts and its lower half was forked to show it was male.

'Claim it!' the people sang then, joining Lhien in a slow shuffling dance. 'Claim it as your own.'

Now it was Aghri who proffered him a stone pot, one brimming with scarlet paint. Taking a mouthful, he spread his hand beneath the figure and blew the paint out in a fine spray.

'He has put his mark to his shaman lineage,' Lhien sang as he stepped back and left behind a perfect imprint of his hand. 'He has pledged himself to the great dance.'

The people responded by raising the torches high above their heads, the smoky light falling eerily upon their upturned faces.

'Name him,' they sang, just as they had sung for Josie. 'Name him in honour of the fire spirit.'

Ivan waited passively, expecting Lhien to mark his face with broad red stripes, which again was what had happened at Josie's ceremony; but instead she merely pointed towards the pocket of his ragged jeans where he kept the steel knife.

It took him a moment or two to realise what must happen next. And why. In the case of the hunters, already stained with the blood of their prey, red paint, symbolical of blood, was enough. For himself it was different. Only actual blood – *his own!* – could bind him eternally to the long shaman tradition.

Nervously, with the people continuing to chant, he drew the knife from his pocket and opened it. This was something he had hoped to avoid; something he had flinched from twice before. He knew that now, however, there could be no running away. To fail yet again was unthinkable, like turning his back on his true self. After that there would be nothing, the days empty and devoid of meaning. Devoid, too, of the warmth and companionship recently accorded to him by the clan. And gritting his teeth, his eyes tightly closed, he raised the knife to his shoulder.

His secret terror was that his hand would refuse to obey. In spite of that the knife barely trembled when he rested the blade on his bare skin. His mind, in fact, felt crystal clear, unclouded by even a hint of panic. This is who I really am, he thought calmly, this is me ... and pressed down.

What surprised him most was how little it hurt –
a slight stinging sensation was all. And also how
easily the steel clove the skin, the blood welling up
black-red in the dim light.

He turned towards Lhien, a trickle of blood
already coursing down his arm.

'With this, your own life-blood, I name you,' she
chanted, and dabbling her fingers in the fresh wound
she marked first his face and then the painting.
'From this day forward you are Rhemi Laan, fire
dancer. This is your spirit name and you will answer
to none other.'

She shook her rattle for the last time, and there
was a great shout from the people who jostled against
him, laughing and breathing his new name into his
ear.

The sun had risen when they emerged from the
cave, the trees free of mist, their multi-coloured
leaves shivering in the cool wind that blew down
from the heights.

Rhemi Laan, Ivan thought wonderingly as he
stood in the sunlight: *Rhemi* – mouthing the single
word to the soft blue of the sky. How strange and
unfamiliar it felt, and yet how right. As if it had been
fashioned for him years earlier, in some forgotten
time, and only now summoned from the dark.
'Rhemi,' he repeated, whispering it aloud now,
letting the breathy sound of it issue out into the
brightening day. Yes, there was an aptness about it;
it fitted him perfectly, mirroring the person he had
become inside.

'So how does it feel having a brand new name?'
Josie asked, breaking in upon his close thoughts.
'Pretty strange, hey?'

'Yes and no,' he confessed. 'The name itself,

it's … it's sort of foreign sounding and familiar all at the same time. Like I just remembered it from another life.'

'Yeah, I had much the same feeling. Now, when you call me Josie, I find myself glancing over my shoulder, looking for someone else.'

'For your old self, d'you mean?'

She nodded. 'I suppose Josie'll always be there in the background, as a kind of second self or shadow. Not that I mind,' she added with an uneasy laugh. 'Just as long as she doesn't try and take over. There's nothing for her here.'

'Nor for Ivan,' he replied. 'He's someone I know, that's all. Like an invisible friend. The one who was always hankering for the ship to come back.'

While they were talking, the rest of the clan had gathered around the fire for their morning meal.

'Come Rhemi! Come Utha!' they sang out. 'Forget these moon words. They belong only to the air. You are creatures of the earth now.'

Joining in the general laughter, they took their places at the fire where fresh barley-cakes were scooped from amongst the ashes.

'Here, Rhemi must eat,' Aghri said, shyly using his name for the first time, and handed him a steaming cake.

He bit into it, more out of politeness than anything else. He was still too excited by the events of the morning to feel hungry, and at the first opportunity he lured Aghri to the fringes of the forest, wanting to be alone with her.

As they took the path down to the lake, however, they were joined by Josie and Lheppo – Lheppo still weakened and pale from his recent ordeal.

'See, I am a child again,' he said with a laugh. 'I

261

must stay close to the camp while others go off and hunt.'

'You'll have the rest of your life to hunt in,' Josie replied.

'Only if you are there at my side,' he said, and reached for her hand.

'I'll be there,' Josie assured him quietly.

'And you?' Aghri asked, turning to Ivan. 'Will you also be here with me through the long passage of the seasons?'

There was a seriousness about her question which demanded a serious answer, and he hesitated, searching for the right words to express his feelings.

'Do you still long for your moon home?' she whispered, misinterpreting his silence.

'No,' he said, shaking his head adamantly, 'we will all stay together, just like this. The moon casts no shadow on us now.'

They were almost the last words he spoke before they reached the lake shore. Only a screen of nearly leafless saplings stood between them and the shore-line, and as they stepped through, Ivan stopped dead, a sudden 'Uh!' of surprise forced from his lips.

'Rhemi? What is it?' Aghri was gazing up at him in concern.

Josie and Lheppo had also stopped, puzzled by the way he just stood there, saying nothing.

'Anything the matter?' Josie asked, reverting to English.

He tried to speak, but couldn't, and had to try again.

'Look . . . !' he managed at last, and pointed to the sandy spit that jutted into the lake.

From where they stood they had a clear view of the message he had left in the sand back in the early autumn, before setting out for the heights. Until that moment he had forgotten it even existed. Although the saplings were now cracked and silvered by the frosty nights, the general outline of the SOS was still legible. And even more legible was the message beside it, picked out in stones.

'Damn them!' Josie breathed from close beside him. 'Damn the bastards to hell!'

Ivan blinked hard several times, like someone clearing dust from his eyes, but when he looked again the message was still there, unchanged.

'WAIT,' it read.

Part 5

THE RETURN

26

Winter came to the lakeside camp within a matter of days. One morning Ivan emerged from the cave to find sleet falling from a dull sky. Driven by gusty winds it soon stripped the canopy bare and deposited a sodden carpet of leaves on the forest floor. Two nights later that carpet froze so hard that it crunched underfoot when Ivan and Aghri went to the lake for water. And shortly after dawn on the following day they awoke to a cave filled with a pale and ghostly light.

Ivan thought for a minute that the ship had arrived and was shining its underlights down onto the clearing. So did Josie, who slipped from beneath her fur covering and walked uncertainly towards the cave mouth, her face nearly as devoid of colour as the wash of light on the surrounding walls. Yet when Ivan joined her seconds later, there was no silver shape overhead: only a steady fall of featherlike snowflakes which had already frosted the bare branches of the trees and settled centimetres deep in the clearing.

'God, it's beautiful!' Josie whispered, gazing in

wonder at the purity of this new-born world. 'There's nothing like this in the future. Not our old future anyway. That's why I hate the thought of leaving.'

Ivan nodded, Josie's tangled emotions not so very different from his own.

'The ship'll come for us all the same,' he said quietly, 'whether we want it to or not. They've located us now and they won't give up. One morning we'll wake, just like this, and it'll be them.'

She brushed distractedly at her face. 'I don't want to think about that now.'

'Why not?'

'Because.' Her voice was flat, telling him nothing.

'That's no kind of answer.'

'For me it is,' she said, and shivered in the wintry chill, both hands clasping her shoulders. 'One day at a time, that's all I can deal with.'

'And when *the* day arrives? When we have to make a choice? What will you do then?'

But he was talking to himself because she had already fled back to Lheppo's arms and the warmth of their communal bed.

Ivan didn't blame her for avoiding the issue. He had little or no idea of what his own future held at that stage, so who was he to demand a decision from Josie? Like her, he found it easier to shelve the whole question – to slip back to his warm fur bed and to Aghri's comforting presence.

'The sky demons have blessed us with snow,' Aghri whispered, snuggling against him. 'Their frozen breath will blow through the land for many moons.'

He knew that this was her gentle way of warning him about the long winter ahead; but having witnessed the dazzling scene outside, he didn't feel particularly worried by the idea of the cold days going on and on for months. In one respect he wanted them never to end, for the spring never to arrive, because the passage of time merely brought the moment of choice closer – a choice that would have to be partly wrong, no matter what he decided. And the same was true of Josie. For as they had both agreed, they each possessed two selves now; and when the ship arrived, one of those selves would have to be forsaken.

That was a far more daunting prospect than the winter could ever be, and so in a sense he clung to the cold days that followed. Revelled in them almost. Clad in heavy furs and stout leather boots (his ragged cotton clothes abandoned for good), he spent hours learning the songs that recounted the legendary history of the clan and of the people at large. Each animal in the forest, he discovered, claimed a kinship to the Neanderthal people, and so did most of the forest plants. Even the patterning of the starlit sky and the changing shapes of the clouds held meaning for them.

'We are the land, and the land is us,' Lhien taught him, 'and the sky is our shelter.'

From Aghri he learned other kinds of truths, such as the importance of play. Not the simple play of children, but a new carefree attitude that turned the heaviest work into something pleasurable. Clearing the drifted snow from the cave mouth after a bad storm, she never grew bored or surly. Instead she translated her boredom into songs and laughed at herself as she chanted them aloud, their steady rhythms making the work lighter and easier to bear.

It was the same when they were caught in a blizzard one day, the wind so hard and chill that they had no hope of making it back to camp before nightfall. Ivan's immediate response was to curse the weather and struggle on. It was Aghri who showed him a better way. Thanking the skies for their blessing of snow, she burrowed into the nearest drift, hollowing out a cave for them to shelter in; and once inside she made up a song about the magnificence of the storm, her throaty melody matching the shriek of the wind.

When Ivan told Josie about it afterwards, she gave him one of her mocking smiles.

'Sounds like count-your-blessings stuff to me,' she said. 'My mother was always full of it. You know, forever telling me to look on the bright side of things.'

'No, it was different from that,' he explained. 'For Aghri it was no big deal being stuck out there in the storm. It didn't seem to worry her, not the way it did me. She ... she sort of *trusted* it.'

'You mean she didn't think the storm could hurt her?'

'Not a chance. She knew all along we were in a tight spot. She was the one who started digging, to get out of the wind. But she didn't see it as an enemy or anything. Brother wind, she called it, as though it was part of the clan and she enjoyed having it around.'

'Enjoyed? How the hell do you enjoy a blizzard?'

'Well, maybe "enjoyed" is the wrong word. What I'm trying to say is that she didn't mind it being there. She accepted it. You see what I'm getting at?'

'Frankly, no,' Josie admitted. 'On the other hand that's the way things are here. For Lheppo too. He sees everything as joined together. Nothing's separate. "I am the hunt," he said to me the other day.'

'What do you think he meant?'

'I'm not sure. I can't explain it in words anyway.

Sometimes, though, when we're out in the forest together, tracking an animal through the snow, I get this feeling that we're all tied to each other by an invisible string which is tugging us onwards.'

'Yeah, but onwards to where?'

'I'm not sure about that either,' she confessed. 'All I know is that I can forget who I am once the hunt gets going. There's just the ... the wind and the bare trees and the tracks in the snow that seem to go on and on. And my own heartbeat. I can hear that all the time, except it's not mine any longer. It's more like a drum beating away in the background. There's one other thing too. When I've been slogging through the snow for hours, I swear I can scent the animal up ahead. You've seen Lheppo and Kharno raise their heads and scent the breeze. Well, it's the same for me. Suddenly the smell of it is just ... just there, as real as the tracks and the trees and everything else.'

As she struggled to express her feelings, a dreamy look came into her eyes. It was as though the very process of self-forgetfulness she was trying to describe had stolen upon her unawares. The forest might almost have been calling to her – drawing her to itself with that invisible string she had referred to. And not surprisingly, some half hour later, she and Lheppo set off on yet another hunt, intent upon cramming as much as possible into those brief winter days.

Perhaps that was the secret of Josie and Ivan's life there in the early part of the winter: the intensity with which they experienced every moment, as if every moment might be their last and they had to make the most of it.

Even the early winter dusks failed to dull their

spirits. Sheltered in the cave amongst the rest of the clan, and with a roaring fire in the cave mouth to ward off the dark and the biting cold, they entered most fully into the culture of the people. By then they had grown blind to the squalor of their surroundings. The magical play of shadow and light on the cave walls, the reassuring scent of heavily greased bodies, the songs and the laughter – these were the things that engrossed them.

And of course the dancing.

For Ivan more than Josie, dance was the single most important feature of their present existence. Without it the stories were not much more than a gabble of words. As far as Ivan was concerned, the old legends came truly to life only when they were acted out – the swish of Lhien's feathered cloak or the rhythmical stamp of feet like a physical connecting link between this wintry present and the long-lost world of the past. He was in his element sitting in the warm fireglow, with one or more dancers gyrating around him, their limbs slick with sweat and grease, their shadows flitting spirit-like from wall to wall.

Only one thing was preferable: to perform the dance himself. Then, like Josie when she was caught up in the hunt, he came close to forgetting who he was. The dance seemed to purge him of himself and carry him off to a realm where words such as 'I' and 'you' had no meaning. As he dipped and spun in time to the song's rhythm, the cave ceased to be and the eternal forest crowded in around him, peopled not by members of this or any other clan, but by the eternal spirits, the true makers of the world. With Lhien's voice droning out some story which he already knew by heart, he would make brief contact with the bird spirit, or the sky demons, or the treacherous soul of fire or ice, those twin forces that ruled the seasons.

'Rhemi,' the people would chant when he collapsed after one of his dances, close to exhaustion. 'Rhemi Laan, the burning one, has been amongst us. He has reached through the winter cold and spoken to us this night.'

★   ★   ★

If he, the legendary fire dancer of old, had been the only one lured there by Ivan's presence, all might have been well. Those long dark nights might have shortened into spring and then summer without any trace of heartache. But as Ivan had known all along – the knowledge like a guilty secret lurking at the back of his mind – the clan was due for a visit from a very different kind of visitor.

The ship.

Sure enough, when he and Josie were least prepared, it arrived.

Nearly two months of the winter had passed, and a blizzard was raging in from the lake at the time. The wind had risen soon after dawn, and although it was still only midday, the cloud had dropped so low and the air was so thick with snowflakes that it felt more like dusk. In such conditions the clan made no attempt to leave the cave, unless it was to collect wood for the fire. Many of them, Ivan included, had hardly stirred from their beds. Secure beneath their thick furs, most were dozing or muttering lazily amongst themselves, content to wait out the storm. Which was why it took so long for anyone to listen past the shriek of the wind to the ship's dull roar.

Kharno, attuned to the sights and sounds of the forest, was the first to sound the alarm.

'Listen!' he barked out, and throwing off his furs he leapt to his feet.

There was a slight lull in the wind, and they all heard it then: an even throb of engines which seemed to vibrate through the ground beneath them.

Josie sat bolt upright and clutched at her breasts, gazing in shocked disbelief out into the storm-swept day. Lheppo gave a soft groan and hid his eyes, not daring to look at her. Everyone else was silent, waiting, even Ivan, who lay straight and still in his bed, his eyes clenched against the whirl of white past the cave entrance.

'Will you go to them?' Aghri asked at last, her fearful whisper barely audible above the mingled noise of ship and wind.

He took a deep breath. 'I must ... must ... ' he stammered out, and ground to a halt.

He must what? What precisely did he *have* to do? He was free, wasn't he? Free to do whatever he pleased. If he really wanted to, he could stay right there and ignore this summons from the future; he could drift back to sleep and let them go away empty handed.

Well, *was* that what he really wanted?

He looked to Josie for guidance, and saw in her face only a mirror of his own uncertainty. The ship's engines, meanwhile, continued to throb, calling to him like the voice of some mechanical beast that had been marked with his blood.

He might have rejected it even then had it not been for the flare. There was a far-off explosion, a bright fizz and flash, and a scarlet flare lodged in the snow of the clearing, its fountain of light so lurid that the whirling snowflakes took on the likeness of bloody droplets.

'Aah, the sky bleeds!' Lhien moaned, and flung herself face down on the cave floor.

The rest of the clan either followed her example or hid beneath their furs, the children wailing in terror.

Clutching onto Ivan's arm, Aghri gazed imploringly into his eyes. 'Don't let them turn their anger upon us,' she pleaded. 'Nor on our mother earth. Tell them to hold back their red spears.'

Lhien added her voice to Aghri's: 'Speak to them in their own tongue, you who know the ways of the moon folk.'

He rose hesitantly from his bed, only to be detained by Josie.

'Don't go,' she muttered.

Having set himself upon this course, however, he found it harder still to turn back, and he quickly struggled into a fur tunic, leggings, and boots.

'You're making a mistake,' Josie called after him as he stepped around the fire and made for the cave opening, but by then her voice was too faint, too lacking in conviction to match the relentless summons of the ship's motors.

Outside he was greeted by a gust of wind that flattened him against the rock wall and blocked his nose and eyes with a stinging flurry of snow. Struggling against this sudden onslaught, he staggered out into the clearing, his face stained a bloody red by the now sputtering flare. High above, just visible through eddying waves of snowflakes, he could make out the huge shape of the ship. He waved one hand in a half-hearted salute, and it began its descent, the thrust from its motors creating so much turbulence in those stormy conditions that the ground snow was sucked skywards, and for some minutes he was caught in a complete white-out.

Temporarily blinded, reeling in this chaos of wind and downdraft, he heard an amplified voice call to him, half the words lost in the ongoing din.

'Where ... other one? Report ... two people.'

He gestured towards the cave. 'She's here, we both are!' he shouted back, but the words were plucked from his mouth and hurled into the trackless forest.

The ship sank lower, branches breaking from the canopy at the forest's edge and careering drunkenly across the clearing. One struck Ivan in the back and forced him to his knees, the power of the wind making it impossible for him to rise. Close at hand the flare was near the end of its life; while the wind and snow together seemed intent on smothering him. He could hardly see the ship now, though it hovered at tree height, its blurred outline all but blotted out by the storm's fury.

Through slitted eyes, one curved arm shielding his face, he saw something dark and sinuous snake down from the ship's underside. A rope! With a sling at one end, which danced at about head height a dozen or more paces to his left.

'Prepare ... board,' the voice blared out, and he hunched his shoulders and lurched to his feet.

The first step was easy, but after that the wind had him in its grip and he had to fight his way forward, to where he was almost within reach of the sling. Another step or two and he could have raised his hand and hung on. But at that instant the flare died, the wind rose beastlike from the lake, and the surrounding space became a solid thing, more snow than air. He did in fact reach upwards, and something grazed across his numbed fingertips. He had only to stretch a little higher and close his hand ... but he didn't.

Or was it a case of couldn't? Of lacking the will?

He was never quite sure about his true motive, the moment of choice speeding past like the wind – that one fleeting opportunity gone even as he blinked and blundered on, groping in the emptiness. For driven by another powerful gust, the ship had again collided with the canopy. Branches crashed down around him, adding to the confusion, and in a welter of noise and turbulence the ship rose through the storm.

' ... back soon,' he heard the voice announce.

Then he was lying face down in a fresh drift of snow, the ship having slipped away into the time routes.

He picked himself up slowly. The wind sounded much quieter now that the engine noise had faded – as though all at once, its task complete, the storm had decided to abate. Through a thinning stream of snowflakes he made his way back to the cave and crouched for a minute or two, warming his hands at the fire.

No one spoke, every eye upon him. Aghri's cheeks were tear-stained – he noticed that in particular – but he could think of no words to console her.

'Well, have they gone?' Josie asked, reverting to English for the first time in weeks.

She was sitting just as he had left her, bare breasted and hollow eyed. With her wild tangle of hair and greased breasts and shoulders, she looked to him like some primitive priestess caught in the act of mourning.

'They've given up for the time being,' he told her, 'but they'll be back. They think they're the lords of heaven and earth, you know that. They won't let something as ordinary as a storm mess up their plans.'

And Aghri, her face distraught: 'Do not speak in this language of the moon. Tell me only that you have sent them away, that they are gone never to return.'

But he could no more lie to her than he could to himself.

'No, the sky demons took mercy on us, that's all,' he said quietly. 'It is they who brought the storm and sent them away, to give us a little more time amongst the people.'

27

The winter was well advanced, and in spite of the hunters' best efforts the clan had made deep inroads into their store of food. Only a little grain remained from the autumn harvest, and much of the dried fish and meat had also been eaten. In an effort to boost their diminishing stores, the hunters' wives had taken to setting woven traps for any small rodents still foraging in the forest; and whenever the weather permitted, Ivan and Aghri spent their days out on the lake, fishing through holes in the ice.

On just such a day, with the morning sky a clear white-blue and the sun glittering on the snow-laden trees, Ivan was preparing to set off when Lhien confronted him.

'It is time for you learn the old language of our ancestors,' she said, and placed a hand on his arm, so that he gave up coiling the plaited line he was busy with and returned her earnest gaze.

'That is a task for many seasons,' he reminded her, for with Lhien's help he had already tried to master some of the more difficult sounds. 'And as you know, my days here may be short.'

'So you will leave when the moon folk come again?'

'I don't know,' he answered honestly.

'Then learn our old tongue,' she pressed him. 'It is the only pathway to our ancient songs. Without it you cannot understand the lore of the people and the magic that binds them to the land. The stories of our beginning will bind *you* here if you let them into your heart.'

'What about the stories of my own people?' he asked. 'How will I forget those?'

'The power of the old tongue will cast them out,' she assured him. 'It will make you whole again, and you will grow to be a great shaman. In seasons to come others will make up songs in your honour. You will dance your way into the legends if you will only stop and learn.'

He was about to answer when Aghri entered the cave. She was ready to set out, a stone ice-pick and a short three-pronged spear cradled in the crook of her arm.

'You cannot hold him here with words,' she said shortly. 'I have tried and failed. His heart is as hard as the blade of his knife.'

Lhien shook her head sadly. 'We will mourn for you if you leave us, Rhemi. Remember that.'

He needed no such reminders. Aghri's reproachful glances were already more than he could bear, and he hurried from the cave, out into the brittle freshness of the morning.

Laden with their fishing gear, he and Aghri took the path to the lake. It had snowed overnight, and their boots continually broke through the crust, the freshly packed snow squeaking at every step.

They spotted no other footprints until they reached the lake's edge where the unmistakable spoor of a deer crossed their path and headed off around the eastern shore. Alongside the deer's delicate prints were much heavier tracks which Ivan recognised as Lheppo and Josie's.

Aghri bent down and sniffed at the tracks, like some cautious denizen of the forest who knew what it was to be hunted. 'The chase is on,' she said. 'I think we will eat fresh meat tonight.'

'Fresh fish too,' he added hopefully, and stepped out onto the frozen surface of the lake.

Near to the shore the ice was thick and firm, but some three or four hundred metres out it thinned enough to protest beneath their weight. There was a sharp crack from underfoot, and Ivan looked questioningly at Aghri.

'Don't worry, Rhemi,' she said, laughing at his nervousness. 'I won't drown you.'

Soon the ice seemed to give at every tread.

'This is the place,' she announced, much to his relief, and dumping the rest of her gear, she unrolled a rush mat.

Kneeling on the mat, she cleared the snow from a patch of ice and set about making a small hole. It was a delicate process which involved marking out a circle with the heavy stone-headed pick. The regular 'tap, tap' of the pick rang out across the lake for some minutes before the circle dipped and floated free.

As she prised it out to reveal a ring of milky blue water, Ivan knelt beside her and baited their plaited line. There was no hook at the end: only a woven sphere of leather about the size of his fist – the weave so loose that when he crammed it full of thawed meat, shreds of the meat poked out through the gaps. That was their lure, which he lowered a metre or so beneath the surface, while Aghri stood ready with a trident-like spear.

'We must call on the water demons to bless us,' she reminded him, and together they broke into song, their voices interlocking as they chanted out the story of how life had come to the once empty waters of the lake.

Long before they reached the part where they thanked the water demons for their bounty, the first of the day's fish had begun circling the bait – a silvery shape more than half as long as Ivan's arm. As it moved in, following the woven ball which Ivan teased towards the surface, Aghri plunged downwards with the spear, the line attached to its haft running out between her mittened hands.

Seconds later the fish lay flapping on the ice beside them. Ivan would have left it there to gasp out its few remaining minutes of life, but Aghri scooped it up and bit it between the eyes, killing it instantly.

'Mercy is what we ask of the bird spirit,' she explained, touching her hand to the spot where the figurine nestled against his chest. 'And mercy is what we must give in return.'

Within the hour another fish had joined the first; and by late in the afternoon a dozen or more glittering bodies littered the ice around the hole.

'Enough,' Aghri declared, and rose stiffly from her kneeling position. 'We have done well today. The water demons have smiled on us.'

Unused to this kind of labour, Ivan rose more slowly, his joints stiff and sore. As he rocked from side to side, flexing his knees, he heard a hailing cry; and turning his back to the setting sun he made out two figures in the near distance. They were following a path down through the trees towards the eastern shore. The lead figure was obviously Lheppo, with what looked like the carcass of a deer slung around his neck; and behind him, though still some way up the slope, was the much slighter figure of Josie.

'Meat!' Lheppo sang out hoarsely, and hefted the carcass above his head.

Aghri answered by snatching up the biggest of the fish and raising it skywards – an action she would later see in magical terms, as a kind of voiceless challenge. For even while she stood there, her arm aloft, the fish like an arrow of silver in the fading sunlight, so the ship returned for the second time.

One moment the sky was empty, a hemisphere of vacant blue, unblemished by so much as a cloud; the next moment the ship had flashed into being. High above them to begin with, it descended in a long clean arc towards the forested area around the camp, where it swooped and hovered, the roar of its engines echoing through the windless day.

Even before it abandoned the camp and tilted sideways, aiming now towards the lake – the pilots apparently aware that they had drawn a blank – Ivan waved his arms and set off at a run. Or rather he tried to, but still stiff from kneeling for so long, the best he could manage was a stumbling walk.

Not so Aghri. Dropping the fish, she charged into him from behind and sent him sprawling. Bewildered, he struggled to his knees, but by then she had grabbed the stone pick and smashed it down onto the ice which groaned and fractured in lightning-shaped zig-zags all around him. He had no option now but to pitch forward and stretch his arms and legs wide in a desperate attempt to spread his weight.

On every side he could hear the furtive whisper of fresh cracks snaking out through the surrounding ice; while directly overhead the ship banked and roared.

'Aghri!' he bleated ... uselessly, for again she brought the stone pick slamming down – and again, until the cracks widened and icy water welled up from below.

He thought she would leave him then, see him slowly sink beneath the surface rather than give him to the ship. Instead she threw herself down, covering his body with her own.

'They abandoned you!' she hissed above the roar of the ship's motors, the downdraft flattening her hair against his face. 'You told me so!' And when he fought with her, the two of them wrestling together in the slick of water that covered the ice: 'They have no honour! How can you go with them knowing that?'

He threw her off and tottered to his feet in time to watch the ship tilt slightly forward and head for the firmer ice over near the shore. Behind him the sun had reached the horizon, casting his shadow across the lake to where Lheppo had dropped the deer and gone charging back up the slope. Ivan noticed with surprise that Josie hadn't moved, an unnatural stillness about her, as if she were nothing more than a painted shape amongst the trees.

Run! he wanted to shout – longing for someone to do *something* – because Aghri was grappling with him again, both arms wrapped fiercely about his waist. As he tried to pull free, they both lost their footing and toppled sideways, down into the slop of water and snow.

He thought they were gone then: the way the ice shrieked under the impact like a creature in pain, and dipped alarmingly. It righted itself, but they were floundering in ankle-deep water now – water so chill that it took his breath away.

Somehow he managed to roll clear of her just as the sun sank from view and dusk descended on the lakeland scene. Shaking from the cold, and with Aghri whimpering beside him, he gazed despairingly towards the shore: to where the ship, in an attempt to land on the narrow spit of sand, had clipped the edge of the ice with its landing gear and broken through. For a few tense moments he thought it would tip sideways and founder completely; but in a shower of shattered ice it righted itself, steadied, and zoomed skywards where it vanished as abruptly as it had appeared.

Gingerly, with Aghri close behind, he crawled through the freezing slop until the ice firmed beneath him. Somewhere off in the distance Lheppo was hallooing to them, but for the present all he could do was lie on his back and gaze at the shadowy emptiness of the sky. The first star appeared, and a second, before he could bring himself to rise. He was seriously cold by then, his fur tunic stiff with ice from its recent soaking.

'I needed to talk to them, that was all,' he said wearily – the only words he had uttered since the ship's departure.

Aghri, who had begun beating her arms against her body to keep warm, paused long enough to click her tongue in disbelief. 'No, you would have abandoned us,' she said, 'the way the moon folk abandoned you.'

He shook his head. 'Maybe I'd have gone, maybe not. It's hard to say. What I wanted was the right to make up my own mind, to choose for myself.'

But it was too cold to go on arguing, and he was already walking away when she answered him.

'And the child? Would you also choose for this unborn life inside me?'

He spun around, stunned, staring at her in the deepening twilight.

'A child? Are you sure?'

'I have counted the moons. There is no mistake.'

'And ... and ... '

'By summer's end a child of the earth and sky will dwell amongst us,' she assured him quietly.

He could think of nothing to say for a while, rocked by the unexpectedness of it all. A child of the earth and sky! Living proof that the past and the distant future could meet and meld; and equally, that the gene pools of two separate peoples could combine. As yet it was too early for him to feel either depressed or elated by the news. He was still in shock – his mind drawn back to a conversation he had had with Josie months earlier, about time loops and the ultimate purpose of their presence there.

'Does this child sadden you?' Aghri asked, troubled by his silence.

'No ... ' he stammered, 'it's just ... just ... '

But how could he explain to her what he felt? How almost as wondrous as the fact of the child was the realisation that time was more than a river that flowed onwards. It could also eddy and turn back upon itself.

'Come,' she said, and urged him towards the shore, for he was shaking with a mixture of cold and excitement.

Yet chilled though he was, he had to convey to her something of his feelings. He owed her that much at least.

'This child you carry,' he said through chattering teeth, 'it is more than just ours. It is also a gift from the moon folk. Whether I go or stay, it will be a blessing to you and to all the people.'

'I know this,' she said simply, and hurried him off through the falling dark – across the barren waste of the lake and up to the cheering light and warmth of the cave.

He was seated before the fire, some of the heat returning to his chilled body, when Lheppo and Josie arrived. There was a thud as the deer was dropped at the cave mouth, and Lheppo strode dark-faced to his sleeping-hollow where he curled up, miserable and alone. Josie, who had followed him in, hesitated for a moment and then crouched at the fire with Ivan.

'Why didn't you go to them?' Ivan asked in English.

'Why didn't you?'

'I tried, but Aghri got in the way.'

'It was more or less the same for me. I'd have had to get past Lheppo first. If I'd been on my own ... ' She shrugged non-committally. 'That's what's bothering Lheppo now. He's learned to read my face. He knows that things might have turned out differently if he hadn't been around.'

'Meaning you'd have left?'

'Or stayed,' she countered. 'Who can say?' And she was about to rise when he caught at her wrist.

'There's one other thing I reckon you should know,' he murmured, dropping his voice though he continued to speak in English. 'After the ship had gone, Aghri told me she ... she's pregnant.'

He was anticipating a startled response, similar to his own down on the lake, but Josie merely sighed and settled back beside him. 'Aah, yes,' she answered vaguely.

'You sound as if you already knew.'

She nodded. 'I did ... kind of.'

'How?'

'Can't you guess?'

'I suppose you worked it out from all that time-loop stuff we discussed up in the mountains.'

She waved the suggestion aside. 'No way. Guess again.'

This time she turned and looked straight at him, and Ivan realised that Lheppo wasn't the only one able to read her face.

He glanced quickly from her to Aghri and back again. 'You mean you ... you're also ... ?'

She gave him a crooked smile and placed one hand on her stomach. 'Yeah, worse luck. But then that's what we're here for, isn't it?'

28

Perhaps because of her stocky frame, Aghri's pregnancy brought little change to her day-to-day existence, and as the winter wore on she went about her regular tasks just as before. For Josie, however, it was different. As the days lengthened and the ice on the lake began to break up, she grew ever more listless, weighed down, it seemed, by the life inside her. Soon she found it impossible to go off hunting with Lheppo; and after that she turned in upon herself, barely stirring from the cave unless she had to.

Nearly as worried about her as Lheppo, Ivan took to coaxing her out whenever the weather was fine, as he did one morning at the very start of spring, with the birds calling through the forest again, and tiny buds braving the last of the snow.

Together they took the well-worn path to the lake where they sat on the sand in the crisp sunlight.

'You know, I still don't find it easy to believe in time loops,' he confessed, returning to a conversation they had had many times in recent weeks.

She didn't answer, gazing moodily across the lake

to where the wind left mare's-tail patterns on the surface of the water.

'What I find hardest to come at,' he went on, 'is the idea that the past feeds upon the future. It's all sort of ... the wrong way round. I mean, it doesn't make any kind of sense. How can we become our own ancestors? How can our children also be our forebears?'

'They can, believe me,' she said shortly, and felt for her stomach, which had become a habitual gesture with her now.

'Okay,' he conceded, 'but what's the point of it all?'

'Maybe there isn't a point,' she said wearily. 'Maybe that's just the way time works, and we were unlucky enough to get in the road.'

'In other words, the accident with the ship had to happen, but it could have been anybody who got tipped out.'

'Something like that,' she agreed unhappily.

'But if that's the way things are, why are you so resentful? Look at this place, it's fantastic. Remember how you used to feel about it back at the start of winter. You didn't mind being here then. You weren't even sure whether you wanted to leave or not.'

'That was before I became a breeding cow for the future,' she pointed out, and again felt for her stomach. 'Now there's nothing here for me any more.'

'There's Lheppo.'

She turned suddenly towards Ivan, more animated than he'd seen her in weeks. 'Lheppo's not enough,' she burst out. 'I ... I love him, but he's still not enough. I need to hunt as well. It's what I'm good at; what I was born for. Once the child comes, I'll be tied to the caves like all the other women.'

'Aghri doesn't seem to mind about that.'

'Yeah, but Aghri hasn't lived in the future.' She indicated the surrounding wilderness. 'This is all she knows.'

'What about when the child's older? You can hunt again then.'

'Do you think I'll be lucky enough to stop at one child?' she answered scornfully. 'Judging by my luck so far, I'll end up with a whole string of them. By the time I'm free I'll be too old and worn out to *walk* through the forest, let alone run.'

'I see what you mean,' he said, feeling helpless in the face of her plight.

'And there's another thing,' she added, unable to stop now she had started. 'I resent like hell being pushed around.'

'By Lheppo, d'you mean?'

'No, by all this time-loop stuff we're caught up in. I didn't *ask* to be dumped here; I didn't *ask* for my genes to be passed on to the people of the future. I was given no say in my own destiny, and I really hate that.'

'Like you said before, it's the way things are,' he said resignedly.

'You reckon?' A shrill note of rebellion had entered her voice, uncharacteristic of her these days. 'So your answer is to take it all lying down? To roll over like a tame dog and give up?'

'What else can we do?'

She scrambled to her feet with an agility he thought she had lost, her face set and determined as she gazed with undisguised longing at the cloud-flecked sky.

'Me? I'm going to grab my life back the very first chance I get. You'll see.'

*   *   *

As it happened, she was given precisely the chance she was hoping for less than a week later, when the ship arrived for the third time.

There was an abrupt roar in the mid-morning stillness, and its bulky steel shape appeared directly over the camp, blocking out the sunlight, its downdraft scattering the embers of the fire across the clearing.

All the hunters were off in the forest, and Lhien was the only one with the presence of mind to try and drive the ship off. As it sank lower and a rope sling snaked down from a small open hatch in the underside, she snatched up a spear and hurled it straight at the hatch. The spear missed its mark, the stone point splintering against steel plates, but that was warning enough for the pilot who banked sharply and sheered away to a spot further down the hillside.

Already Lhien was back in the cave, searching for fresh weapons in case the ship returned; and that was when Josie made her move. Unnoticed by everyone but Ivan, she sidled along the outer rock wall of the caves and vanished into the forest.

'Josie!' Ivan shouted, and set off in pursuit.

He soon lost sight of her in the dense spring growth, but he knew which way she was headed, and he too made directly for the now muted throb of the ship's engines, which sounded from down near the lake.

He reached the shoreline first. The ship, as he had guessed, was anchored in the shallows on the western side of the bay, in the spot where he and Josie had been pitched into the water nearly a year earlier. Even as he burst out onto the sandy beach, so a hatch opened in its side, a little above the waterline, and someone stared out at him: a weird-looking man with a curiously flat face which seemed almost boneless ... until Ivan remembered with a faint sense of shock that this was a normal kind of face in the future, and that what he had been expecting were the heavy Neanderthal features he had grown used to.

Was this what he, Ivan, looked like? he wondered briefly, unable to suppress a shudder of distaste. This boneless flabby thing?

Before he could pass judgment on himself, the bushes above the shoreline rustled and shook, and Josie stepped onto the sand, her cheeks flushed with anticipation.

'Get out of my way,' she said breathlessly. 'You're not going to stop me now.'

'I don't want to stop you. I want you to think first, that's all.'

'I haven't done anything else but think all winter,' she said, and pushed him aside so roughly that he stumbled and fell into the shallows.

He picked himself up, dripping wet, and scooped his shoulder-length hair away from his face. Over to his left he was aware of the man shouting and gesturing for them to hurry, but he kept his eyes firmly on Josie who had begun wading across the bay.

'What about the future?' he called after her. 'You go back there now and you could endanger it. You're carrying a child that's half Neanderthal, for God's sake!'

She turned to face him in the thigh-deep water. 'My kid's also half like me, remember. Like *us*!'

'All the more reason to think about what you're

doing,' he countered. 'The modern half of your child is what will change the course of history. You could at least stay until after it's born.'

'Oh yeah? And what do I do then? Just walk away and leave it here?' She laughed cynically. 'Come on, Ivan, get real. The fact is, history doesn't need me any more, because there's your and Aghri's kid to take care of the future. If our theory about time loops is right – and remember it may not be – then that one kid's enough to preserve the loop without me being around. Or you either, come to that.'

'Me?' He had known all along that the decision was his too, but up until then he had avoided the issue, sheltering behind the pretence that Josie's choice was the one that counted – that it was her child he had to think about first.

'Listen,' she said, switching to a note of appeal, 'it's been great here, a wonderful adventure. I'd be the last person on earth to deny that. But we've reached our use-by date. We've done what we were put here for. There's nothing to stop us heading out.'

Ivan was about to answer when there was a splash from over near the ship as the man dropped into the water, a rope around his waist, and waded towards Josie.

'We came here to rescue you,' he shouted, 'not listen in on a debate. Now let's move!'

Josie turned on him with a fury he was totally unprepared for.

'You butt out, d'you hear me! We're the ones who've been waiting, not you. For a whole goddamn year! So just keep out of this and give us what time we need.' Then to Ivan, a sly smile on her face: 'What d'you say? Are you coming with me or not?'

Stated like that, the choice was so simple really – so stark and clear-cut that he wondered why he had been heart-searching about it for so long.

'I think I'll stay,' he said, and felt a sudden rush of elation.

'You sure?'

'There's nothing much in the future for me,' he explained. 'Just a humdrum life and one relative – and she's not blood related. Whereas here ... ' But it was impossible, under those conditions, for him to list all the things which held him to this lakeland scene: Aghri and their child, his status as a budding shaman, the sheer beauty of this unspoiled world, and above all the vitality and mystery of the people and their ways.

'I'd be a fool to myself if I walked out on all this,' he added. 'I won't say I don't sometimes miss the comforts of the future. I do. I always will. But they're not enough to lure me back.'

'Look, would somebody mind telling me what's going on?' the man broke in, and made a tentative grab for Josie's arm, but she shook him off and waded ashore.

'You asked me to think before I acted,' she said seriously, and rested both hands on Ivan's shoulders. 'Well, I'm asking the same of you. Think what your life here will be like. You'll be an old man at forty – that's if you're lucky enough to live that long. With no medicine, no basic hygiene, every day could be your last. You could be killed by some animal in just a few minutes from now, on your way back to the cave. Is that really what you want?'

'That's only half the equation,' he said quietly. 'There are also the things this place offers me. A whole new identity for a start, one I'm really happy with. I'm *somebody* here. You should understand that better than anyone!'

She nodded. 'Yes, maybe I do. Though I still wish you'd change your mind.'

'In my place, would *you* change your mind?' he responded.

'I'm not in your place.'

'What about you then?' he said, shifting the focus back to her. 'If things were different – if you could go on hunting and be as free as Lheppo – would you leave or stay?'

She frowned, thinking. 'I'd still leave,' she said at last, her voice flat and final.

'In that case there's nothing more to say.'

And taking her head in both hands, he touched his forehead to hers in the Neanderthal sign of farewell.

As she straightened up, there were tears in her eyes; and in his too, when she turned away and waded across to the ship.

From the shore Ivan watched her arguing fiercely with the man in the water, both of them gesturing in his direction.

'Here!' he heard the man cry in amazement. 'In this primitive hole! He must be crazy!'

A woman had also appeared in the open hatch, her strangely boneless face as alien to Ivan as the man's. 'I hope you know what you're doing,' she called out. 'It's a hell of a job finding this tiny pocket in time, and that makes these trips expensive. We can't keep coming back on the off-chance that you'll change your mind.'

'Then you'd better make this the last trip,' he assured her, hoping he sounded as resolute as he felt.

'You don't want to think again? Because our job isn't to force you to come with us. Though God knows why.'

'No, this'll do me,' he said with a shake of the head. 'Talk to Josie, she'll explain.' And he backed away up the beach, giving the ship plenty of room to take off.

The woman looked at the man, shrugged, and between them they helped Josie clamber in through the low opening. Josie was barely on board when the pitch of the engines changed and the woman reached for the lever that controlled the hatch.

'What shall I tell Lheppo?' Ivan called hurriedly, having to shout above the rising engine noise.

Josie's hand moved to her stomach and a shadow of regret passed across her face. 'Tell him I'm ... I'm sorry. And to ... to take care.'

'Is that all? You know Lheppo, he'll find it hard to go on without you.'

She was crying openly now, both hands clinging onto the hatch to prevent its closing. 'I know,' she called back despairingly. 'It'll be the same for me. But I can't change things ... I can't ... '

Ivan didn't hear the rest, the engine noise too loud. His last glimpse of the youthful Josie, etched upon his memory ever after, was of a ragged but unmistakable member of the people flanked by two slack-faced aliens. Then the hatch swished closed, and with a roar the ship lifted clear of the lake.

That first rush of air and spray nearly knocked him over, and he had to clutch onto the nearest bush to keep his balance – watching as the ship climbed into the sunlit sky ... wavered for a split second ... and vanished.

He was alone! Even more alone, in one sense, than he had been in the mountains when he had fled from the hunt. Except that this time he was fleeing from nothing. This was his choice – a choice about which he had no regrets. He was aware of that already, a feeling of calm replacing the agitation he had experienced in those last seconds of farewell.

He looked around, and noted with approval the sparkling waters of the lake, the shimmer of the fresh-leafed forest at his back. This was his rightful place. His life. From now on he would be Rhemi Laan, fire dancer, and no one else.

To mark the importance of the occasion, he performed a few shuffling dance-steps in the sand. They were a rehearsal only, for the great dance he would perform around the fire that night – a dance that would somehow capture both the tragedy and the triumph of the ship's departure.

Satisfied, he turned towards the upward path and saw someone watching him from the cover of the trees. Aghri. Her heavy-boned face, with its tattooed brow ridge, utterly familiar to him. Even beautiful.

'You have stayed,' she said softly.

'Yes, I've stayed,' he agreed with a smile.

And looping his arm through hers, he walked with her up towards the caves.

A STORY
UNTOLD

———————•———————

It happened only two-and-a-half years later, in the dying days of autumn, when the clan was on its way home from the great gathering. Just before they reached the pass, there was a flash in the sky, and a small blue craft of a kind Rhemi had never seen before landed about fifty metres away on the grassy plain.

'Don't go to them,' Aghri pleaded.

Hearing the anxiety in her mother's voice, two-year-old Tipphu began to cry.

'Hush now,' Rhemi said, the bones and teeth clicking together in his long hair as he bent down and wiped the tears from his daughter's cheeks. 'The moon folk won't hurt you.' Then to Aghri: 'Come with me. You have nothing to fear from them any more.'

Leaving the rest of the clan huddled around the sleds, she and Rhemi approached the ship.

The hatchway stood open when they reached it, and a woman in her early to mid thirties watched them from the dim interior. Even when she moved forward into the light it took Rhemi a little while to recognise her.

'Utha!' he said surprised, his mind automatically settling on the name given to her by the people.

'It's a long time since anybody called me that,' she said in English – and for Rhemi there was a brief delay as he struggled to decipher the unfamiliar sounds of his former language.

'You ... you look ... well,' he said awkwardly, having to search out the half-forgotten words.

'So do you. How much older are you now? Two years? Three? I wish I could say the same. You've hardly changed at all ... except for the scars maybe.'

He fingered the burn marks on his brow. 'They ... they show ... who I have become.'

She smiled, not at all mockingly – the smile of a much older, more mature woman.

'Ah yes, I see.'

'So ... so what are you doing here?' he asked, the English words coming more easily to him now.

'I've brought something for you. Or should I say someone? My son.'

As she spoke, she gestured with one hand, and a boy of about fifteen stepped through the hatchway and down onto the plain. Despite his neat appearance and modern dress, he looked pure Neanderthal, short and thick-set, with a brow ridge that completely shadowed the soft grey of his eyes.

'I ... am ... Eric,' he said in the language of the people – his meaning clear enough, but his accent and intonation all wrong.

'I taught him a few words and phrases,' Josie explained, reddening, 'the bits and pieces of the language I could remember. It's just that it all faded so quickly, and on my time scale I've been away for over fifteen years.'

Baffled by all the foreign talk, Aghri offered Eric

302

her broadest smile. 'He is a handsome boy,' she said admiringly, unaware as yet of who he was.

'Yes,' Rhemi agreed, 'he is a boy to be proud of.' And in English, to Josie: 'He looks a lot like his father.'

'So much for my dominant modern genes,' Josie commented with a laugh, and ruffled her son's hair. 'But talking of Lheppo, how is he these days? I often think of him.'

The inquiry itself sounded casual and relaxed, yet Rhemi couldn't help but notice the way her eyes skittered across to the sleds, and how a tiny frown mark appeared in the middle of her forehead.

'Things have been bad for Lheppo,' he told her honestly, and saw the frown deepen. 'He hasn't hunted for the past two years or more. Not since you went off in the ship. Most of the time he sits and broods.'

Josie turned her head away for some moments, saying nothing, and when she turned back her face was clear again.

'Well, having his son here may make a difference,' she said with false brightness. 'I hope so, because if Eric's going to master the hunt he'll need as much fatherly guidance as he can get.'

'You mean you're giving him up?' Rhemi asked in amazement. 'You're leaving him here for good?'

'What else?' Some of Josie's youthful bravado showed through. 'I kept him with me until he was old enough to survive in this kind of environment. Now it's Lheppo's turn to look after him.'

'But why bring him here at all?' Rhemi shook his head in bewilderment. 'And why choose this time, only two years after you left? It'll be hard for the clan even to understand who he is. From their point of view he's too grown up to be Lheppo's son.'

'I wanted him to meet people like Lhien,' she admitted. 'I was scared that if we arrived after fifteen of *your* years had elapsed, some of them might be dead.'

'I still don't see why you want him to end up here,' he insisted. 'In a place you turned your back on. Don't get me wrong,' he added, addressing Eric. 'You're welcome amongst us. The clan will find a place for one of its own kind, I can tell you that right now. But a huge step like this! I find it hard to credit that you'd choose to abandon everything for a land and a people you scarcely know.'

'You did,' Josie pointed out.

'Yes, but I didn't just step off a ship and decide to stay. I was dumped here. By the time I got the chance to leave, it was too late. This was where I belonged.'

'Maybe Eric belongs here too,' Josie put in quietly.

'How d'you mean?'

Again she ruffled the boy's hair. 'Just look at him. Like you said, he's his father's son. Physically he doesn't fit back in the future. *He* knows that, I know it, and so does everyone else.'

'And for that reason you think he'll be happier with us?'

'There is another reason,' she said carefully, and exchanged a quick glance with her son. 'One that Eric and I have discussed quite a lot. You see ... ' She hesitated and then plunged on. 'According to the experts – and God, how I was grilled by them after I got back – your genes alone may not be enough to sustain the time loop. Oh, and by the way, everyone accepts the idea of time loops now, and all the contradictions that go with them. That's why, years ago, you weren't forced to come back with me. Anyway, for this loop to hold we probably need a bigger gene pool. More variety. Another genetic strain, for instance, in case one dies out, because if that modern strain was lost, there'd be no future world as we know it.'

'So is that really why you've come? To boost the gene pool?'

'We didn't just come,' she explained. 'We were *sent.*'

'What's the difference? You're here. You're willing to give up your son for the sake of the future.'

'For his sake, too.'

Rhemi looked directly at Eric. 'How do you feel about this?'

'I feel this is where I belong,' he answered stoutly, 'where I'm meant to be.'

'You sound like your mother.'

'Why shouldn't I?' he responded, a little of Lheppo's fierceness showing in his eyes. 'She taught me who I am.'

'And who are you?'

'I am half Neanderthal,' he said, his tone a mixture of pride and defiance. 'I have a claim upon this place, and it has a claim on me.'

Aghri chose that moment to push between them. 'What did he say?' she asked eagerly.

'He said that ... that this is now his home,' Rhemi replied, translating freely.

'So the moon folk have renewed their blessing,' Aghri cried in delight, and leaning forward she kissed Eric's hand, greeting him as she would any long-absent member of the clan.

'I thought I could count on Aghri,' Josie said with a stiff-lipped smile.

'Yes, but not necessarily on Lheppo,' Rhemi told

her, and nodded to where he continued to squat sullenly beside the sleds, refusing to glance in their direction. 'Your leaving the way you did, without so much as a goodbye, really got to him. He felt totally betrayed. I'm not sure he'll accept anything from you ever again.'

'Not even the gift of our son?'

'Maybe not.'

She turned away as she had before, saying nothing for a while.

'What if I convince him that I really *did* care?' she said at last. 'That running away hurt me as much as it did him? Would it make a difference?'

Rhemi looked doubtfully at this sterner-faced version of Josie; a woman now so much older than himself; one who gave no sign of having cried in years, least of all of having cared.

'It might make him change his mind,' he conceded. 'But how on earth can you convince Lheppo of something like that?'

'Tell him ... ' She took a long searching breath. 'No, start off by explaining to him that Eric is our son. You're the shaman, you can convince him if you try. You can say something about children growing up faster on the moon. It doesn't really matter what excuse you come up with as long as he believes you.' She paused once more. 'Then tell him that our son bears the proof of ... of who I am and what I felt.'

'What sort of proof? I don't understand.'

She stepped into the sunlight for the first time, and he saw with surprise that there *were* tears in her eyes, there was no denying it.

'I thought you would have noticed by now,' she said, and pointed to her son's ear, where a tiny silver droplet dangled from the fullness of the lobe. 'As I remember,' she went on sadly, 'Lheppo called this a moon tear. Am I right?'

Before Rhemi could answer, Aghri, who had understood nothing of their exchange, clicked her tongue in ready sympathy. 'The boy carries the sign of the moon folk's grief,' she sighed, reaching out to touch the droplet with the tips of her fingers. 'According to the legend, the moon spirits weep because they are parted from us, the true people.'

'I didn't manage to follow that,' Josie confessed. 'You'll have to translate for me.'

He did so as freely as he had before. 'She says that . . . that Lheppo will accept the boy when he sees the sign.'

'So he'll forgive me?'

'Yes, I think maybe he will. I really do.'

But she had ducked back inside the dusky interior of the ship, and already he was speaking only to a dimly seen shadow from another world.